A Dilemma for the Duke

Barrington's Brigade
Book 2

Ruth A. Casie

DRAGONBLADE PUBLISHING, INC.

© Copyright 2025 by Ruth A. Casie
Text by Ruth A. Casie
Cover by Dar Albert

Dragonblade Publishing, Inc. is an imprint of Kathryn Le Veque Novels, Inc.
P.O. Box 23
Moreno Valley, CA 92556
ceo@dragonbladepublishing.com

Produced in the United States of America

First Edition April 2025
Trade Paperback Edition

Reproduction of any kind except where it pertains to short quotes in relation to advertising or promotion is strictly prohibited.

All Rights Reserved.

The characters and events portrayed in this book are fictitious. Any similarity to real persons, living or dead, is purely coincidental and not intended by the author.

ARE YOU SIGNED UP FOR DRAGONBLADE'S BLOG?

You'll get the latest news and information on exclusive giveaways, exclusive excerpts, coming releases, sales, free books, cover reveals and more.

Check out our complete list of authors, too!

No spam, no junk. That's a promise!

Sign Up Here

www.dragonbladepublishing.com

Dearest Reader;

Thank you for your support of a small press. At Dragonblade Publishing, we strive to bring you the highest quality Historical Romance from some of the best authors in the business. Without your support, there is no 'us', so we sincerely hope you adore these stories and find some new favorite authors along the way.

Happy Reading!

CEO, Dragonblade Publishing

Additional Dragonblade books by Author Ruth A. Casie

Barrington's Brigade Series
A Marriage for the Marquess (Book 1)
A Dilemma for the Duke (Book 2)

The Ladies of Sommer-by-the-Sea Series
The Lady and Her Quill (Book 1)
The Lady and the Spy (Book 2)
The Lady and Her Duke (Book 3)
The Duke's Lost Love (Novella)

Pirates of Britannia Series
Donald
Hugh
Graham
The Pirate's Jewel
The Pirate's Redemption

The Lyon's Den Series
The Lyon's Gambit
The Lyon's Alliance

Barrington's Brigade – the Story

*From duty to devotion to their King, their Country,
and the women that they love.*

Against the dramatic backdrop of the Peninsular War, the lives of six courageous retired officers unfold in a world markedly different from the one they knew. These seasoned men soon realize that their most significant challenges extend far beyond the battlefield.

United by an unbreakable bond and led by their revered commander, Lord Barrington, these officers proudly don the title of "Barrington's Brigade." Their commitment transcends the chaos of war as they pledge unwavering support not only to Barrington's service for England but also to each other. Together, they embark on a journey to overcome both the visible and concealed scars of war, navigating a society on the brink of profound social and cultural transformations.

Amidst their quest for peace and normalcy, they uncover a sinister criminal element: the Order of Shadows, a clandestine organization that thrives on manipulation and power. This shadowy group poses a new threat, weaving a web of deceit and danger that these men must unravel to secure justice and protect their king, country, and those they love.

Tied by a loyalty beyond question, these extraordinary comrades stand ready to support each other in times of need. A distinctive gold coin becomes the symbol of their unwavering brotherhood, commemorates their unbreakable bond, and serves as a unique calling card—summoning their assistance whenever it is presented.

Step into a world where honor, loyalty, and love intertwine as the remarkable men of Barrington's Brigade and the women who captivate their hearts traverse the intricacies of Regency society while battling the dark forces of the Order of Shadows, forging their paths to their happily ever afters…

Chapter One

2 September 1822
Sommer-by-the-Sea

"REALLY, LORA," SAID Lady Harriet, "you must make a decision soon." Lady Lora Preston sat in a plush chair in the Rostov Tearoom, her gaze drifting beyond the rim of her teacup to the world outside. Sunlight filtered through lace curtains, casting intricate shadows on the painted blue walls framed by white wainscot panels. Her glance shifted to the petite vase of autumn flowers and the crisp white linens topped with lace overlays that draped the table. She sipped her tea as the soft hum of whispered conversations and the gentle clinking of fine china created a soothing symphony around her.

Lora's close friend and confidant, Lady Harriet Lockford, was in an affectionate, teasing mood. A sly smile played on her lips as the waitress approached, setting a fresh pot of steaming tea between them before she slipped away.

Lora took a deep breath, allowing the rich aroma of black tea, warm bread, and freshly baked scones to fill her senses and for Harriet to continue.

"How many seasons have gone by without you securing a proposal?" Harriet pressed, her eyes following the waitress's retreating figure before settling back on Lora.

"If we count this year." Lora's finger tapped thoughtfully against her cheek as she gazed at the exposed wooden beams overhead. A playful pause lingered between them, the corners of her mouth hinting at a concealed smile. Harriet, nee Manning, daughter of the renowned Dr. Bertram Manning, now blissfully wed to Asheton, Earl Lockford, had taken it upon herself to become Lora's ardent matchmaker, a role she embraced with zeal and genuine care.

Lora, the daughter of the Earl of Fallsmith, was a striking woman with an elegant presence. Her chestnut hair cascaded in soft waves down her back, each strand catching the light to reveal subtle hints of auburn. Her vivid green eyes sparkled with intelligence and a hint of mischief, a gaze that seemed to pierce straight into the soul.

Encouraged by her parents to nurture her independent spirit, Lora carried herself with confidence and compassion. There was an undeniable poise, a reflection of her noble upbringing, tempered by a warmth that drew people to her. Her laughter could ease the sternest of dispositions, and her unwavering determination was a beacon to those fortunate enough to call her friend.

And yet, beneath the polished exterior, there was a restlessness, a yearning for something more than the predictable social engagements and parade of suitors. Perhaps it was this silent quest for a genuine connection that kept her heart unclaimed, a secret she harbored even from dear Harriet.

"That would be three." She glanced at Harriet before she picked up the menu. "Proposals are not the problem. The issue is who they're from." A fleeting image of Lord Davenport's incessant boasting about his horses flashed through her mind, prompting an amused smirk. "I suppose I prefer quality over quantity."

"You don't belong on the shelf." Harriet hovered the teapot over her cup and then refreshed it. "You are smart, witty—"

"I do have all my teeth, that should be worth something," Lora interrupted without raising her head from the menu, smiling all the while. "You should speak to my father. He is of the same opinion as you." She peeked over the menu. "I should take bets on who will be the first to find me a suitable suitor."

"Oh. Lora, be serious. I warned you that if you didn't take this seriously, your father would find a suitor for you."

She didn't need to glance at Harriet. They both knew her father could only be held off so long, and with his recent illness, he had mentioned suitors to her more than once.

"What about Lord Penton? He is quite the catch." Harriet lifted a sugar cube with the delicate silver tongs but, after a brief pause, returned it to the bowl.

Lora wrinkled her nose at the mention of the man's name. "Absolutely not. He is as dull as dishwater."

"Earlier this week I saw you in the park with Mr. Charles Hastings. What is Mr. Hastings like?"

Lora paused for a moment, gathering her thoughts. "He's quite the gentleman, Harriet. Polished and articulate, with a charm that's hard to ignore. He shows a genuine interest in my work with the clinic, always asking thoughtful questions, and offers astute suggestions. He is considerate. He carries himself with a quiet confidence and has an air of distinction about him. It's refreshing to spend time with someone who seems to genuinely care about the causes I hold dear. Still, there's an intriguing sense of mystery about him, something that keeps me curious… and perhaps a little wary. I can't quite put my finger on it, but there's something about him that feels… not entirely genuine."

Harriet's brow furrowed slightly, her curiosity deepening. "Not entirely genuine? That's a bit concerning," she said, her tone thoughtful. "It's good to trust your instincts, Lora. Sometimes, they pick up on things that aren't immediately obvious."

Continuing on her line of inquiry, Harriet shifted to another potential suitor. "What about Sir Edmund Law?" She took a sip and glanced at Lora over the rim of her teacup. "He has a fine estate and a respectable lineage."

Lora shook her head, still reading the menu. "Too pompous. I could never abide his constant preening." She glanced over the top of the menu. "I liked you better before you became Lady Lockford. When you were Harriet Manning, an aspiring female doctor—"

"I spent all my time at the clinic. Now, I spend my time between my dear Asheton, our son Colin, and finding you a husband. And do not change the subject. If none of these fine gentlemen interest you, tell me, what do you want in a man? And by the way," she pointed to the menu in front of Lora. "There aren't that many items on Tatiana's menu."

"He must be intelligent, of course." Lora placed the menu on the table and began ticking off the traits of her perfect man on her fingers. "And kind, with a sense of humor."

"And handsome," Harriet added with a wink. "Don't forget that."

Lora smiled. "Yes, and handsome. But more importantly," her smile faded as she leaned toward Harriet, her eyes narrowing with a severe glare, "he must be fair-minded, respect my independence, and support my work. And he must understand and agree that my endowment is mine to manage."

Harriet was about to respond when her eyes widened slightly. Someone had entered the room. Her voice took on a teasing tone as she stared over Lora's shoulder. "This ideal man of yours must also be tall, broad-shouldered, with an air of command about him. I would think dark hair, piercing blue eyes, and a smile that could charm the birds from the trees. A confident man, yet with a warm gaze that," Harriet leaned in close and whispered, "would curl your toes. Would that suit you, my friend?"

ACROSS THE ROOM, Adam, Viscount Wesley, Lora's brother, spotted the newcomer and stepped over to him. "Rockford. I didn't know you were in Sommer-by-the-Sea."

The gentleman turned with a welcoming smile. "Wesley. I

thought it was your voice. Good to see you." Rockford removed his glove and extended his hand. Adam grasped it firmly.

"How are you fairing? It's been ages since we last spoke." Adam's voice held a hint of nostalgia.

Rockford chuckled, a warmth spreading through him at the sight of his old friend. "I'm well, thank you. It has indeed been too long." He glanced around the room, memories flooding back. "Evergreen Lodge seems just as I remember it."

Adam nodded, his expression softening. "We spent many summers here, didn't we? You, Lora, Barrington, and I, we were quite a team."

Rockford's eyes twinkled with the recollection. "I remember. Those were carefree days. We'd race through the gardens, daring each other to climb the tallest trees."

"And the nights we'd spend under the stars, dreaming of adventures," Adam added with a grin. "It's hard to believe how much time has passed."

"Yes," Rockford agreed, a touch of melancholy in his voice. "Eton took me away, and life has taken us all in different directions. But it's good to be back, to see familiar faces and places."

Adam clapped him on the shoulder. "It's good to have you back, old friend. Sommer-by-the-Sea hasn't been the same without you."

Rockford smiled, a sense of belonging settling over him. "I missed this place and the people in it. And I look forward to catching up with everyone."

"How are things in London?" Adam asked with genuine interest. "Busy with estate matters and my duties in Parliament. And you? How is your family?" Rockford slipped his gloves into his pocket, a flicker of curiosity crossing his face.

"Everyone is well, though Father's health has been a concern. Lora and I have taken on many of his responsibilities." Adam rested his hand gently on the back of a nearby chair.

Rockford tilted his head thoughtfully. "I've heard she is active with Dr. Manning's project to expand his clinic."

"She is. She's unearthed some surprising issues while working to get the project approved." Adam's face lit up. "But enough about that. What brings you to Sommer-by-the-Sea? Business or pleasure?"

"A bit of both, actually." Rockford adjusted his coat, a flicker of unease crossing his features. "Barrington invited me to join him here to discuss some matters, but I'm also taking the opportunity to enjoy seeing old friends."

"Sommer-by-the-Sea has a charm all its own." Adam placed a reassuring hand on his old schoolmate's shoulder, a warm smile spreading across his face. "I prefer the atmosphere here, far more appealing than London's incessant activity and noise. The serenity here gives one room to breathe and think."

"Indeed." Rockford slowly exhaled, the lines in his face softening. "It has a certain tranquility that's hard to find elsewhere."

"I stopped here to speak to Lora. She's having tea with Lady Harriet Lockford, and then I plan on making my way to the apothecary. Barrington is in the same direction. If you don't mind, I'll accompany you." Adam scanned the room and found his sister and Lady Harriet. "I just need to give Lora a message. Why don't you come with me? She'll be glad to see you."

Rockford followed Adam's gaze to where Lora and Lady Harriet sat and nodded. "I'd be delighted. It's been too long since we've spoken."

⊰⊱

LORA CHUCKLED, A sparkle of amusement in her eyes. "The picture you present is too good to be true. Who is this paragon of manhood?" She shook her head as she chuckled. "Really, Harriet. No one could be that perfect."

"Lora, Lady Harriet." Adam tilted his head in a nod.

Harriet smiled like the cat who ate the canary as Lora turned to face her brother.

Adam gestured toward the approaching figure. "Lora, you remember Garrett, Duke Rockford." His gaze shifted to her tablemate. "Rockford, this is Lady Harriet Lockford, wife of the Earl of Lockford."

Lora looked up and met Rockford's gaze, a flicker of recognition softening her features. "Why, of course? Your Grace." She inclined her head gracefully. "It has been a long time."

Rockford's smile broadened, warmth radiating from his steady gaze as he held Lora's eyes for a moment longer than necessary. "Indeed, Lady Lora. It is a pleasure to see you again." There was a hint of nostalgia in his voice as a flicker of unspoken memories passed between them.

In the midst of exchanging pleasantries, Lora couldn't help but think of the carefree young man who had charmed everyone with his reckless adventures and daring escapades. She remembered the laughter he incited, the thrill of his presence like a gust of fresh wind through the stifling halls of society. But the man standing before her now was different. There was a depth that hadn't been there before, a sense of duty and responsibility. It was etched into the lines of his face and reflected in his steady gaze. He was no longer the devil-may-care youth she remembered but a man who had clearly grown and changed, shaped by the passage of time, unspoken burdens, and the scars of war.

Adam bent to his sister's ear. "I need to speak with you about the clinic. There's some urgent news that requires your attention."

Lora's eyes widened in surprise. "What kind of news?"

Adam glanced at Rockford and Harriet, then back at Lora. "It's best we discuss it in private."

Lora took a deep breath, her mind racing. What could have happened? She turned to Rockford and Harriet. "Please excuse me for a moment. Your Grace, would you be so kind as to keep Lady Harriet company until I return?"

Rockford nodded. "It would be my pleasure."

She didn't miss the hint of curiosity that flickered in his eyes as he took a seat.

"Lady Harriet, how is your father?" Rockford asked, all his attention directed at Harriet. For a moment, a very brief one, Lora thought she saw the mischievous boy she once knew.

Adam led her away, his expression growing more serious with each step as they moved to a private corner of the room. Once they were out of earshot, he turned to her, his voice low and urgent.

"A message is being prepared to send to the king opposing the expansion of Dr. Manning's clinic."

"Opposing the clinic?" Lora's heart skipped a beat. "But why would anyone do that? It's been doing so much good."

His fingers raked through his hair, leaving it tousled as he exhaled a slow, deliberate breath. "There are several reasons. First, some local physicians and apothecaries see the clinic as a threat to their livelihoods. They believe it undermines their practices and takes away their patients."

She felt a surge of frustration. "That's rubbish. The clinic serves people they don't want near them, the poor who can't afford their fees. We provide care to those who have nowhere else to turn."

"Exactly," Adam agreed, "but they see it differently."

"What do you mean?" Lora's eyes narrowed.

"Some believe the clinic's focus on treating the poor fosters dependency and idleness, undermining the social order by encouraging reliance on charity rather than honest work."

"That's absurd." Lora's eyes were as dark as a storm brewing over the North Sea. "Most of the injuries we treat are from people working themselves to exhaustion. Some are hurt because of the dangerous conditions they're forced to endure. The clinic helps them heal so they can return to work."

Adam placed a reassuring hand on her shoulder. "I know, Lora. But there's also a third issue, which is both an opportunity and a challenge. On the one hand, your work has attracted the attention of individuals with significant influence in court."

"We've worked hard for that recognition."

"I agree, but on the other hand, some influential people are concerned that the clinic's success is drawing too much attention to social inequalities. They fear it could lead to calls for broader reforms, which they are not willing to entertain."

Lora took a deep breath, her determination growing firmer. "We can't let them succeed in undermining our work. The clinic is vital to the community."

"Absolutely," Adam said without hesitation. "We must rally those who agree with us to our cause and present an undeniable case to the king. Every moment counts, and we cannot afford to fail."

A rich chuckle from Rockford drew Lora's attention. She turned to Adam with a slight smile. "We best get back."

As they approached the table, Adam touched Lora's arm, slowing her pace. "Lora, you should consider speaking to Rockford about this. His position as a Member of Parliament could be very beneficial in responding to those against us. He is the Deputy Under-Secretary of State for the Home Department. He's responsible for managing domestic affairs, including law and order, immigration, and for our cause, the important one, public health."

"Rockford?" Lora shook her head, glancing at her brother. "I can't associate him with being serious about something this important."

She knew her brother well enough to recognize when he was trying to push her in a direction she didn't want to go. She took a deep breath as Rockford stood and held out her chair.

She nodded her thanks, looked into his eyes, and stopped, fixed in place. For a moment, the serious words exchanged with her brother faded. She couldn't help but admire Rockford's dark hair, the way it fell just so, those piercing blue eyes that seemed to see into her soul, and that irresistible smile, capable of charming the birds from the trees.

Chapter Two

"LADIES, IF YOU'LL excuse us." Rockford and Adam stepped out of the tearoom and were greeted by the crisp autumn air. The tree lined streets of Sommer-by-the-Sea were busy with activity. Shops and market stalls lined the cobblestone streets on Westmore Commons, the hum of conversation mingled with the scent of fresh baked bread and roasted chestnuts. Meanwhile, townsfolk went about their daily routines, greeting each other with friendly nods. Altogether, it created a comforting, cozy atmosphere.

"Unless you've drastically changed, you don't strike me as a man to take a seaside holiday. What's brought you here?" Adam asked, stepping aside to avoid a woman carrying packages.

An autumn breeze caught the trees, sending a cascade of red, orange, and yellow leaves raining down.

"Barrington's request. Even though I am retired from the service, when your former commanding officer invites you to visit, you *visit* as quickly as possible." A hint of a smile played on Rockford's lips.

Adam nodded. "I can imagine. Barrington has always had a commanding presence."

Rockford fingered the gold coin in his pocket, a tangible reminder of his duty. "He sent me this three days ago." He removed the coin from his pocket and showed it to Adam. "My *invitation*. Barrington is a man of few words."

Adam turned the coin over in his hand, his thumb brushing

lightly over the engraved initials. "BB, for Barrington's Brigade." There was a note of respect in his murmured voice. "I've heard tales about the Brigade's exploits." He handed the coin back to Rockford, fully aware and in awe of Rockford's sense of loyalty and responsibility.

"Yes, some were adventures." Rockford tucked the coin back in his pocket. "Without a militia near Sommer-by-the-Sea, the magistrate often turns to Barrington for help. Even though we're no longer in the service, we all took an oath to answer his call whenever we are needed."

Adam's eyes widened. "And each of you received a coin?"

"Yes," Rockford nodded. "Barrington's father, Duke North-wood, gave them to us the evening Barrington walked into the drawing room on his own for the first time, his mother by his side. Each of us helped him recover. The coin symbolizes our commitment and now serves as a silent call to duty."

Adam looked thoughtful. "It's quite a responsibility. No, let me rephrase that. It's an outstanding honor."

"That it is," Rockford agreed. "As the second son, Barrington has the privilege and means to take on such commitments. It works well for him. And here," Rockford looked around, "Barrington prefers North Sea and the cliffs of Sommer-by-the-Sea to the formality of London." Rockford glanced at the shops, the people, and the masts of the large ships at the dock in the distance. "And so do I."

"I agree. Sommer-by-the-Sea is a beautiful place. I prefer it in the summer, although I do look forward to London during the season," Adam said as they approached the apothecary. "Here is where I leave you."

Rockford glanced at the bottle glass window. He raised an eyebrow, concern flickering in his eyes. "If you don't mind me asking, are you ill?"

Adam paused, debating whether to share more. After a moment, he sighed. "Thank you for your concern, but no, thankfully, I'm not ill. It's about Lora's project."

"The clinic?" He glanced at the apothecary. "I do not understand the connection."

"She's facing some serious opposition. Someone is preparing to send a message to the king asking him to oppose the expansion. I wouldn't be surprised if they attempted to shut the clinic down completely. Lora feels she must take action to counter it."

Rockford's expression grew serious. "What reasons are they giving for their opposition?"

Adam exhaled, rubbing a hand over his jaw. "It is not one grievance but several, each tangled with the next. Some physicians and apothecaries claim the clinic threatens their livelihood, though it serves those who could never afford their services to begin with."

Rockford's gaze flicked toward the apothecary's shop. "That is why you're here."

"Yes. He once supported the endeavor, but something has changed. I intend to hear his reasoning directly."

Rockford crossed his arms. "Surely that alone does not warrant a message to the king."

Adam shook his head. "No. Others claim the clinic upsets the natural order, encouraging dependence on charity. And then there are those who care nothing for the clinic itself but fear the wider implications. If one successful reform is allowed to flourish, it may embolden calls for more."

Rockford's expression darkened. "So it is not truly about the clinic at all."

"No," Adam agreed grimly. "It is about control."

"That is your most damning reason." Rockford considered this for a moment. He nodded, determination clear in his eyes. "In my capacity within the government, I can advocate for the clinic's expansion, build alliances, and counteract the opposition's arguments with solid evidence and public support."

Adam nodded. "Your influence and connections in London could be crucial in presenting a strong case to the king. Dr. Manning's reputation with the Royal College of Physicians and the clinic's initial success should also work in our favor."

Rockford's expression softened. "I'll see what I can do. I have heard the odd comment or two. In general," he quickly added, "not concerning Dr. Manning's project. We must take care. If there is opposition and it's organized, we'll need a solid plan."

Adam's face lit up with relief. "I don't know how to thank you. I've been concerned that Lora would do something rash."

Rockford placed a reassuring hand on Adam's shoulder. "You don't need to thank me. Lady Lora's dedication is admirable, but I understand your concern. She never was one to sit still when she thought action was necessary. I'll do my best to help protect the clinic and support her efforts."

Adam's tension seemed to melt. He reached out to Rockford, firmly clasping his forearm. "I appreciate it, Rockford. Truly. With your help, I'm certain we can secure the clinic's future. I admit I need to see to Father's holdings in Brighton and was concerned about being gone under these circumstances."

"You gather the information you need," Rockford nodded toward the apothecary, "I'm off to Barrington's."

"Before you go, our family is hosting a gala in several weeks at our estate. We would be honored if you would join us.

"Thank you." It had been a long time since he'd been to Fallsmith Manor. He silently chuckled. A long time indeed, another lifetime since he filched a tart from Mrs. Kelly's kitchen. The thought of the warm, sweet aroma of apple tarts tickled his memory and made his mouth water. "I would be delighted to attend."

"That's wonderful." Adam clapped Rockford on the shoulder. "You take care."

Rockford nodded, his expression serious. "I will, my friend. Farewell."

Adam's expression grew serious. "One more item. I know I mentioned it before. Lora is taking the clinic issues personally. If you become involved, be gentle with her. She's passionate and driven. This project is close to her heart."

"That doesn't surprise me." He chuckled as a distinct picture of a very independent young girl came to mind. "I'll keep that in mind. You have my thanks for the warning."

Adam touched the brim of his hat and headed toward the apothecary's door.

Rockford continued along South Wickham and up King's Way to Barrington's manor, his mind swirling with thoughts. He admired Lady Lora's dedication to the clinic, but his mission required his full attention. Barrington had called him to Sommer-by-the-Sea to uncover who was influencing government officials, and Rockford couldn't afford any distractions. He would, of course, do what he could, but despite a pang of regret, he pushed thoughts of the clinic aside. Helping Lady Lora felt right, but his duty to Barrington came first.

As he approached the entrance of Sommer Chase, Barrington's home; Sanderson, the butler, opened the door.

"Good afternoon, Your Grace. Welcome back to Sommer Chase. Lord Barrington is in his library."

"Thank you, Sanderson. It is good to see you. I'll find my way."

"Very good." The butler let him pass and closed the door behind him.

Rockford made his way through the familiar halls of Sommer Chase, his footsteps echoing softly on the polished floors. He entered the library and was immediately at ease. Large familiar cases filled with books stood on two walls and surrounded the fireplace on the third. A sideboard with goblets and decanters adorned the fourth wall. Over the sideboard hung a map of the area.

Reese Barrington's bearing spoke of a man who carried the weight of leadership with quiet confidence. Fair and just, he was respected not only as a commander but as a protector who stood shoulder to shoulder with his men. During the Peninsula War, Barrington was the first to charge into battle and the last to leave the field, ensuring no man was left behind.

The scars of war marked him, both physically and emotionally. Severely wounded in action, he fought relentlessly to regain his strength, his determination allowing him to recover with only a limp and a few noticeable scars. The most pronounced one carved across his right cheek, discreetly softened by the clever trim of his valet's handiwork.

His jet-black hair, now streaked with silver, lent him an air of distinguished wisdom, while his sharp Nordic blue eyes seemed to see straight to the truth of a person. Whether in the crisp lines of a uniform or the understated elegance of casual attire, Barrington's presence commanded respect, his every move a reflection of the discipline and resolve forged in battle.

"Rockford, welcome." Barrington rose from behind his desk, stepped forward, and extended his hand. "It's been too long. I trust London hasn't worn you down?"

Rockford shook Barrington's hand firmly. "Not yet. The sail from London was pleasant enough, though I could have done without the endless political debates." He smirked slightly. "How have you been?"

"Busy, as always," Barrington said with a knowing nod. "And, unfortunately, dealing with a rather pressing matter." He gestured toward the chair by the fireplace. "Please, make yourself comfortable."

Rockford settled in as Barrington took the seat beside him.

"I'll get right to the point," Barrington continued. "There has been some thievery of late. A highwayman of all things. We haven't seen one in this area for a while, but his activities have become brazen. He is a picky thief, targeting only couriers carrying messages for the King."

"He only targets the royal courier." Rockford paused. How odd. "No one else?"

Barrington shook his head. "No one else. He is very selective."

Rockford leaned forward, his interest piqued. "Selective? Do we know what information the messages he's intercepting contain?"

"He's a clever one," Barrington admitted. "We sent decoy messages, he ignored them. Even when we hid the message to the king among council documents, he took only that and left the rest for us to find."

A smile tugged at the corner of Rockford's mouth. "Decisive and deliberate, this highwayman isn't just after money or random opportunity. He's hunting something specific. A man with a purpose." He leaned back, fingers steepled as his mind worked through the implications. "The message to the king... that he ignored a decoy and targeted the real one... This suggests an inside source. Someone who knows what to look for and when."

"It's possible there's a connection to recent events in the area, including the opposition to the clinic project."

Rockford's eyes widened in surprise. "The clinic project? That's quite a leap."

"Perhaps," Barrington conceded. "But we can't rule anything out at this point. We need to investigate further." Barrington drummed his fingers on the arm of the chair. "As you mentioned, we, too, have concluded that the thief must have someone informing him on who to stop and who to let pass."

Rockford's eyes narrowed. "Do you have anyone in mind?"

"There are a few who could be helping him," Barrington replied. "But we need solid evidence before we dare approach anyone."

"I understand your predicament. It is definitely a sensitive one."

"The route through Baycliff Woods provides several convenient areas for our highwayman to strike. We've found no pattern to where he stops the courier. We thought to send the courier with an escort but all that did was make the culprit more creative. He struck at night and left a note. We decided to change the couriers but that didn't help either. We need to stop him once and for all. I called you here because I need someone with your skills and connections to lead this investigation."

Rockford glanced at the map, his mind already working through the possibilities. "With a secret informer working on this from the inside, we'll need to be careful."

"Agreed," Barrington said grimly. "And with the king arriving on October 21st, we have little time. His visit was unexpected, but Parliament insisted on his presence to address concerns over recent political unrest. If this highwayman is after more than mere coin, His Majesty could be walking into a trap."

Rockford's mind raced. A highwayman with such precision and foresight wasn't just a thief, this was someone with a mission. The note left behind suggested a brazen confidence, almost as if he enjoyed taunting his pursuers. But taking only certain messages? That pointed to something deeper. Someone's betrayal.

Was the highwayman working alone, or was he a pawn in a larger scheme? If there was an insider, the stakes were even higher. Who stood to gain from disrupting royal correspondence, and, more importantly, why?

The king's visit wasn't just a deadline. It was a clue. If this highwayman had a greater motive, October 21st might reveal his endgame. Rockford would start with Barrington's list of potential informants. Someone knew too much, and he would find out who.

"Political unrest. Nothing else?" Rockford asked.

A hint of intrigue appeared in Barrington's eyes. "There are whispers of various reasons. Some say it's political, others suggest economic interests or even a personal retreat. It's an unusual visit, indeed."

Rockford stared at Barrington intently as the urgency of the situation became clear. "Understood. Adam Wesley spoke with me about the clinic project."

"Yes, the planned clinic improvements have been a beacon of hope for many. However," Barrington sat back and drew a deep breath, then released it slowly. "Wesley is correct. It's also drawn significant opposition."

"Wesley mentioned that some influential people are writing against the project. They must not have sent anything off yet. If they had, it would have crossed my desk. His Majesty has me review anything related to health issues. He also went over the reasons for the resistance to the project. What more do we know about this opposition?"

Barrington hesitated before answering. "We have reason to believe someone is working hard to convince property owners and influential people to oppose the clinic by playing on their concerns."

"Yes," Rockford was glad he had stumbled upon his old friend. "Those being competition, fear of creating a dependent population, and spreading social unrest."

"Adam is well versed in the issues. He's planning to go to Royston Mills to talk to the textile mill owners. Dr. Manning's clinic services the mill workers and their families. Uncovering the highwayman's identity is one of our top priorities."

Rockford glanced at the map, a thought forming. "Do you think there could be a link between the highwayman's activities, the opposition to the clinic, and the project I'm working on in London?"

Barrington looked thoughtful. "It's possible. The issues involve influential people and sensitive information. We need to consider all possibilities."

"I'll see what I can find. If there's a connection, we'll find it." He glanced at Barrington, a smile playing on his lips. "At first, I thought your invitation was to make me look more guilty than people already think I am. Leaving London at the height of the scandal doesn't exactly put me in a good light."

"There was no way to avoid it."

"I never thought our contrived monetary malfeasance scandal would come in handy here. Whoever is behind the highwayman may try to compromise me or invite me to participate, thinking they can use me to their advantage. We couldn't have planned this better."

Barrington's eyes lit up with interest. "That's clever. They might be more willing to reveal their plans if they think they can get your cooperation. Until we know who is involved, you must be careful."

With a surge of determination, he turned to Barrington. "It appears I'll be helping Lady Lora, after all."

Barrington's expression softened. "Your involvement could make all the difference."

"You're difficult to say no to." They both chuckled.

"There is one final item."

Rockford stared at his former commanding officer. The man was a master of strategy. What else could there be?

"We must agree that we will not disclose the identity of the secret informer under any circumstance. Everything could be lost if we reveal their identity before we have all the evidence to bring it to the King.

"On my oath." Rockford put his gold coin on the table and slid it toward Barrington.

Barrington nodded and slid the coin back to him.

"Your word is all I need. Return this to me when our mission is completed. Now, let me show you the information I've been able to gather so far."

⇢⟫⟪⇠

LATER THAT EVENING, Rockford arrived home with the day's discussion still buzzing in his head. He spotted a sealed envelope on his desk as he entered his study. The Fallsmith family crest was unmistakable.

He picked up the envelope, broke the seal with a practiced hand, and read the elegantly scripted invitation.

The Right Honorable, The Earl and Countess of Fallsmith,
requests the honor of your presence
at a Gala to be held at
Fallsmith Manor
on the 20th of September 1822
at 7 o'clock in the evening
Hosted by Lady Lora and Viscount Adam Wesley
RSVP by the 10th of September

A smaller note was tucked inside, written in Adam's familiar hand.

Rockford,

My apologies for the late notice. The family hopes you can attend.

Adam.

A slight smile touched his lips. "That will be an interesting evening." He placed the invitation on his desk along with other correspondence that needed his response.

Chapter Three

20 September 1822

A S ROCKFORD'S CARRIAGE rolled along King's Way, he gazed absently at the passing countryside, his mind consumed by the events of the past fortnight. It had been over two weeks since his return to Sommer-by-the-Sea, and he had wasted no time immersing himself in the investigation. Whispers of his scandal in London had followed him here. Small towns thrived on gossip, and while he paid it little heed, he couldn't entirely dismiss the way it sharpened the townsfolk's curiosity about his movements.

The elusive highwayman had not struck during this time, even though the royal courier had been dispatched four times. Peculiar. Coincidence? He doubted it, especially given that his prime suspects had conveniently left town on each occasion.

Meanwhile, the village buzzed with chatter about Dr. Manning's clinic expansion. The gossip grew more heated by the day. Opposition to the project seemed to be mounting, and Rockford suspected the very people he was investigating were behind it. Every conversation he overheard held a hint of something deeper as if the entire village spoke in a code he was only beginning to decipher.

Rockford leaned back against the carriage seat and considered his next move. The pieces were all there, he just needed to fit them together. Helping Lady Lora with the clinic might do more than earn her gratitude. If the resistance to the clinic was connected to the larger plot he was investigating, then aiding her would not only be the right thing to do but also a strategic advantage.

Then, there was the scandal trailing behind him. As a duke, he enjoyed certain advantages. People still engaged with him, even if with caution. Yet their wariness worked to his benefit. Once they believed he was compromised, the people he was after would lower their guard, inadvertently revealing secrets they'd otherwise keep hidden. He could already feel the undercurrents shifting, each interaction a subtle maneuver in a larger game he was determined to win.

His carriage turned into the gate and down Fallsmith Manor's drive. It had been some time since he was last here, and the sight of the imposing structure brought back a flood of memories.

The manor stood imposingly at the end of a long, tree-lined drive, its solid stone and brick facade projecting strength and permanence. The architecture confirmed the Fallsmith family's wealth and influence, with ivy climbing its sturdy walls and large, mullioned windows reflecting the sun's setting. An image of the manicured gardens came to mind, and the gate in the back stone wall that opened onto a path that meandered along the cliff's edge. There was a perch where you could look out over the vast expanse of the North Sea.

Rockford recalled the evenings spent here, the grand gatherings and quiet moments alike. As the carriage drew closer, the elegance of the portico came into view. When the carriage came to a stop, Rockford stepped out and paused, noting with a touch of nostalgia that the manor stood just as it had the last time he'd visited. Venturing inside, he found everything as he remembered, the rich mahogany paneling, the black and white checkerboard marble floor with the Fallsmith family medallion in the center of the pattern. The intricate design was a hammer and anvil encircled by gilded rays of light. Around the edge, the family motto, *Strength Forged in Honor.*

"Good evening, Your Grace. It is good to see you again. Welcome back to Fallsmith Manor."

"Good evening, Axbridge. It is good to be here." He leaned in. "I'll have to stop by and catch up on the local goings and comings."

The very formal butler glanced at him and smiled. "Will the whiskey be pilfered from your father, Your Grace?"

"Not this time. I've upgraded to pilfering my own stock." Rockford grinned. "I've learned a thing or two since my youth, Axbridge."

The butler's lips twitched, barely suppressing a smile. "I shall believe that when I see it, Your Grace."

He followed Axbridge into the bustling ballroom. The room was alive with movement and sound. The light of the crystal chandeliers overhead danced across the gathering. The music played softly, but Rockford's attention was elsewhere. He surveyed the crowd, noting familiar faces and potential allies. Laughter and conversation blended into a hum that filled the space, but he listened for particular voices, snippets of conversations that might interest him. For him, this gathering was more than a social event. It was an opportunity.

As Rockford made his way around the room, Lord Fallsmith approached him with a welcoming smile. "Rockford, it's been far too long." The earl extended his hand. His hair had greyed since Rockford last saw him, but his eyes still held the same sharp intelligence.

"Indeed, it has," Rockford firmly shook Lord Fallsmith's hand. "It's good to see you again, my lord."

Lady Fallsmith joined them, her elegant gown rustling softly. "Your Grace, you haven't changed a bit," she said warmly, her eyes reflecting genuine pleasure. "Perhaps a bit taller and less mischievous. We've missed your visits."

Rockford chuckled as he bowed slightly. "Lady Fallsmith, the pleasure is mine. I've missed being here as well."

"We must sit together. I'm eager for you to bring me up to date with what you've been doing." Lord Fallsmith said. "With my brandy, not your father's."

Rockford and the earl both laughed. "I will see to it," Rockford said.

"I was so surprised when Adam mentioned you had returned," Lady Fallsmith went on.

The conversation went on for several more minutes. Lord Fallsmith gave a warm chuckle. "Well, Rockford, I trust you'll find plenty of familiar faces here tonight. Do take the opportunity to reacquaint yourself."

Lady Fallsmith nodded, her smile gracious. "Indeed, Your Grace. And if there's anything you require, you need only ask. We won't keep you from mingling."

As he nodded and moved further into the room, he felt a sense of ease wash over him. Despite the years that had passed, the warmth and hospitality remained unchanged. He allowed a small smile to play at the corners of his lips. How easy it is to forget one's roots when you're away.

He scanned the crowd, looking for familiar faces, particularly Adam and Lady Lora. He nodded, greeting old acquaintances, his gaze sharp as he took in the subtle dynamics at play.

As he continued to weave through the gathering, Rockford spotted Lady Lora approaching him. Her emerald gown shimmered with every step, catching the light in a way that seemed almost deliberate. Her eyes sparkled, drawing him in with an energy that he could only describe as confident. Yes, that's what it was. Confidence. It was in the graceful sway of her stride, the proud lift of her chin, and the way her shoulders squared as though the room revolved around her. Conversations paused as she passed, people eager to acknowledge her. She had grown, he realized, not just in beauty but in a presence that commanded attention without effort.

"Lady Lora. How has your evening been?" His voice was smooth and inviting. "Would you join me for a turn around the room?"

She returned his smile, taking his offered arm. "The evening has been quite delightful, though I must admit, your presence adds a certain charm."

Rockford chuckled softly, guiding her through the crowd. "You flatter me, my lady."

She hesitated, choosing her words carefully. "I believe our last conversation was rather... tense. I apologize. I was... preoccupied with some troubling news."

Rockford's smile widened slightly. "No apology is necessary. We all have our moments."

Lora walked beside him in comfortable silence for a moment before speaking softly. "I hope you won't think me impertinent, but I wanted to ask after your well-being."

He glanced at her, a hint of curiosity in his eyes. "That's most kind of you. I assure you, I am quite well."

She hesitated, choosing her words carefully. "It's just that... I've heard some whispers recently. Rumors that concern you. They troubled me, and I thought it best to speak with you directly."

Rockford maintained a neutral expression, but someone who knew him well would see the flicker of something deeper in his eyes. "I see. Rumors have a way of spreading—often without merit, don't they?"

"For that, I am glad." She met his gaze. "I have always held you in high esteem. Even when you pulled my hair."

His eyes widened. "Only after you tied the legs of my breeches in knots while I was swimming in the lake."

She smirked. "Ah, but you were quite the sight trying to undo them."

Rockford chuckled. "You were wise to keep your distance. If I remember, my thoughts were... less than noble."

"Yes, best leave it there." They walked on in companionable silence.

"Those summers at the lodge were some of the best," she mused.

"Simpler times," he agreed. He glanced at her, warmth in his gaze. "Perhaps we should visit again."

She shot him a knowing look. "Only if you promise not to swim in the lake this time."

He leaned in, voice low. "No promises."

Lora laughed. "Then I suppose we'll just have to see what happens."

Rockford's grin was full of mischief. "It appears some things never change."

She tilted her head. "And here I thought dukes were fearless."

"Oh, we are." He offered his arm. "But even a duke knows better than to underestimate Lady Lora Preston."

She laughed again, genuine and light. "Perhaps I've gained a reputation."

"One that's well-deserved."

She rested her hand lightly on his forearm. "Shall we continue? There are some new faces you might be interested to meet."

"Lead the way." Rockford gestured gracefully. "I'm at your disposal."

They continued their stroll through the ballroom, weaving elegantly between clusters of guests. The soft glow of candlelight bathed the room in a warm ambiance. The music, a combination of strings and pianoforte, blended into a cheerful melody that underscored the murmur of conversations.

The fragrant blooms strategically placed throughout the rooms and hallways added a subtle sweetness to the air, with the heady aroma of roses and honeyed notes of jasmine. The crisp, clean scent of lilies provided a refreshing contrast, and lavender added a calming, herbal undertone. Amid the floral symphony, a faint trace of lemon and smoke lingered, unexpected, yet easy to overlook.

As they walked, Rockford leaned in slightly. "I must admit, it's refreshing to be back here. London has its charms, but it lacks the... authenticity of Sommer-by-the-Sea."

Lora glanced up at him. "It's a place that's filled with nostalgia."

"Indeed," he nodded in agreement. "Tell me, who among our

old acquaintances are present tonight?"

She pointed discreetly with her fan toward a distinguished gentleman speaking animatedly near the fireplace. "Lord Penton is here, still regaling anyone who'll listen with tales of his travels."

Rockford smiled. "Some things truly never change."

"And over there," she continued, "are Lord and Lady Atherstone. Their daughter Amelia has just returned from a season in London."

"Ah, to be young and enamored with the ton," he mused.

Lora gave him a sidelong glance. "You speak as though you're ancient."

"Merely experienced," he replied with a wink.

Lora shook her head and chuckled. They paused briefly to greet a passing couple, exchanging pleasantries before moving on.

"How have you truly been, Rockford?" Lora asked softly as they resumed their walk. "It's been ages since we've had a proper conversation."

He considered her question for a moment. "Busy, as always. The responsibilities of the position, you know."

She nodded. "I can only imagine."

"But enough about me," he said, steering the conversation. "I've heard of your involvement with the clinic's expansion. That's quite an undertaking."

Her eyes brightened. "It's a cause I believe in deeply. Access to proper medical care is something everyone deserves."

He admired the passion in her expression; it lit up her face and made her even more beautiful. "Your dedication does you credit."

Lora's smile widened at the compliment. She turned her gaze briefly toward the crowd.

As they moved through the ballroom, a sharp, clipped voice rose above the hum of conversation. Rockford's attention snapped to a group of men near the fireplace, their hushed but urgent tones setting them apart from the polite chatter around them. One man jabbed a finger toward another, his expression taut with frustration. Another shook his head sharply, his lips pressed into a thin line as if restraining his temper.

Their well-tailored coats and commanding stances suggested they were politicians, or at least men accustomed to wielding influence. Whatever their dispute, it was no idle discussion. Rockford glanced back at Lora, her voice still echoing in his thoughts, but his curiosity pulled him toward the gathering storm brewing by the hearth.

Lora noticed his momentary distraction and followed his gaze, leaning in slightly. "They seem quite… engaged, don't they?"

Rockford nodded. "Indeed. It appears they're discussing something of great importance." He wondered what had them so excited.

"There is Lady Grantham. We must say hello." Lora gestured near the fireplace. Rockford glanced at her, noting her expression. She seemed genuinely curious, not mischievous.

"By all means." With a subtle squeeze of her arm, he guided her closer to the group, keen to catch a bit of their conversation without drawing too much attention.

"…this highwayman is ruining everything we've planned." The snippet of conversation reached his ears, piquing his interest.

"Interesting," Rockford murmured under his breath, his gaze never wavering from the group. It seemed there was more at stake tonight than mere social pleasantries.

"We must act now." The man's agitation grew. He was at the edge of panic. "I say we confront him tonight, armed and ready."

Rockford watched as the others walked the man out onto the terrace. "Fear clouds judgment," his voice barely perceptible above the din of the ballroom. The truth of his words resonated with him as he considered their next move.

Lora turned to him, her eyes filled with concern. "What are we going to do? This highwayman seems unstoppable."

Rockford maintained his composure. "If I were in their position, I'd focus on a strategic plan," he said in a calm and steady manner. "First, they need to concentrate on finding the solution rather than dwelling on the obstacle. Panicking and rushing into action will only make things worse. It could get them killed. Second, they need to gather more information, think several steps ahead, and set a trap to outsmart him. Rushing into action without a clear path most often leads to disaster."

Lora nodded slowly, absorbing his words. "You're very good at this." There was an appreciation in her voice he hadn't heard before.

"It's the second best thing I do." He gave her a smile that could charm the birds from the trees.

"Dare I ask what is the best thing you do?" She bit the inside of her cheek to prevent from smiling.

He leaned close and whispered, "I'm a gentleman, my la-dy…but I do have my moments."

Lora's eyes twinkled with amusement, and a subtle smile played on her lips. He observed the blush creep from her neck onto her cheeks. "I do enjoy a man with moments, Your Grace."

"Good evening, Your Grace, Lora." Lady Harriet and several others passed by them, their faces alight with excitement.

"Lora, you must come at once," one of them said urgently. "Lady Dorset wishes to speak with you about the clinic."

Lora glanced at Rockford, a question in her eyes.

He gently untucked her hand from his arm. "You go ahead," he said with a reassuring smile. "I'll be here."

With Lady Lora whisked away by her friends, Rockford was momentarily alone. He made his way towards the terrace. With any luck, the men would still be there.

The cool night air was a welcome contrast to the warmth of the ballroom. Rockford stepped onto the terrace, his eyes adjusting to the dim light. He spotted the group huddled together, their voices low but urgent.

He positioned himself near a stone pillar, close enough to catch fragments of their conversation without drawing attention to himself.

"…must find a way to deal with him," one voice hissed. "If he continues, he could expose all of us.

"Do you think he knows about the gun shipments?" another voice, laced with anxiety, asked.

"It's possible," a third voice replied, a hint of caution in his tone. "We need to be cautious."

"And the documents," a different voice interjected. "If there were intercepted…"

"Which documents?" someone demanded sharply.

"The correspondence you altered addressed to the royal council," came the hushed response.

"If that falls into the wrong hands," the first voice said, "there is a good chance they will see it was forged…"

Forged royal documents? Arms shipments? Correspondence? Financial Records? Rockford's heart quickened. He needed to know more, but the conversation shifted.

"Keep an eye on Hastings," the cautious voice said. "He's been asking too many questions. We can't afford any mistakes, not with the arms trade involved."

Rockford strained to hear more, but the men went off in different directions, their expressions tense. As Rockford turned to re-enter the ballroom, he nearly collided with Barrington.

"There you are. I was beginning to think you had disappeared." Barrington stepped aside, allowing him to enter.

"Just needed a breath of fresh air. Do you know the men who just left the terrace?"

Barrington looked toward where Rockford gestured. The men had already been absorbed into the crowd. "No, I didn't get a clear look at them." Barrington glanced at him. "Why do you ask?"

They walked into the ballroom. "They had some interesting information."

"Here?" Barrington's eyes widened in surprise, and then slowly, his expression turned into an approving glance. "We can't talk here, obviously. Meet me tomorrow at my club. We can talk there."

Rockford nodded as they made their way to the refreshment table.

⟫⟫⟫⟪⟪⟪

"LADY DORSET'S QUESTION was simple enough to answer. Of course, the project is going forward." Lora stood with Harriet, the others dancing or at the refreshment table.

"You're to have a rest from the clinic and all its happenings tonight. At least pretend you're having a good time." Harriet paused. She wasn't fooled. She stepped closer, lowering her voice. "You seem preoccupied. What are you chewing on?"

Lora sighed, glancing around to make certain no one else was within earshot. "Father spoke to me before our guests arrived."

Harriet raised an eyebrow. "There is more to this story. What did he tell you?"

Lora, who had been looking out at the dance floor turned to Harriet. "He's leaving for Brighton in the morning, and he made it quite clear that when he returns, he expects to know the name of my suitor."

Harriet's eyes widened in surprise. "Oh, Lora. I feared this would happen."

"Yes, I know. You have tried to spare me this embarrassment." He let out a deep sigh.

"The first thing we are going to do is let him see you having a good time dancing the night away."

Lora laughed. "You're right. Get him wondering who I'm going to choose."

Harriet smilid, a mischievous glint in her eyes. "Exactly. Now, I haven't seen you on the dance floor all night. There are several eligible gentlemen here tonight," Harriet said as she scanned the room. "Shall we find you a charming dance partner or two?"

Lora smiled politely, though her thoughts were still on Rockford. "Who do you have in mind, Harriet?"

Harriet's gaze landed on two gentlemen engaged in conversation. "There's Lord Penton. He seems to be wherever you are. And there is Mr. Whitfield. He comes from quite a charming and excellent family. You should get on the dance floor unless you want your father to take action. Would you like me to introduce you?"

Lora hesitated, her gaze drifting back to where she had last seen Rockford. "Lord Penton can travel all he wants. He is still as dull as dishwater. He came up to me earlier. I suppose it wouldn't hurt to meet Mr. Whitfield. I understand he is the owner of one of the new mills on the Sommer River."

Harriet beamed and quickly led Lora over to him.

"Lady Lora, may I introduce Mr. Whitfield. He is new to Sommer-by-the-Sea, most recently from Royston." Harriet turned to the gentleman. "Mr. Whitfield, this is Lady Lora Preston."

Mr. Whitfield bowed respectfully as the music started. "It is an honor to meet you, Lady Lora."

"The pleasure is mine, Mr. Whitfield. Welcome to Fallsmith." Lora inclined her head gracefully.

"Lady Lora, I hoped you would honor me with a dance." He held out his hand.

Lora put her hand in his. "Excuse us, Lady Harriet."

"By all means," Harriet said with a satisfied smile as Lora and Mr. Whitfield took to the dance floor.

"Lady Lora," Mr. Whitfield began, "have you had the chance to visit the new botanical gardens in town? They've recently added some rare orchids that are quite stunning."

Lora's eyes lit up with interest. "I haven't had the pleasure yet, but I've heard wonderful things about the gardens. I passed by when a shipment of flowers and exotic plants arrived for the new hothouse. Do you enjoy botany, Mr. Whitfield?"

"I do, indeed," he replied. "There's something quite peaceful about spending time among the flowers. It's a welcome respite from the busyness of daily life."

"I can imagine," Lora nodded. "I've always found nature to be very calming. Do you have a favorite bloom?"

Mr. Whitfield thought for a moment. "I'd have to say the camellia. It's an exotic choice from the Orient, but there's something timeless about its beauty and elegance. And you, Lady Lora?"

"I've always been fond of lavender," she replied with a smile. "The scent is soothing, the flower is a lovely color, and it reminds me of home."

As they continued to dance, Mr. Whitfield glanced around the room. "It's been a long time since I've been to Sommer-by-the-Sea."

Lora smiled. "Have you had the chance to reconnect with anyone this evening?"

"A few acquaintances, yes," he said. "But I must admit, meeting you has been the highlight of my evening."

Lora blushed slightly. "You're too kind, Mr. Whitfield."

As she glided across the dance floor with Mr. Whitfield, his words became a distant murmur, hardly penetrating the haze of her thoughts. The room swirled around her in a blur of colors and laughter, but her attention was drawn beyond her partner's shoulder. There, at the edge of the ballroom, stood Rockford. Although his tall figure stood partially in the shadows, his gaze was unmistakably fixed on her, piercing through the crowd with an intensity that sent a thrill racing up her spine. The world seemed to slow, the music fading as their eyes locked across the distance.

In that charged moment, he gave a subtle nod, a gesture so slight that it could have gone unnoticed by anyone not utterly captivated by him. Her heart skipped a beat, then fluttered wildly like a captive bird yearning for release. A warm flush bloomed in her cheeks, spreading through her like fire leaving her both exhilarated and unsteady. The air between them felt tangible, stretched taut with unspoken words and lingering possibilities.

Lora barely noticed when Mr. Whitfield spun her gracefully, his polite smile not reaching the depths of emotion she sensed from Rockford's mere glance. *What is he thinking?* she wondered, her mind racing. *Does he feel this compelling pull as I do?* The questions tumbled in her thoughts, igniting a spark of anticipation and desire she hadn't allowed herself to acknowledge until now.

As the dance drew to a close, she found herself breathless, not from the waltz, but from the profound connection that had passed between her and Rockford in those fleeting, stolen moments. The awareness lingered and left her longing for more.

Chapter Four

ROCKFORD'S GAZE SHIFTED from Lady Lora. He spotted Sir Reginald Medburn near the terrace door in a heated discussion with another guest. The flickering light from the terrace torches cast shadows on their faces, accentuating the intensity of their exchange. He made his way over, catching pieces of their conversation about local land disputes. As he approached, the other gentleman excused himself and walked away.

Medburn was a man of average height. His neatly trimmed grey hair and sharp dark eyes suggested a man of authority and wisdom. The lines on his face spoke of years spent in negotiation and leadership, each wrinkle earned with experience and resilience. Rockford knew that behind Medburn's calm exterior was a man who could be both shrewd and fair. It was a combination that had earned him respect and, at times, fear among his peers.

"Sir Reginald," Rockford greeted with a polite nod. "It's been a while."

Medburn turned, his expression softening as he recognized Rockford. "Rockford, indeed, it has. How have you been?"

"Busy with parliamentary duties," Rockford replied. "I couldn't help but overhear your discussion. Land disputes can be quite challenging."

Medburn sighed. "The proposed expansion of the clinic requires additional land, which the local council plans to acquire through compulsory purchase."

"No wonder the landowners are upset. They will be forced to sell even if they don't want to, and without the ability to negotiate the selling price."

Medburn shook his head. "There is that, but there are concerns that the increased activity and noise will disrupt the quiet nature of the area. But their bigger issue is the potential for lowering the property values."

Rockford nodded thoughtfully. He understood their concerns. "I see. It's a delicate balance between public good and private interests. Have there been any proposals to address these concerns?"

Medburn shrugged. "Some have suggested relocating the clinic to a less populated area, but that would defeat the purpose of making it easy for those in need to get to it. Others suggest paying the landowners more money and making improvements to the area to lessen the impact, but it's a fiercely debated issue."

As Rockford nodded thoughtfully, he noticed Lord Barrington approaching with Mrs. Bainbridge by his side. Medburn followed Rockford's gaze and smiled politely.

"Good evening, Barrington, Mrs. Bainbridge," Medburn greeted them as they came up beside them.

"Good evening, Sir Reginald," Barrington replied with a nod. "Rockford, Mrs. Bainbridge demanded she greet you."

"If you'll excuse me, I must attend to another matter." Medburn turned to Rockford. "It was good speaking with you."

"Of course, Sir Reginald," Rockford replied. "Thank you for the conversation."

Medburn bowed slightly and stepped away, leaving Rockford, Barrington, and Mrs. Bainbridge to continue their discussion.

"Mrs. Bainbridge, it's a pleasure to see you." Rockford inclined his head respectfully.

Mrs. Bainbridge returned the smile, her eyes twinkling. "Your Grace, the pleasure is mine. How have you been?"

"Busy with parliamentary duties, as always," Rockford replied. "But it's good to be back in Sommer-by-the-Sea. And you, milady?"

"Quite well, thank you. The community has been busy, as you can see," Mrs. Bainbridge said, gesturing to the lively ballroom.

Rockford nodded. "Indeed. I was just speaking with some of the guests about the expansion of Dr. Manning's clinic. It seems to be the topic of the day. What are your thoughts on the project?"

Mrs. Bainbridge's expression grew thoughtful. "I believe it's a noble endeavor. Dr. Manning's work has been invaluable to the community. However, there are concerns."

Rockford sighed. "Yes, I've heard quite a bit tonight. It's a complex issue, but I'm hopeful a way can be found to address them and support Dr. Manning's needed work."

"Honoria, Lord Barrington." Lady Beatrice glided towards the refreshment table with an effortless grace, her gown sweeping elegantly across the floor. She paused, her smile warm yet composed, as she inclined her head in greeting.

"Lady Beatrice, you know Duke Rockford." Mrs. Bainbridge motioned toward him with a slight nod.

"Of course." Lady Beatrice smiled warmly at Rockford. "It's always a pleasure to see you, although it has been some time." She glanced at Rockford and Barrington with a coy smile. "Would you gentlemen mind if I stole Mrs. Bainbridge away? Just for a short time." She pinched her forefinger and thumb together to emphasize the brevity.

Mrs. Bainbridge glanced at him and Barrington. "Excuse me. I shant be long."

As the ladies took their leave, Barrington leaned toward Rockford. "There's been an odd fellow around town. Sanderson mentioned noticing him a few times."

Rockford raised an eyebrow. "Oh? Should we be concerned?"

Barrington shrugged subtly. "That's difficult to say. He's been seen at the tavern and around gatherings but keeps to himself.

Seems to disappear before anyone gets a good look or has a chance to approach him."

"Interesting," Rockford glanced at the empty corner. "He blends into the background?"

"Exactly," Barrington agreed. "Just something to be aware of. With everything happening around the clinic and the recent rumors, it's wise to stay cautious."

Rockford nodded. "Agreed. We'll keep a wary eye out for him."

Before the conversation could continue, the soft rustle of silk caught Rockford's attention. Lady Lora approached, her eyes bright and inquisitive. Rockford turned to her, allowing a warm smile to soften his features. The enigma would have to wait. He welcomed the distraction of her company.

"Lady Lora." He offered her a warm smile. "Would you care for some punch?"

"Thank you, Your Grace," she replied, accepting the cup he handed her. "Are you enjoying yourself?"

"Quite." He gave her his best neutral stare.

"I haven't noticed you on the dance floor."

Rockford turned to her, his neutral stare tuning into a playful glint in his eye. "Would you do me the honor of a dance?"

Lora's eyes sparkled with delight. She put the cup down. "I would be delighted, Your Grace."

"You'll excuse us, Barrington." Rockford didn't wait for a response. He offered her his arm, and they made their way to the dance floor. The music swelled, and they moved gracefully in time with the melody.

"You dance beautifully," he said. "You're no longer stepping on my feet, I see."

"Thank you, Your Grace. And you've finally learned to lead properly," she replied with a smile.

Rockford chuckled, appreciating the lighthearted banter. It felt natural and easy, a pleasant contrast to the more serious matters occupying his mind. As they danced, he found himself lost in the rhythm. The warmth of Lady Lora's hand in his and the grace with which she moved made the moment feel almost timeless.

As they glided across the floor, Rockford's gaze swept briefly over the assembled guests. His eyes met those of Lord Fallsmith, Lady Lora's father, who stood at the edge of the ballroom. The older gentleman watched them with a discerning eye. When their gazes connected, Lord Fallsmith gave a subtle nod, a hint of approval in his expression.

Rockford felt a surge of satisfaction at the unspoken acknowledgment. This moment was unlike any he had known before, uncomplicated, effortless, right.

Here, with Lady Lora, everything felt right. He was drawn to her not just by her beauty but by her spirit and intelligence. She was a woman who could stand at his side, not behind him. For now, there was only the dance, the music, and the woman in his arms.

He was disappointed when the music ended, the moment slipping away too quickly. They bowed to each other, lingering just a heartbeat longer than propriety dictated before he escorted her back to Barrington. As they approached, he noted Mrs. Bainbridge's return, her familiar smile suggesting she had been watching with keen interest.

Their conversation was light, but a subtle shift in the air caught Rockford's attention—an undercurrent of unease threading through the hum of the ballroom. It wasn't until he noticed the small breaks in conversation around them that he turned.

A figure moved through the crowd with deliberate steps.

Charles Hastings carried himself with a confidence that bordered on arrogance, his sharp gaze sweeping the room with shrewd intensity. The guests seemed to part slightly as he approached, their conversations softening, their glances wary, as if reluctant to draw his notice. He paused briefly at the edge of their group, studying each of them with a calculating gaze before he spoke.

Hastings was a tall, well-dressed gentleman, his self-confidence so polished it bordered on artificial, crafted to conceal a more calculating nature. His dark, neatly styled hair and sharp brown eyes lent him an air of precision, each glance cataloging weaknesses he could use in the future. His strong jawline and easy smile could disarm those around him, but to Rockford, it was merely a mask.

What are you concealing, Hastings? Rockford pondered, his suspicion of the man deepening with each encounter, Paris during the war, twice in London, and now here. As he endeavored to unravel the layers of what he was up to, he was well aware that he had to keep a vigilant eye on him. There was something amiss about the man, something that didn't tally.

"Good evening," Hastings greeted, his tone smooth but with an edge that set Rockford on alert.

"I must say," Hastings continued, "you both make quite the striking pair on the dance floor."

"Hastings," Rockford acknowledged with a nod, his expression neutral. "It's been some time."

"Indeed, it has," Hastings replied, his voice carrying a hint of something more. "I've been quite busy with various endeavors, but attending such splendid events is always a pleasure."

Lora smiled warmly. "Mr. Hastings, it's good to see you. Are you enjoying the gala?"

"Very much so, Lady Lora," Hastings said, his gaze lingering on her. "Your parents have truly outdone themselves. I've had the pleasure of calling on you quite often recently, and their hospitality is always impeccable."

Rockford's eyes narrowed slightly as he observed Hasting's smooth demeanor. The surge of protectiveness for Lora rose coupled with a gnawing suspicion.

Hastings turned to Rockford. "And I must commend you, Your Grace, on your resilience. Not many could handle the pressures of both London and the countryside with such ease."

Rockford's jaw tightened slightly, the sharpness of Hastings' words cutting deeper than he cared to admit. Memories of whispered scandals and sidelong glances within the ton flickered in his mind, rumors of intrigues that kept London's elite gossips busy for weeks but he forced them aside. He hadn't realized the gossip had reached Sommer-by-the-Sea. All the better. But Hastings' attention to Lora? That wasn't in the report he received, just that he was socializing in circles far above his station. For now, he straightened his posture and met Hastings' gaze with unwavering calm, determined not to give the man the satisfaction of a reaction. "Adaptation to duty is a necessity that some understand better than others, Mr. Hastings," he replied smoothly, his gaze steady.

"Quite right," Hastings agreed, his smile never wavering. "I've heard whispers of your recent endeavors in London. Scandals can be so trying, can't they? But I'm sure a man of your stature knows what to do."

Rockford regarded him coolly, a faint, mocking smile playing at the corners of his mouth. "Whispers are the preoccupation of idle minds," he said. "I choose not to lend them credence. It's fortunate that one's true character isn't defined by the fleeting amusements of the gossiping crowd." He paused, allowing his words to settle. "I trust you find more substantial matters to occupy your time?"

"Indeed." As the music began anew, Hastings turned his attention back to Lora. "Lady Lora, may I have the honor of this dance?"

Lora glanced at Rockford, seeking his silent counsel. He offered a reassuring nod, though a flicker of something unreadable passed over his features. Turning back to Hastings, she mustered a polite smile. "Of course, Mr. Hastings."

Hastings took Lora's hand and led her onto the dance floor. They moved gracefully to the lilting melody, their figures weaving among the elegantly dressed couples. Standing at the edge of the ballroom, Rockford watched them intently. The subtle barbs Hastings had delivered echoed in his mind, stirring an irritation he rarely allowed himself to feel. His fingers absently traced the faint scar concealed beneath his sleeve, a relic of battles past, the old wound seeming to throb in tandem with his rising tension.

As he observed Hastings and Lora, the pieces began to fall into place. Someone was stirring people up against the clinic expansion project Lora was involved with, and Hastings' name had been mentioned in connection with the unrest. And now, here he was, dancing with her, the very source of her troubles.

He fought to maintain his composure. Seeing Lady Lora in Hastings' arms evoked a mix of protectiveness and an unsettling emotion he was reluctant to name. Hastings' hand rested on her waist with an ease that bordered on impropriety. His fingers splayed just a fraction too intimately.

A rush of heated anger shot through Rockford, igniting a flame he struggled to quell. He knew all too well that Hastings delighted in provocation. He reveled in any sign of unease. Rockford refused to grant him that satisfaction. Yet, observing Lady Lora smile graciously at Hastings, unaware of the man's true nature, gnawed at him. The thought that she might be drawn into Hastings' web unsettled him intensely.

Beside him, Barrington followed his gaze, his expression darkening. "Hastings knows exactly what he's doing," he muttered, his tone edged with frustration. "He's testing your patience. If we're not careful, he'll manipulate the situation to his advantage before we realize it." He fell silent for a moment, then added, "The scandal is spreading faster than we anticipated, just as you hoped. Hastings is taking the bait."

Rockford gave a terse nod. "Indeed. Hastings revels in sowing discord, a talent he perfected in London. And you're correct. He aims to provoke me, but I won't oblige him."

"Good," Barrington said firmly. "We need to stay the course. We might not get another chance before the king arrives. The more he spreads the scandal, the more likely the highwayman will contact you, which will bring us closer to exposing the corruption."

"Absolutely," Rockford agreed, though his attention drifted to the dance floor. Hastings whispered something to Lady Lora, causing her to laugh softly. The sound, usually so delightful, now struck him as vulnerable. His gaze remained fixed on them, every movement, every gesture under his vigilant scrutiny.

Turning away, Rockford stared into the inky blackness beyond the window, his thoughts unraveling into dangerous territory. Barrington's words echoed in his mind: *We might not get another chance.* He had fought countless battles, but this war was different, waged in parlors and ballrooms, where missteps were more lethal than swords. Every decision carried unseen consequences.

Memories of treachery resurfaced, the sting of betrayal still fresh despite the years. It had happened during the war, a trusted ally turning against him in the heat of battle, leading men to their deaths. The irony wasn't lost on him now. He was contemplating a similar deception, not against an enemy, but against a trusted friend he held in high regard.

Lora.

His grip tightened on the glass in his hand. Duty had always been his compass, but now it pointed directly against the one person who had reignited a light in his life. The thought clawed at him, each step closer to betrayal pressing relentlessly on his conscience. Protecting her meant deceiving her. A cruel irony.

But could he do it?

He swallowed hard, the bitterness of the truth settling in his gut. If Hastings was aware that he was suspicious of him, the man wouldn't hesitate to use Lora against him. If she remained unaware, she couldn't be manipulated. If she believed in the ruse, Hastings would have no reason to suspect otherwise. But would she ever forgive him for it? Would he forgive himself?

He exhaled slowly, the weight of the decision pressing against his chest.

"I intend to draw Hastings out, Barrington," Rockford said at last, his voice low but firm. "He already sees me as a rival, and I'll use that to uncover his plans. If I court Lady Lora, I can stay close enough to protect her while forcing Hastings to reveal his hand."

Barrington studied him, concern flickering across his features. "And when she learns the truth?"

Rockford hesitated. He had no answer for that.

"She may never forgive me," he admitted finally, his voice quieter. "But if it keeps her safe, I'll endure it."

Barrington shook his head. "You can't let Lady Lora or anyone else know about this plan. We have no idea who is betraying us."

"I know." Rockford paused, the gravity of his decision settling heavily on his shoulders. More was at stake than the clinic's expansion or stopping a mere highwayman. Someone had infiltrated the highest levels of government, and he and Barrington were the last line of defense. But Lady Lora… she was fiercely proud. In her eyes, he would become the betrayer, the one who shattered her trust.

Barrington's voice cut through his thoughts. "Is there no other way? Think of what this will cost her. What will it cost you?"

Rockford clenched his fists. "Do you think I haven't considered that? Hastings won't hesitate to use her against me if he suspects the truth. If sacrificing her trust spares her from becoming a pawn in his schemes, then it's a price I must pay." He met Barrington's gaze, desperation flashing before steely determination took over. "If our positions were reversed, you'd tell me we have no choice but to press on."

Barrington raised his glass, the liquid catching the dim light. "To the journey ahead."

"To the journey ahead," Rockford echoed. The words struck like a blow, conjuring unbidden memories of Captain Edward Langley. Langley had spoken that very phrase the night before the ambush, the betrayal that left scars far deeper than the one hidden beneath Rockford's sleeve.

His gaze drifted to Lady Lora, moving gracefully in Hastings' arms. The sight twisted something inside him. The memory of Langley's treachery merged with the looming reality of what he was about to do. Lady Lora glanced his way, her face lighting up with a radiant smile, the kind that had warmed him to his core. It was a silent beacon of her trust, a trust he was about to fracture.

Rockford held her gaze for a fleeting moment, the impact of his decision pressing harder than ever. "I'll see you at your club tomorrow," he murmured to Barrington, though his focus was no longer on the conversation. Each word felt like a stone sinking into his chest.

Without waiting for a response, he turned and strode toward the exit. Each step carried him further from her light, plunging him into the darkness of the night beyond. The lively melody of the ballroom faded into the rhythm of his pounding heart.

Stepping into the cool night air, Rockford inhaled deeply, the chill biting through his resolve. The path he had chosen would shield her, yes, but it would also fracture something irreparably. As the shadows of the estate loomed before him, the truth struck like a dagger: in saving her, he was losing himself.

Chapter Five

21 September 1822
Morning

THE MORNING SUNLIGHT peeked through the curtains in Rockford's study, a single ray crept across the room and landed squarely on his face, rudely waking him from oblivion. He threw his arm over his eyes to block the sun. It was less painful than trying to move. His head already ached. The last thing he wanted was to face the day. What a tangled mess. He'd rather be back in London facing that turmoil.

There was no turning back now. He tried to swallow, but his throat was as dry as the Sahara Desert. He lay still for a moment as pieces of the previous night's events came together.

The late evening passed in a whirl of blurred faces and distant laughter, the lively gala dissolving into the background. Later, in the quiet of his study, he sought comfort at the bottom of a crystal decanter. The fiery burn of the whiskey was a welcome penance, a searing reminder of the choice he made. One drink bled into the next, each sip further dulling the edge of his anguish yet deepening the hollow ache within him.

Images of Lady Lora drifted through his thoughts, her trusting smile, the way her eyes shone with unspoken feelings. The memory cut through the lingering haze, the weight of his decision pressing harder against him. He rubbed a weary hand over his face, regret settling heavily on his shoulders.

The silence of the room was suffocating, broken only by the

faint crackle of the dying fire. His fingers brushed against the glass on the desk, but as he lifted it, the dull clink against the wood told him what he already knew, it was empty. Just like last night's choices.

With his eyes still closed, he pressed his fingers to his temples, trying to will away the pounding in his skull. The mission was too important for him to be laid low by excess and self-pity. With a groan, he ran both hands down his face and forced his eyes open just as his valet entered, moving with practiced efficiency as he carried a tray into the room.

"Good morning, Your Grace."

"There's no need to shout, Jeffers." Rockford squeezed his eyes shut.

"Sorry, Your Grace," the valet whispered. "I've brought you a prairie oyster and some strong tea. It should help with the headache."

Rockford waved his hand gratefully. He wouldn't dare try to move his head. "Thank you, Jeffers. I'll need all the help I can get today."

Jeffers set the tray down on the desk. "This should help as well, sir." He lightly placed a compress on Rockford's forehead.

"Bless you. That feels good." The pounding in his head was nothing compared to the ache in his chest. Every heartbeat was a painful reminder of what he planned to do. The cool compress on his forehead provided little relief against the storm raging inside him.

After a few minutes, Rockford sat up and glanced at the clock. It was nearly time to meet Barrington at the club. Rising from the sofa, he steeled himself for the challenges ahead. There was no room for doubt or regret now.

This is to protect her, he reminded himself as he and Jeffers climbed the stairs to his room to clean up and prepare for his meeting.

As Jeffers laid out his clothes, Rockford's thoughts drifted back to his time in the military. The memory of that April day in

France remained vivid, the damp earth heavy with recent rain, the acrid bite of gunpowder clinging to the air, and beneath it all, a faint, fleeting sharpness he couldn't quite place, tangled with the lingering smoke. Crouching, their footsteps were muffled by the underbrush as they advanced through the outskirts of the eerily quiet city of Toulouse, the tension wound tight. He scanned the area, scrutinizing the sparse trees and the distant silhouette of the city. He and his second in command, Captain Edward Langley, had meticulously crafted the attack plan, ensuring they accounted for every detail, including the potential weakness of their right flank. To ensure success, he would lead the troops on the right flank, but Langley reasoned the men needed him to manage the entire plan. Langley stepped up and volunteered to take the right flank.

All week long, they advanced only to be pushed back. Now, with their new plan, he moved his men forward and found there were no defenses in sight. As Langley had noted, the morning mist that clung to the ground would hide them. Suddenly, out of the mist, the deafening roar of cannon fire shattered the silence.

"Ambush!" someone shouted, but it was too late. The French were upon them, rifle balls whizzing past, tearing through the foliage and flesh alike. Rockford's voice cut through the chaos. "Defensive line! Take cover. Return fire!"

He moved swiftly, rallying his men and directing them to safer positions. Rockford himself took a position at the front, his pistol ready. He fired at the advancing enemy, his aim steady despite the chaos around him. "Hold the line!" he shouted, his voice unwavering.

As he assessed the situation around him, Rockford saw a gap in their right flank. Where was Langley? As Rockford moved closer, Langley was nowhere to be seen. A sense of unease settled over him. He quickly put another officer in command and moved to investigate.

Creeping through the underbrush, Rockford kept low, his senses on high alert. The sounds of battle raged around him, but he focused on finding Langley. He had to be alive. They had served together for the last two years. He couldn't think the worst, but by god, he would carry his friend on his back to get him behind their line if necessary.

As he neared the edge of the clearing, he heard voices and found cover behind a tree. Slowly, he moved until he could see the men and stopped. He saw him, Langley, standing with a French officer. They were talking and pointing towards specific areas of English's defenses, areas Rockford had discussed in confidence with Langley.

Betrayal. The realization hit him like a bullet to the chest. His blood ran cold. He watched for a moment longer, confirming his worst fears, before hurrying back to his men. There was no time to lose.

"Regroup!" he shouted as he reached his troops. "Follow me!"

The men responded instantly, their trust in Rockford unwavering. He led them in a swift counterattack, fiercely pushing back the French. Despite their efforts, some of his men had fallen. There was no time to mourn. Rockford focused on saving as many as he could and turning the tide of the battle.

His pistol fired one last shot before the chamber clicked hollow. With a muttered curse, he slid the weapon back into its holster. Scanning the battlefield for an opening, he knew he'd have to rely on his wits now, directing his men where they were strongest while keeping the enemy off balance.

Langley rushed to him as his troop gained ground, his face a mask of confusion. "What's happening? This isn't what we planned!"

"Neither was your betrayal," he growled, his rage all consuming. "Why, Langley?" Rockford demanded, his voice taut with anger and hurt. "Why deceive us?"

Langley stared at him, his gaze cold. "You wouldn't understand. There's more at play here than your narrow sense of duty."

"You're endangering everything we fought for! What have

you done?" Rockford shouted over the din of battle. He drew his sword. "How could you betray us like this?"

But Rockford, consumed by anger and the need to protect his men, didn't wait to listen. They clashed violently, their swords flashing in the chaos. Langley's blade struck with precision, slicing across Rockford's forearm before he could fully deflect the blow. Pain shot through him, warm blood seeping into his sleeve, but he gritted his teeth and pressed forward.

As the fight reached its peak, Rockford had Langley at his mercy. "Explain yourself now, traitor!"

Before Langley could speak, an explosion rocked the battlefield. The force of the blast knocked them both to the ground, dazed and disoriented.

When Rockford regained consciousness, Langley was gone. The enemy had retreated, and the battle had shifted, but the questions remained.

"Langley!" Rockford shouted, but his voice was swallowed by the sounds of war. He scanned the area desperately, but there was no trace of his former friend. The pressing advance of French troops forced him to rally his men, pushing thoughts of Langley aside for the moment.

By the day's end, the British forces had held their position, but at a high cost. As Rockford walked among the wounded and the fallen, exhausted, he pushed on. Reports came in. Captain Edward Langley was missing in action. Official records would later note his disappearance, but the truth of his betrayal remained a burden that Rockford alone carried.

He filed a report detailing Langley's treachery, but without concrete evidence or a body, his superiors received it with skepticism. Rumors spread quietly among the ranks. Some whispered that Langley had been captured, and others suggested desertion. The ambiguity shrouding the event left lingering doubts.

The unresolved nature of Langley's fate gnawed at Rockford. The failure to bring a traitor to justice haunted him, a phantom lingering at the edge of his conscience. And now, as he faced the possibility of deceiving Lady Lora, the parallels pressed heavily on his soul.

Duty had always been his guiding star, but his feelings for Lady Lora had now clouded his path. The thought of deceiving her was unbearable, yet the thought of failing in his mission was equally daunting.

Rockford's mind snapped back to the present as Jeffers handed him a fresh shirt. "Your Grace, is everything satisfactory?"

He nodded absently, his hand unconsciously tracing the scar on his forearm, the one left by Langley's blade. "Just lost in thought, Jeffers," he murmured. "Thank you."

As he dressed, Rockford steeled himself for the day ahead. The echoes of the past began to quiet.

"Jeffers, order my carriage," he instructed.

"Of course, Your Grace." Jeffers inclined his head before exiting the room.

Rockford took a deep breath, gazing out the window as the morning light fully embraced the day. As he descended the stairs, the burden of both past and present rested on his shoulders. Yet, beneath it all, a flicker of hope remained. The truth would prevail someday, and the shadows of his actions would finally be dispelled. He hoped. They had to.

Chapter Six

THE SOMMER RIVER Club, with its plush velvet chairs and polished mahogany tables, was a haven of quiet sophistication, a stark contrast to the busy streets outside. Rockford found Barrington seated in a private corner, a stack of documents spread out before him.

"Good morning, Rockford." Barrington looked up from his papers. "I trust you rested well?"

"Well enough." Rockford sat across from his friend, signaling the footman for a drink.

Barrington put down the papers and gave Rockford his full attention. "Indeed. Are you absolutely certain about this? Misleading Lady Lora is no small matter. We must be certain there's no other way."

Rockford leaned forward, the gravity of his decision written on his face. He took a deep breath, knowing he had to justify his course of action to Barrington and himself.

"I've considered every possibility. The stakes are too high to waver now," His voice steady despite the turmoil deep in his heart. "If we don't act before the king arrives, the consequences could be disastrous."

Barrington sat back in his chair, crossing his arms. "Go on."

"The rumors are spreading faster than we anticipated, faster than we can control," Rockford explained, his tone edged with urgency. "That's exactly what we intended. It paints me as someone vulnerable, someone the true culprit might believe they can manipulate.

"Hastings has expanded my role in the scandal to being an even greater rogue. He spun the story so convincingly that even those outside his circle are starting to believe it. If we don't act before the king arrives, the scandal we created will no longer be just a tool, it will become the distraction that allows real corruption to thrive. Worse, it risks drawing His Majesty into a carefully woven web of deceit, forcing him to act based on falsehoods rather than truth. A single misstep in his judgment could destabilize the government, weaken our allies, and leave the crown compromised.

"I cannot allow that." His jaw tightened. "If playing the role Hastings has given me ensures we get to the truth, then that is the role I must play. Even if it costs me everything."

Barrington's brow furrowed, but he nodded. "So we stay with the plan."

"Precisely. Hastings must believe he's winning, but we need to act quickly," Rockford crossed his arms, his gaze fixed. "The chaos would only increase with His Majesty here."

Barrington leaned forward slightly. "And Lady Lora?"

Rockford's jaw tightened. "She's in danger because of Hastings. His efforts to undermine the clinic already threaten her work, but if he sees the Fallsmith fortune as an opportunity, that could make her an even bigger target. The only way to protect her is to stay close, and we both know she won't willingly accept our help if she knew the truth."

Barrington remained quiet, his expression stern as Rockford stood. "I see your point. Now that we know Hastings is involved, the scandal is more than just a means to lure him out. It's becoming a weapon our enemies could use against the monarchy. If public trust erodes, it's nearly impossible to regain. We can't let that happen."

"It's also our duty to prevent this from touching the king." Rockford leaned closer, his voice low. "Allowing this to escalate, would be a failure on our part."

"Exactly." Barrington paused, letting his words sink in before continuing.

"Acting now gives us the element of surprise. If we wait, Hastings and his allies could entrench themselves further, and it will be even harder to dismantle their plans."

Barrington nodded slowly, his expression thoughtful. "You've clearly thought this through."

"And then there's the legacy we'll leave behind," Rockford added quietly. "Resolving this scandal sets a precedent for dealing with corruption, securing the future of the kingdom. We can't afford to hesitate."

Barrington let out a long breath, the tension easing slightly from his shoulders. "Very well. We proceed as planned. But know this, Rockford, deceiving Lady Lora will be the hardest thing you'll ever do. Make sure you're ready to face that."

Rockford nodded, the gravity of his decision clear in his expression. "I am. For her sake and for the kingdom, I am. Now, let me tell you what I overheard last night."

The footman set a cup of coffee on the table. Rockford took a sip, then leaned closer to Barrington, lowering his voice. "The highwayman is targeting specific items, documents and shipments of arms, that could be linked to the corruption we've been investigating in London."

Barrington leaned forward, his expression sharpened. "What kind of documents?"

"Royal correspondence and financial records," Rockford replied grimly. "Worse, some of the royal documents have been forged."

Barrington's usual composure slipped. "Forged royal documents? If those reach the wrong hands—"

"They'll undermine trust in the monarchy itself," Rockford finished. "Recovering them is critical. The financial records implicate high-ranking officials, exposing just how deep this network runs."

Barrington nodded, his expression dark. "If the wrong people intercept those documents, it could be catastrophic."

"Exactly. And with the king arriving in four weeks, there's no time to waste."

Barrington exhaled, his mind already working through the possibilities. "We have some avenues to explore. Lord Whitfield has been unusually secretive, and there is something questionable about Sir Becket's financial dealings."

"And Hastings," Rockford added. "His rise among the wealthy and powerful is suspicious at best. We need to dig deeper into his connections before it's too late."

Barrington tossed the papers onto the table with a scowl. "Hastings isn't just a pawn. He's facilitating these transactions, an intermediary for corrupt politicians, brokering deals in exchange for wealth and influence. He's profiting from both sides of the scheme."

Rockford took another sip of coffee, his mind racing. "If he's this deeply entangled, bringing him down could unravel the network." He exhaled sharply. "But we'd need more than just suspicion. We need proof that his involvement ties back to the forgeries and the missing documents."

"Exactly," Barrington agreed.

Rockford's gaze darkened. "And Lady Lora? Hastings' interest in her isn't just social, is it?"

Barrington's expression turned grim. "No. He's after her fortune. The endowment from her grandmother is substantial. Marrying her would give him direct access to that wealth."

Rockford's posture stiffened. "How do you know this?"

Barrington let out a dry chuckle. "Because Hastings was careless enough to say it himself. I overheard him talking to Mr. Whitfield near the cliffs, both of them had been drinking. Hastings let slip that he had 'inside knowledge' from a banker about her endowment. He spoke as if her fortune was already his to claim."

Rockford's jaw clenched. "Then he's not just using the scandal to ruin me. He's maneuvering to trap her."

LORA'S DAY BEGAN as any other. She rose to a cup of hot cocoa brought in on a tray by Teresa. As she went about her morning routine, her thoughts drifted to the previous night. Dancing with Hastings had been pleasant enough, but it was her moments with Rockford that lingered. She couldn't explain why she felt so strongly about him. They had known each other since childhood. Perhaps that was the reason. Familiarity.

Finishing her cocoa, she dressed, took her pelisse and reticule, and headed downstairs.

"Your carriage is waiting as you requested, my lady," James said, opening the door and escorting her outside.

She took a deep breath, savoring the hint of a second summer mixed with the first chill of autumn. As James helped her into the carriage, she settled onto the seat, but her thoughts refused to do the same.

Rockford's words from last night lingered in her mind, weaving themselves into her growing uncertainty. Hastings had been attentive, charming even, yet something about him never felt quite real. Rockford, on the other hand... he had always been a contradiction, distant one moment, frustratingly mysterious the next. And yet, when she was with him, the world seemed sharper, more alive.

By the time she arrived at Lockford Hall, her thoughts were no clearer.

Soon, she was seated at Harriet's breakfast table, stirring her tea absentmindedly. "I'm conflicted about Rockford and Hastings," she admitted, staring into her cup. "They're so... different."

Harriet looked up, her eyes filled with gentle concern. "Different, how?"

"Rockford is steadfast and reliable, but often infuriatingly overprotective," Lora said with a sigh. "He reminds me of Father, always trying to steer my decisions."

"And Hastings?"

"He's intriguing," Lora said, her eyes brightening. "Charming in a way that feels refreshing. When we spoke after the gala, he showed genuine interest in the clinic and even suggested ways to secure funding."

Harriet furrowed slightly. "What sort of ways?"

"Loans for such projects can be arranged if one knows the right people," Lora explained. "He offered to introduce me to people who would be interested."

"Lora," Harriet said carefully, setting her cup down, "isn't it rather forward for him to discuss financial matters with you?"

"Perhaps," Lora admitted as she met her friend's gaze, "but he seemed sincere. It's hard not to be intrigued by someone who shares my passion for the clinic."

"Even so," Harriet cautioned, "gentlemen don't usually broach such topics with a lady he's just met. It might be wise to exercise caution."

"You think he has ulterior motives?" Lora asked, a hint of defensiveness in her tone.

Harriet hesitated. "Not necessarily, but with your inheritance and standing, some men may see more than just your admirable qualities."

Lora traced the rim of her teacup, her gaze distant. "I know. That's why I want someone who respects my independence and supports my work."

"Someone like Rockford?" Harriet suggested softly.

Lora gave a bitter laugh. "Rockford challenges me, yes, but he keeps so much to himself. He left the gala without a word. It's as if he's hiding something."

"Have you considered speaking with him about it?"

"Every time I try, there's a wall between us," Lora said, frustration creeping into her voice. "Hastings, though… he makes me feel appreciated. Listened to."

Harriet reached across the table, her hand covering Lora's.

"Just promise me you'll be cautious. Sometimes, people say what they believe you wish to hear."

"I suppose you're right," Lora murmured. "I shouldn't be too quick to trust."

"Exactly. And if you have doubts, take time to consider them carefully. Don't let anyone rush you."

"Thank you, Harriet." Lora managed a smile. "Your counsel means so much to me."

"Now," Harriet said warmly, "shall we walk in the gardens in town? I haven't been there in a while."

"I'd like that," Lora agreed. "It would be nice to clear my head." She put down her teacup. "I understand there are rare camellias in the botanical garden."

"Then it's settled," Harriet said, her eyes brightening. "We'll make a day of it. We may even stop at Madame Pembroke's shop. I understand she has some new gowns."

Chapter Seven

21 September 1822
Afternoon

ROCKFORD WALKED DOWN the steps of the Sommer River Club. Last evening's overindulgence lingered as a ghost of memory, but the tension between his satisfaction and unease gnawed at him. Barrington had offered him a chance to step away from this project, yet an unseen force compelled him forward. Help Lady Lora? To what? To loathe him? To witness her torment? To be the architect of her suffering? He paused for less than a heartbeat before moving on. No, none of that was true. He would find a way to support her through the aftermath. To prove he truly cared. To protect her.

Enough. He breathed in the crisp afternoon air, a stark contrast to the tense atmosphere he had just left behind. His mind turned to the importance of the information he and Barrington had discussed. The scandals surrounding George IV had seemingly ceased when he was coronated. Yet, he couldn't fathom what these documents might contain that could surpass the infamy of forbidding his wife from the coronation or his long-standing affair and illegitimate children. The weapons were something else.

Rockford sought a momentary escape as he stepped into the bustling Westmore Commons, letting the atmosphere distract him from his inner turmoil. Market day was bustling with vibrant stalls displaying a riot of colors and the lively chatter of vendors and customers filling the air. Aromas of freshly baked bread and sizzling street food wafted through the crowd, offering a welcome reprieve from his thoughts. For now, he wanted to lose himself in the vibrant atmosphere, to let the energy and life around him lighten the burden of his mission, if only for a few moments.

"Your Grace." The woman dipped a slight curtsy with a smile as she passed by.

"My Lady." Rockford touched the brim of his hat in salute, returning her smile before continuing on his way.

He had always found these excursions in Sommer-by-the-Sea pleasant and invigorating, a welcome contrast to the commotion of London streets. Now, in the early autumn, the town and its surroundings enjoyed the wind off the North Sea. Perhaps later, he'd walk along the cliffs. If he concentrated, he could almost hear the thunder of the waves and see the rushing surf. Yet, the warmth of the afternoon sun did little to chase away the persistent chill of uncertainty that had settled in his chest. The mission's shadow loomed no matter how he tried to push it away.

As he walked, he tipped his hat to a few familiar faces, exchanging polite greetings. He stopped at a haberdashery stall drawn by a display of finely crafted hats. One in particular caught his eye, a stylish hat with a unique feather tucked into the hat band.

He picked it up and tried it on, turning toward the shop window to inspect the fit. As he adjusted the brim, his gaze flicked to the reflection in the glass. A gentleman stood a short distance behind him, his attention seemingly on the same display.

The man gave a brief, appreciative nod, perhaps in approval of the hat, before shifting his gaze and continuing down the street. Rockford set the hat back in its place. He strolled on, passing the bookstall, when a familiar figure among the crowd caught his attention.

His heart gave a small, unexpected jolt.

"Lady Lora," he greeted, inclining his head. "A pleasant surprise to see you."

⟫⟫⟩✷⟨⟪⟪

THEY BEGAN TO walk on together, weaving through the bustling stalls. Lora glanced at the various vendors, then back at Rockford. "It's such an active place. I imagine it must be quite different from your usual surroundings."

Rockford smiled. "Indeed, it is. But I enjoy the change of pace."

Lora hesitated for a moment, then continued, "You mentioned you were visiting Lord Barrington. How long will you be staying in Sommer-by-the-Sea?"

Rockford paused, considering his response. "For a few more weeks, at least. There are some matters I need to attend to here." He glanced around and then refocused on her. "But I must admit, being here seems… perfect."

Lora kept her eyes fixed on him, a hint of nervousness in her voice. "I've always loved it here. There's just something special about it, don't you think?" She smiled, perhaps a bit too widely, and her chatter was more than usual, filling the space between them.

He noticed how she was so focused on him, not even looking where she was going. When the door to the fabric store swung open, he gently held her back, narrowly avoiding a mishap. She glanced at him, a grateful smile on her lips.

"Thank you, Your Grace," she said softly.

"Of course," Rockford replied, his tone warm. She didn't utter a word for several minutes.

"Did you enjoy the gala?" she eventually said, giving him a side glance.

"I definitely did." He gave him a side glance. "The article in the Sommer Chronicle was nothing but accolades." He nodded. "They mentioned how the event was '*a dazzling display of elegance* and generosity, bringing together the finest of society for a noble cause.' It was truly a night to remember." He leaned toward her. "Should I go on?"

Her laugh bubbled with delight. "Please, spare me. I believe Mama read the article to me several dozen times this morning. The Chronicle was quite generous. Mother was pleased. She enjoys creating the autumn event and is already planning one for the winter. You must attend."

"If I am still in Sommer-by-the-Sea, I will make every effort to be with you as long as you save a dance for me." He leaned close to her. "Now that I've learned to lead, I must practice and show off my skills."

Lora's eyes sparkled with amusement. "You're going to be quite the sought-after dance partner," she teased, her earlier nerves giving way to genuine laughter.

Her laughter, soft and unguarded, eased the tension gripping him. Rockford found himself drawn to her warmth, her charm a momentary reprieve from his worries. The vibrant display of flowers ahead provided an easy excuse to linger. "Do you have a favorite flower?"

"Lavender." She glanced at the assortment and didn't look at him. But he noticed her purse her lips trying to hide her smile. "The scent is so soothing, and the color is lovely."

Rockford nodded. "Ah, a muse for poets and dreamers, a gentle lullaby that calms the spirit." He turned and caught her eye. "Lavender depicts the depth of emotion and beauty of a tender heart." He paused. "I think lavender fits you very well," he said, his voice low and promising.

Lora blushed slightly as he held her stare. "Thank you, Your Grace. Perhaps we should move on."

"Of course." He picked up her hand and looped it through his arm. They walked on in companionable silence for the next few moments, each lost in their own thoughts. Rockford found himself genuinely enjoying her company, her presence a soothing balm.

"Do you recall the time we snuck into your father's library after dark?" he asked, trying not to smile.

"And you insisted on reading ghost stories by candlelight. I was terrified for weeks!" Lora chuckled.

"It made for memorable nights. I still laugh at how we jumped at every creak and shadow."

"I made you escort me to my room." She shook her head. "How young and daring." She took a deep breath. "But I wouldn't change any of that for the world."

They walked on, each in their own thoughts for several minutes.

"Lady Lora," he began, breaking the silence. "As a member of the Health and Home Care Committee, I wanted to thank you for your dedication to the clinic. Your commitment to this work is truly admirable, and it's inspiring to see such passion and devotion."

Lora looked up at him, her eyes shining with gratitude. "Thank you for your kind words. Your impression means a great deal to me. The clinic is my way of serving the community, seeing to what, for some, are their basic needs."

Rockford's smile warmed. "Your work is truly admirable."

Lora's expression lifted with quiet pride. "Thank you, Your Grace." She hesitated for a moment, then continued, "Actually, I've been contemplating how to accelerate the project. It needs more financial support to prove to others that it's not just my idea but is a project that interests others enough to provide funds to move it forward. I've even been approached with an offer for a loan."

Rockford's smile faded, his protective instincts taking hold. "A loan? Loans must be repaid with interest, Lady Lora."

Lora nodded slowly. "Yes, I am aware, but the proposal is tempting."

He rubbed the scar on his forearm, his instincts on alert. "Interest payments can double a project's cost, leaving you, or an investor, trapped." The idea of someone exploiting her naivety left a bitter taste in his mouth.

Lora's eyes widened slightly as she absorbed his words. "I hadn't considered the long-term implications of taking on a loan with high interest." She paused, her expression thoughtful. "I'm grateful for the explanation, Your Grace. It's clear that I need to explore other avenues for funding."

Rockford's chest tightened as regret warred with duty. Every instinct screamed to protect her, even if it meant stepping further into her life, a step he knew might complicate everything.

"There are other ways to raise funds," he said thoughtfully. "You could organize a charity event. It would bring the community together and raise the necessary funds. It may also be a way to allay the fears and concerns that appear to be circulating about the clinic's expansion. An event could serve to move the project forward."

Lora's eyes lit up with renewed hope. "That's a wonderful idea. A charity event could indeed make a significant difference. We could create an outstanding event."

"*We?*" Rockford hesitated, realizing he hadn't intended to involve himself further. But the opportunity to support her, and keep a closer eye on her dealings, was too important to ignore. "I'm glad you think so. *We* can discuss the details over tea if you'd like." They reached the end of the market.

Lora nodded enthusiastically. "I would appreciate your help. This afternoon?"

"Most definitely," Rockford replied with a smile. "Until this afternoon, Lady Lora," he said, inclining his head.

"Until then, Your Grace." As he walked away, the warmth of her smile lingered, but so did his unease. He couldn't shake the sense that this charity event might reveal far more than either of them expected.

Chapter Eight

21 September 1822
Teatime

ROCKFORD ARRIVED WITH a large bouquet of lavender, roses, dahlias, and chrysanthemums, all in shades of purple. He engaged the bell pull, and when the footman answered the door, he handed him his calling card.

He was ushered into the drawing room. Lora's eyes widened in surprise at the sight of the flowers. "Your Grace, these are beautiful! Thank you."

"I thought you might enjoy them. You did say lavender was your favorite."

Lora took the bouquet, her smile radiant. "Please, make yourself comfortable. I want to bring these to Mrs. Kelly."

Alone, Rockford took in the room. It was furnished with a refined touch. The walls were covered with delicate pink and cream floral wallpaper that included touches of green. A grand fireplace framed with a carved mantel was the focal point of the room. Above it, a large mirror added a sense of spaciousness. To one side was a mahogany tea table with eight matching chairs. A porcelain tea set with a floral pattern, tiered plate of scones, and tart were ready to serve.

Soft natural light filtered through the tall sash windows, illuminating the room and the sage-green curtains framing the view. Rockford glanced outside—then froze.

A man in a dark coat and a hat similar to his stood at the

garden gate, speaking with the footman who blocked Rockford's view of his face. As if sensing his gaze, the man glanced over the footman's shoulder, looking directly toward the window, toward Rockford. Then, without hesitation, he turned and disappeared down the path, the footman calling after him.

"They really are beautiful." Lora entered carrying a vase with the flowers he gave her. She placed the vase in the center of the piecrust table in front of the tall window. He pulled himself away from the window. They sat on the sofa in front of the fireplace. He made a mental not to find out who the mysterious visitor was before he left.

Lora busily poured him tea. "One lump or two?"

"None for me, thank you." He picked up the cup and saucer as she poured her tea and put one lump into it.

"Have you been thinking about the type of charity event we should offer?" She set her teacup down and continued. "I think something with a good deal of interaction, similar to a grand ball. It would attract a good deal of attention and bring in significant donations."

Rockford's mind raced. "What about something unique, something associated with the beauty of flowers?"

Lora's eyes lit up. "A Floral Gala? Lady Harriet and I were talking about her greenhouse. I believe it is too small." She smiled at Rockford. "I understand you have a large greenhouse, at Evergreen Lodge, your uncle's estate, Your Grace. Perhaps that could be made available?" She stared hopefully at him.

Rockford's ties to Sommer-by-the-Sea ran deep, woven through countless summers spent at his uncle's estate. He had formed enduring friendships with Lora and Adam, their bond forged during their youth. But as he grew older, his life took him to Eton and beyond, and he hadn't returned to the village in years.

Rockford nodded, picturing the event. "The greenhouse would be perfect. Upon arrival, each guest could be given a flower, symbolizing the clinic's mission."

Lora smiled, encouraged by his approval. "I thought we might do several events. We could have an art auction and a luncheon. Three separate events that may appeal to different people. The gala would be the final event of the series."

Rockford agreed. "And we could make the gala special and have a few performances throughout the evening. Perhaps a string quartet or the local choir. It would add to the ambiance and make the event even more memorable."

"Yes, and we could have a theme for the gala." He observed Lora's enthusiasm and found it infectious. "Something elegant and timeless, like an Enchanted Garden."

Rockford raised an eyebrow. "An Enchanted Garden? It would certainly make the evening more," he paused, "enchanting."

He watched as the thought flew through her mind. "It would symbolize growth and healing, much like the mission of the clinic."

Rockford gazed at her. The theme was impressive and creative. To her point, it perfectly aligned with the clinic's mission. Connecting the event's aesthetic with its deeper purpose could result in larger donations.

Lora paused, her expression thoughtful. "There's something else I've been considering. Whether the guests give money to the clinic or not, we should ensure they understand exactly how their contributions will be used. Perhaps we could create a pamphlet that outlines the specific projects, the needs of the clinic, and what their contribution will provide. This way, they will know exactly how their generosity makes a difference."

Rockford raised an eyebrow, impressed. "That's an excellent point."

Lora smiled, encouraged by his approval. "Thank you. I believe truth and transparency are crucial for building trust and ensuring continued support."

Lora's sincerity was undeniable. And yet, here he sat, smiling congenially while planning to deceive her. He would cause her pain, that much was certain. What he hadn't anticipated was how much it would cost him.

Rockford nodded. "Your foresight will undoubtedly contribute to the success of this event."

"When should we hold this event? I would think the middle of October. What are your thoughts?" she waited for Rockford.

"I agree. The middle of October would be good."

As they finished their discussion, Lora looked at him with gratitude. "Thank you. I couldn't do this without you."

Rockford smiled warmly. "That is not so." Reaching across the table, he took her hands in his. "These ideas, very good ones, are yours. I only wish some of my colleagues in the House of Lords had your foresight and dedication. I thank you, Lady Lora. It is an honor to work alongside you."

Lora's eyes shone with determination. "I'm looking forward to working with you."

"As long as you don't lock me in the closet." His eyes were full of mischief.

Lora laughed out loud, a large, unladylike laugh. "You still remember."

"How can I forget? You asked me to fetch something in the next room. I walked through the door and the next thing I knew, the door was slammed and the lock was turned and I found myself in a closet."

"I came back an hour later and sat by the door and read to you, but you didn't answer. After a while, I got concerned. I kept calling you but you said nothing."

Rockford nodded, trying not to laugh.

"I admit. I panicked and struggled to open the door. And when I did all I found was a stool with a half-eaten biscuit and you nowhere to be found."

"For days I couldn't figure out how you got out. I searched the closet and found nothing. It wasn't until I confessed to Adam that he showed me where to find the latch for the jib door."

"He was my accomplice."

Her head popped up. "What!"

He looked at the papers on the table. "We vowed never to

tell you."

The warmth in her voice made Rockford hesitate. Planning this event with her had been a pleasant diversion, but it was only that, a diversion. The closeness they shared now would serve its purpose, drawing Hastings out. And when that happened, he needed to be ready.

As he stepped out of the drawing room, Rockford spotted the footman and approached him. "Who was the man at the gate earlier?"

The footman bowed slightly. "I'm not certain, Your Grace. He suddenly left before he told me his name."

Rockford nodded, his brow furrowing in thought. "If you see him again, let me know immediately."

The footman bowed again. "Of course, Your Grace."

As Rockford walked away, his mind raced with possibilities. Who could that man be? He slowed his pace and took a breath. He was being foolish. It was probably a suitor for one of the housemaids.

HASTINGS SAT IN his study, the rented suite of rooms at the Stonefield Inn, the dim light from the oil lamp casting long shadows across the modest room. Papers and documents lay spread out before him, detailing the intricate web he had woven to undermine Rockford and secure his own position. He had been working tirelessly, too much was at stake to falter now.

He leaned back in his chair, a satisfied smile playing on his lips. The recent note, outlining Rockford's involvement with the upcoming events in Sommer-by-the-Sea gave him what he needed. These events would be the perfect opportunity to further his schemes. With the elite of society gathering for various social functions, he could manipulate conversations, gather intelligence, and sow seeds of doubt about Rockford.

Hastings picked up a letter from his desk, reading it over once more. It was an invitation to a clandestine meeting with men who shared his ambition. Hastings scanned the list of influential men who had pledged their support in exchange for his political favors: Earl Marchant, Surveyor General of Ordinance; Viscount Montague, Deputy Secretary of the Board of Control. Hastings' gaze lingered on the last name. Rockford's boss, Edward, Duke Oakdene, Under-Secretary of State for the Home Department. Lord Barrington's brother, how poetic, given their rivalry. No love was lost there.

Gaining their backing was critical to his success. With their influence, he could discredit Rockford and position himself as a trusted ally to the king. Then there is the lovely Lora. Her endowment was a significant prize, and he was determined to win her favor. Her fortune would be his to do as he pleased. He had already begun to charm her but knew he needed to be careful. Rockford's presence was a constant threat, and he couldn't afford any missteps. Removing him as a competitor was the first order of business.

Just then, a knock on the door interrupted his thoughts. "Enter," Hastings called, setting his papers aside.

A messenger stepped in, bowing slightly. "A letter, sir. Need I wait for a response?"

Hastings took the letter. "No, that will be all." He dismissed the messenger with a curt nod. He opened it, his eyes scanning the contents quickly. A slow smile spread across his face.

"So, a gala at Evergreen Lodge," he murmured to himself. "An event that will surely attract the elite." He tapped the letter against his chin thoughtfully. "With the right timing and subtle suggestions, I'll shift the narrative ensuring Rockford's reputation unravels even more."

His mind was already working on how best to manipulate the situation to further his ambitions. He glanced at the clock. It was time to put his plan into action. And if all went well, he would finally have the power and influence he deserved.

Chapter Nine

"MY LORD, THIS just arrived from Lord Barrington." Rockford's butler extended the salver to him containing a note with Barrington's seal.

Rockford took the message and opened it immediately. Barrington wasn't one to send messages at this time of night.

Rockford,

I have come across some troubling information that requires your immediate attention.

His brow furrowed as he read further. Hastings, always Hastings.

We have incontrovertible evidence that Hastings has been making inquiries about Lora's endowment and her involvement with the clinic. His interest seems more than casual, and I fear he may be planning something that could jeopardize her reputation and the success of our efforts.

Rockford's jaw tightened. Hastings' schemes were growing bolder, and now Lora was directly in his sights. He began pacing as he continued reading.

Additionally, I have noticed an increase in suspicious activity around town. There have been reports of strangers loitering near the clinic, asking pointed questions about its operations and funding. Some have even inquired about Lora's routines and the nature of her work. This could be a precursor to something more serious.

Rockford stood still, his grip tightening on the parchment. Strangers asking about Lora? This wasn't mere coincidence, it was a warning.

We need to discuss our next steps and ensure we are prepared for potential threats. Meet me here tonight.

He folded the note carefully and tucked it into his coat pocket. There was no time to waste.

Barrington

Rockford knew he had to act swiftly. Failure meant exposing Lora to harm and watching Hastings' plans unravel everything he had worked for. It was not an option he could afford, for either of them.

"Have my horse brought around," he told his butler as he gathered his papers.

His man quietly left the room. Rockford, papers in hand, stood and headed for the door. It was going to be a long night.

Rockford rode through the quiet countryside, the rhythmic sound of his horse's hooves providing a steady accompaniment to his racing thoughts. Barrington's urgent message was heavy on his mind. Hastings' inquiries about Lora's endowment and the suspicious activity around town were troubling enough, but the potential threat to Lora's reputation and the clinic's success made the situation even more dire.

As he rode, Rockford mentally prepared for the meeting. He needed to approach the conversation with Lora carefully, ensuring she understood the potential dangers without alarming her unnecessarily. He also needed to strategize with Barrington to counter Hastings' plans and protect Lora and the clinic.

Arriving at Barrington's estate, Rockford dismounted and

handed the reins to a waiting groom. He headed to the study where Barrington was already waiting, poring over a stack of documents.

"Thank you for coming," Barrington replied, looking up from the papers.

Rockford nodded, taking a seat across from him. "What have you uncovered?"

Barrington handed him a small stack of documents. "We have testimonies from local merchants who Hastings bribed to withhold donations and supplies from the clinic. They were paid handsomely to ensure the clinic would struggle."

Rockford's eyes scanned the testimonies, his anger mounting. "This is damning. What else?"

"I have detailed financial records showing suspicious transactions between Hastings and several influential figures. These records indicate a network of corruption, with money being funneled to discredit the clinic and sway public opinion against Lora."

Rockford's brow furrowed as he examined the records. "This is worse than I thought. Hastings has been more meticulous than we anticipated."

Barrington nodded. "There's more. A trusted confidant of my brother's has contacted me. He's witnessed Hastings meeting with strangers asking about the clinic's funding. It seems part of a coordinated effort to gather information and possibly sabotage our efforts."

Rockford's eyes narrowed. "Our efforts? This goes beyond just the clinic."

Barrington hesitated for a moment, then spoke. "There's a thread here that ties back to your London mission. We've confirmed that Hastings has been in contact with individuals who we set up to have connections to the 'scandal' you were involved in. These individuals are working under our direction but it's not just about the clinic or Lora—it's part of a larger scheme. We're starting to see that Hastings is likely a key player."

Rockford's mind raced with possibilities. "We need to act at once. The gala could be our opportunity to expose Hastings, but we need conclusive evidence."

"I agree," Barrington said. "We'll need eyes and ears everywhere."

"I'll speak with Lora tomorrow." Rockford sat back in his chair. "She has sharp instincts and might notice things we miss, but we can't risk alarming her or Hastings."

"It's going to be a long night." Barrington pinched the bridge of his nose, trying to ward off the fatigue. He rang for his butler.

Sanderson quietly entered the study. "Sir?"

"Coffee, Sanderson." Barrington glanced at Rockford. "Strong and plenty of it."

"Sanderson," Barrington called out before the man left the room. "A large cup with plenty of sugar." He turned to Barrington. "I thought we would begin by gathering concrete evidence of Hastings' bribery and financial misconduct. Who can we trust to handle that?"

Barrington nodded. "I'll send out a call to Peter Simms and Simon Watts."

"Gold coins." Rockford took his out and flipped it in the air. "Both men are excellent and thorough."

"Yes, they are. They will discreetly collect testimonies and financial records. We must ensure every piece of evidence is secure."

"And I can monitor the gala preparations," Rockford added. "It'll give me access to shipping bills and other documents. I'll keep an eye out for any irregularities."

Barrington agreed. "And plays into your "financial vulnerability." Good. Next, we need to protect key witnesses. My brother Edward can coordinate that discreetly, ensuring their safety and willingness to testify against Hastings."

"Edward can also coordinate with regional authorities," Rockford said.

"I'll secure the clinic's operations," Barrington continued.

"We can't let Hastings' attempts at sabotage succeed. I'll discreetly allocate additional resources to ensure its stability."

Rockford nodded. "And we need to disseminate incorrect information to mislead Hastings about our true intentions. What should we let leak out?"

"We should make him think we're focusing on something minor, perhaps a small funding event for the clinic," Barrington suggested.

"We're planning an art auction." Rockford nodded as he looked over their plans.

"That fits very well. We'll use it to buy time and gather the necessary evidence. Edward can manage this from within Hastings' network."

"Within Hasting's network? I don't understand" Rockford stared at Barrington.

Barrington handed Rockford a list. "These allies understand the stakes and can act discreetly. I'll gather testimonies and track financial records. You'll monitor the gala and shipping documents. Edward will secure the witnesses. Hastings thinks Edward is working with him."

As the meeting wrapped up in the early hours of the morning, Rockford felt a renewed sense of purpose. He glanced at the horizon as the first light of dawn began to break. "We don't have much time, but with a coordinated effort, we can bring Hastings down and finally put the London scandal to rest. Maybe then I can look forward to some peace and quiet."

Barrington nodded. "We've seen to everything. It is a solid plan."

Rockford stood, tucking the documents into his coat pocket. Each step forward brought him closer to unraveling Hastings' schemes, but at what cost?

Chapter Ten

22 September 1822

As THE COUNTRYSIDE stirred to life, Rockford's determination carried him home. Meanwhile, across town, Lora woke to a far less focused morning.

She had tossed and turned throughout the night, her mind racing with thoughts of the charity event and, more persistently, Rockford. Each time she closed her eyes, their conversations, his intense gaze, and the way he genuinely cared about the clinic replayed in her mind. The clinic. Who was she fooling, certainly not herself? The excitement for the event was second to her growing feelings for Rockford.

By the time she finally drifted off to sleep, dawn was already breaking. She awoke with a start, realizing she had overslept. Panicked, she dressed quickly, her thoughts muddled from the lack of sleep.

Looking into her mirror, it was Rockford's image that looked back at her. He stood tall and confident, with his dark hair, piercing blue eyes, and a smile that could charm the birds from the tree. Yesterday at tea, he was intense yet kind, always understanding more than he told you. There was a softness in how he looked at her, a gentleness that made her heart race.

She remembered the warmth of his hand at her waist when they danced or when he tucked her hand in his arm. She closed her eyes and conjured up him stroking her… Her eyes flew open.

His dedication to the clinic was undeniable, but his unspoken care for her left her breathless. The way he listened, truly listened to her ideas and concerns, made her feel seen and valued.

Every glance he cast her way, every fleeting touch, sent a thrill through her, stirring emotions she hadn't felt in a long time. She was drawn to his strength and vulnerability, the complexity of his character that he revealed in quiet moments. He was becoming someone she deeply cared for and couldn't stop thinking about.

She finished dressing, and a knock sounded on her door as she reached for her gloves.

"Come in." She turned as Anna, her maid, entered with a small, ornate box.

"This just arrived for you, my lady."

Lora took the box, her curiosity piqued. She opened the lid, and a faint yet distinct aroma of lemon and smoke mingled with the scent of silk that wrapped a delicate porcelain figurine of a woman in a flowing gown holding a bouquet of lavender flowers. She glanced into the box and found the accompanying note.

Dear Lady Lora,

I heard about your upcoming event and wanted to send a token of my admiration for your tireless efforts and dedication.

Warmest regards,
Hastings

Lora's brows furrowed as she traced the delicate figurine with her fingertips. It was undeniably beautiful, yet something about it unsettled her. The figurine's perfect elegance felt too calculated, too deliberate. She set the gift and note aside, a vague unease prickling at the edges of her thoughts. "Thank you, Anna."

Anna placed the morning correspondence on Lora's desk.

As she climbed into the cabin and began the ride to Harriet's estate, her thoughts drifted back to Hasting's gift. It was beautiful and extravagant, more than she would have expected. Hastings had been particularly attentive, and she couldn't help but wonder about his motives. Was he simply being kind, or was there a calculated purpose behind his gesture?

She had Harriet to thank for her discomfort, warning her that the man might be more interested in her trust than in her.

The ride to Harriet's estate was peaceful, and little by little, her mind settled. By the time she arrived, she decided to keep her guard up and trust her instincts.

The footman ushered her into the cozy breakfast room that looked out at the garden.

"Lora. Good morning," Harriet exclaimed, kissing her cheek. When she pulled away, Harriet took a long look at her. "Good heavens, Lora, you look exhausted!" Harriet exclaimed. "Have you not slept at all?"

Lora tried to smile reassuringly. "I'm fine, Harriet. Really."

But Harriet wasn't convinced. "You don't look fine. Something's clearly troubling you. I could put something a bit stronger into your tea if you like."

Lora sighed and sat down. "That won't be necessary. It's Hastings," she lied. She dare not mention anything about Rockford. "And then there was his gift…"

Harriet's brow furrowed. "A gift? What kind of gift?"

"An extravagant one," Lora replied. "Too extravagant. And there's his offer to help with funding the clinic expansion. It's unsettling."

Harriet leaned closer, her voice gentle but firm. "Lora, trust your instincts. If something feels wrong, it probably is. Perhaps it's time to speak directly with Hastings."

"Perhaps I will. I'm too tired to think at the moment," Lora replied, putting the serviette on her lap. "Actually, I wanted to talk to you about something important."

"Of course," Harriet asked, pouring them both tea.

"We're planning a gala to raise funds for the clinic," Lora began. "And I was hoping you would consider working with me. It's going to be at the Rockford Manor Greenhouse. The theme is an enchanted garden."

"We?" Harriet simply stared at her and waited for her to respond.

"Rockford and me. He, too, thought a loan was a risk. He suggested a charity event to raise funds. The clinic has been in such dire need of funds lately. I haven't told Rockford yet, but I spoke to several shop owners and people who donated in the past, but they seem to have shut their doors to us."

Harriet's eyes lit up with excitement. "I'd be thrilled to work with you! The greenhouse will be perfect for showcasing the flowers. I'm so glad you asked. I'm also intrigued by Rockford assisting you."

Lora smiled in relief. "Thank you, Harriet. Your support means a great deal to me."

Harriet took the cloche off the eggs and passed the platter to Lora. "Lora, I've been thinking. There's this charming young gentleman I'd like you to meet. He's quite dashing and—"

"Harriet, I appreciate your efforts, but I'm far too busy with the gala," Lora said gently. "Besides, I'm not looking for anyone right now."

Harriet tilted her head with a knowing smile. "Not even Rockford? Don't pretend you haven't noticed the way he looks at you."

Lora's cheeks warmed. "We've known each other since we were children, Harriet. He's only helping with the clinic because he believes in its value." She paused, the words feeling hollow even as she spoke them. "That's all there is."

Harriet's smile softened. "If you say so, Lora. Just promise me you won't dismiss what's right in front of you. Sometimes, the best things happen when you least expect them."

They finished their breakfast, discussed more details of the gala, and enjoyed each other's company. As Lora prepared to leave, she felt reassured, knowing Harriet was working with her.

"Must you leave so soon?" Harriet walked her to the foyer.

"Yes, I must. Rockford is coming this afternoon to work on the plans. We're thinking an art auction. And please do not say anything." Harriet playfully shook her head. "Thank you again for working with me. I'll let you know as soon as we have more details," Lora said, hugging Harriet.

"We. I do like the sound of that." Harriet laughed before Lora could chastise her. "Promise me you'll be careful around Hastings. I don't trust him."

"I will. And thank you for breakfast." Lora left Harriet's estate, her thoughts circling between the gala, Hastings' attentiveness, and the quiet anticipation of seeing Rockford again.

Chapter Eleven

30 September 1822

THE PAST WEEK had been a whirlwind of planning, with Rockford and Lora meeting regularly to finalize the details of the art auction and gala. She smoothed her gown and steadied herself. There was still much to do, and Rockford was due to arrive shortly.

"Good afternoon, Your Grace," Lora greeted him with a warm smile. "I'm so glad you're here."

"Lady Lora." Rockford returned her smile as she showed him to a seat in her drawing room. As they settled into the study, Lora felt a subtle shift in the air, an awareness of Rockford that she hadn't noticed before.

He removed some papers from his coat pocket. "I have more people to add to the guest list, a few influential people who should be in attendance."

Lora glanced at the list, appreciating his thoroughness. "These are excellent additions. Some had not occurred to me. I've become absorbed with the menu."

"The menu is entirely your domain," Rockford said with a smile as she handed him what she had put together. "Your taste is impeccable."

"About the guests… I noticed Hastings is on the list." Rockford glanced up from the papers. "Are you aware he's been showing particular interest in the clinic?"

Lora glanced at him, her brow arching. "I've heard murmurs,

yes. He's expressed his support for our project. Is there a reason for concern?"

Rockford hesitated, choosing his words carefully. "I think we need to be cautious. There have been some… inquiries about the clinic's funding and motives. I want to make sure everything moves forward without complications."

Lora studied him, catching the slight tension around his eyes. "There's more, isn't there?"

He met her gaze. "I've heard Hastings may not have the clinic's best interests at heart. I don't want anything jeopardizing your work."

She tightened her grip on the parchment list, a frown tugging at her lips. "I appreciate your concern, but Mr. Hastings has been nothing but supportive. He even offered to introduce me to potential patrons."

Rockford's jaw tensed, almost imperceptibly. "Generosity like that often comes with a price."

Lora tilted her head, watching him closely. Silence stretched between them, thick with unspoken thoughts. "You don't like him."

"It's not about that."

But it was, and she knew it. He was too controlled, too measured, and too careful with his words.

"I just want to make sure you and the clinic are safe," he added.

Lora exhaled softly, her fingers smoothing over the list. "You've done so much already." She hesitated, then looked up at him. "I didn't realize you cared this much."

Rockford looked momentarily taken aback. "Of course, I care. Your dedication is admirable, and the clinic does vital work. Dr. Manning's and Lady Harriet's work has been stellar. You may not be a medic, but you have been a fundamental part of the clinic since its inception."

A faint blush warmed her cheeks. "Thank you. I appreciate your concern." She let out a breath. "There is still so much to do."

He cleared his throat and returned to studying the documents. "Yes, there is. I can oversee the finances. It might alleviate some of the burden."

She considered his offer. She was well equipped to handle the finances as well as the art auction and gala, but his assistance would be a great relief. "That would be most helpful. Managing the details has been… time consuming."

"I'll handle the banking issues. If there's anything unusual, I'll inform you immediately," Rockford assured her as he took the folio with the financial records and reviewed them.

Lora nodded, her worry easing a bit. "I feel relieved already."

He offered a reassuring smile. "Then it's settled. We'll tackle this together."

Their eyes met and the atmosphere seemed to shift. A lingering connection passed between them, charged with an unspoken understanding.

"Do you have any thoughts about the entertainment?" His voice lost some of its formality as he reached for a pen and a blank paper.

Her face brightened. "I was considering a string quartet for the gala. It would add an elegant touch to the evening. There are musicians who played at my family's gala, and I'm certain Harriet may have some thoughts as well."

"An excellent idea." He nodded as he made a note. "And for the décor, I was thinking ivory and gold. Timeless and refined."

She smiled, a genuine warmth reaching her eyes. "You have quite the eye for these things. I'm impressed."

He chuckled softly. "I've attended my fair share of events. One picks up a thing or two."

She leaned forward slightly, her curiosity piqued. "Is that so? Perhaps you have hidden talents yet to be discovered."

"Perhaps," he replied, a playful glint in his eyes.

A comfortable silence surrounded them as they resumed their planning. Yet, beneath the surface, a subtle tension lingered, an awareness of each other that hadn't been there before.

As Rockford spoke, Lora found herself drawn to the cadence of his voice.

Then there was the movement of his lips. They were firm yet inviting, with a natural curve that hinted at both strength and tenderness. A sensuous quality drew her eye, making her wonder what it would be like to kiss him, feel their warmth, taste their sweetness, the very idea sent a shiver down her spine.

She stood abruptly and walked to the sideboard across the room. She needed a moment away from him to collect herself, her mind swirling with the thought of their unspoken connection. "Would you care for some tea or something stronger?"

Rockford followed her. "Tea, if you please."

Lora turned to face him, her heart still pounded. She stared at his lips. Dear God, he had wet his lips, and they glistened. Swallowing hard, she moved her focus to his eyes. What had started as a chill turned into a slow-burning fire. Their proximity, warmth in his eyes, and soft, inviting lips were all too much. Without thinking, she closed the distance between them and pressed her lips to his in a kiss.

For a moment, Rockford was taken aback, but then he responded, his hand gently cupping her cheek. "Lora." He drew her close. His kiss was tender, filled with unspoken emotions and promises.

When they finally parted, Lora's cheeks were flushed, her breath coming in soft gasps. "I... I don't know what came over me," she whispered, her eyes wide with surprise and vulnerability.

Rockford shook his head, still smiling softly. His thumb brushed her cheek, a tender gesture that sent a thrill through her. "You don't need to explain. It was... unexpected but not unwelcome. And this time, I didn't come away with a bruised eye."

She tucked her head into the space beneath his chin. "You called me Lora like you did so long ago."

Rockford smiled, his eyes softening. "I prefer not to remind you of the names you used to call me, ferret, carrot, parrot, but never Garrett. Should I go on?"

Lora let out a burst of laughter and quickly clamped her hand over her mouth.

"We should get back to work." His voice was low with a touch of regret.

She nodded, her heart still racing. They returned to the table, the atmosphere charged with a newfound tension. As they worked side by side, the memory of the kiss lingered but didn't fade, not completely.

"I received this in my morning post," Rockford said after a few moments and handed her a response. "His Majesty is looking forward to attending the Enchanted Garden event on the 21st of October. This is a gentle way of directing us to change our date. He will be attending. His support could be pivotal for the clinic's future."

Lora's eyes widened. "His Majesty?"

"Securing his support could significantly advance the clinic's cause."

She stared at him, a mix of surprise and apprehension. "That's... monumental." Her voice wavered slightly. "What if we fail to meet his expectations?"

Rockford reached across the table, his hand resting gently atop hers. "We'll ensure everything is perfect. I have complete faith in you."

She looked down at their hands, his touch sending a subtle warmth through her. "It's a daunting prospect."

"Great accomplishments often are," he said softly. "But you are more than capable."

Her gaze met his. "You always know what to say to ease my worries."

He smiled, his thumb brushing lightly over her fingers before he released her hand. "I'm glad to be of service."

The afternoon passed in a comfortable rhythm, with discussions of music for the gala as well as the selections for the art auction. But beyond the planning, it was the unspoken moments that lingered, shared glances, fleeting smiles, the quiet understanding between them growing with each passing hour.

As evening approached, Rockford gathered the financial records into his folio. Across the room, Lora remained focused on a final review of the menu, her lips pressed together in thought as she traced a finger down the page. The soft glow of the lamp bathed her in warm light, and for a fleeting moment, he allowed himself to simply watch her.

He cleared his throat lightly, the sound breaking the quiet hush between them, and closed his folio. "Lora. It might be best to keep the king's attendance to ourselves for now."

Lora glanced at him. "Why?"

"If word spreads too soon about his attendance," his expression serious, "it could lead to unnecessary complications, particularly for his safety. Discretion is essential in such matters."

She considered his point and nodded. "Very well, I'll keep his attendance to myself."

As he stood to leave, a flash of a man with a dark coat popped into his mind. "If you notice anything amiss or have concerns, you'll let me know at once."

"I will," she assured him, then added softly, "Rockford, about earlier—"

Before she could continue, he closed the distance between them, his finger gently pressing against her lips. The softness of her skin ignited a longing he had been trying to suppress. "Did I offend you?" he asked, his voice barely above a whisper.

She shook her head, her eyes searching his. "No, not at all."

He brushed a stray curl from her face. The unspoken emotions between them swelled. Without further hesitation, he leaned in, capturing her lips in a tender, deliberate kiss.

This time, he poured all his unspoken words into the connection, the admiration, the desire, the regret. Her hand rested lightly against his chest, and he wondered if she could feel his turmoil.

When they parted, her eyes remained closed for a moment, as if she was savoring the moment. As she opened them, the vulnerability he saw there warmed and shattered his heart.

"Until tomorrow," he murmured, stepping back. His voice carried the burden of promises he wasn't sure he could keep.

She offered a soft smile. "Until tomorrow."

Leaving Fallsmith Manor, Rockford felt as though he was on a precipice. The kiss lingered on his lips, a reminder of everything he longed for, and everything he stood to lose.

Protecting Lora had always been his priority, but now his feelings for her blurred the line between duty and desire. Each step away from her felt heavier with realization that his love could place her in greater danger. The path he had chosen, to protect her by any means necessary, now felt more treacherous than ever. But no risk was too great if it meant keeping her safe.

As THE DOOR closed behind him, Lora touched her lips gently, her fingers tracing the lingering warmth. A swirl of emotions, joy, confusion, anticipation, made her tumble. She moved to the window and watched as Rockford's figure receded into the evening shadows.

What just happened? she wondered, her heart fluttering. The connection she felt was undeniable, yet a hint of uncertainty clouded her thoughts. Memories of their childhood kiss flooded her mind, and she realized she had often measured others by Rockford's loyalty, honesty, and kindness. Now, she understood she hadn't been exaggerating.

One thing was clear, their relationship had shifted in a way she hadn't expected. Though uncertainty lingered, she couldn't bring herself to regret it. Whatever challenges lay ahead, she knew she was willing to face them. The growing emotions that bound them were undeniable, and she wouldn't ignore them any longer. After all, she thought with a faint smile, life's most precious moments often came without warning.

Chapter Twelve

5 October 1822

OVER THE NEXT week, Lora and Rockford delved into the preparations for the upcoming events with unwavering dedication. Each day brought them closer, their shared goals fostering a growing affection.

At the Sommer Art Gallery, they meticulously reviewed several pieces of artwork for the auction. Eventually, a captivating piece, Wivenhoe Park at Dusk by John Constable, was selected. Crispin Montgomery, director of Devonshire and Sommer Art Galleries, proposed hosting the auction at the stunning Sommer Castle and graciously offered to speak to the mayor to make the necessary arrangements.

During their visits to the gallery, Lora found herself stealing glances at Rockford, admiring how his eyes lit up with passion when discussing art. Their fingers brushed as they pointed out details in the paintings, sending shivers down her spine.

Their quest for the perfect music led them to audition three quartets and a small ensemble, ensuring the gala would have the correct music. During one audition, as the music swelled, Rockford extended his hand to Lora, leading her in an impromptu dance. They twirled gracefully, their laughter blending with the notes of the violin, their connection deepening with every step.

Hours were spent with Harriet and Mrs. Turner, Rockford's diligent housekeeper, to finalize the menus for the auction and the gala. The planning sessions were filled with lively discussions, laughter, and the occasional stolen glance.

One afternoon, as they sampled various dishes, Rockford playfully lifted a spoonful of delicate custard toward Lora. She arched a brow but leaned in, allowing him to feed her. The smooth, sweet flavor melted on her tongue, but it was the warmth in his gaze that truly lingered.

"You approve?" he asked, his voice laced with amusement.

Lora swallowed, savoring both the dessert and the moment. "It's lovely," she said, tilting her head. "Though I suspect you're enjoying this more than I am."

Rockford smirked. "Perhaps. But can you blame me?"

Their eyes locked, the playfulness between them giving way to something deeper, an unspoken understanding, a moment suspended in time.

As the days passed, their collaboration evolved into a seamless partnership, setting the stage for what promised to be an unforgettable series of events. Every meeting, every shared smile, and every touch brought them closer, building a foundation of trust and affection that neither could ignore.

Rockford's remorse grew alongside his feelings for Lora, his heart torn between his duty and his desire for her. He was terrified of the moment she would discover the truth—either by his own confession or through a cruel twist of fate. The thought of telling her himself paralyzed him with guilt and dread. How could he explain his actions without destroying the trust and affection they had built?

The fear of her finding out on her own was even more suffocating. Every day he worried that someone would expose his deceit, that Hastings' machinations would come to light, or that Lora would stumble upon the truth accidentally. His fears kept him in a constant state of tension, each moment with her tainted by the looming shadow of his secret.

Yet, he couldn't resist drawing her closer, memorizing the feel of her in his arms, the sound of her laughter, the light in her eyes.

Two days later, Lora's drawing room was abuzz with polite conversation. The scent of fresh scones and bergamot tea lingered in the air, mingling with the soft hum of laughter. The fire crackled in the hearth, casting a gentle warmth that wrapped around the gathering like a familiar embrace.

Rockford watched Lora as she poured tea, her movements graceful, effortless. Every so often, her eyes flicked toward him, a shared glance, a silent understanding. A warmth settled in his chest, a quiet contentment that had woven itself into his days without him realizing it. It was no longer something fleeting, something to be enjoyed in passing, it had become familiar, something he could count on.

Barrington sat at ease, engaged in light conversation with Mrs. Bainbridge, their exchanges filled with easy familiarity. The afternoon carried the kind of unspoken harmony that required no words, only the simple pleasure of good company.

Barrington leaned toward Rockford. "I received word this morning that the highwayman struck again this morning."

Rockford tensed. Barrington placed a calming hand on his arm.

"The pouch was taken. A few miles south, the pouch was found with the documents untouched but the purse gone. This is not the first time this courier has been accosted by the highwayman. He is certain it is the same man. I find it interesting that he's becoming a petty thief."

The butler stepped forward. "Mr. Hastings."

The moment fractured, not abruptly, but with an almost imperceptible shift. Lora's hand hesitated just slightly as she poured, a flicker of something too quick to name before she composed herself.

"Mr. Hastings, please join us for tea." Her voice remained poised, her smile practiced.

The warmth in the room dampened, as if a draft had slipped through an open door. Hastings entered, his presence drawing unseen lines between them. His gaze locked briefly with Rockford's before he inclined his head in greeting.

"Thank you, Lady Lora."

"You wouldn't believe what happened at the last charity auction," Mrs. Bainbridge began with a twinkle in her eye. "Lord Grantham accidentally bid on a painting of a cow, thinking it was a renowned landscape! He was too embarrassed to retract his bid, and now he's the proud owner of 'Bessie in the Field.'"

The room erupted in polite laughter, with Harriet adding, "Ah, poor Lord Grantham! I heard he's planning to donate it to the art auction, where he hopes it will be admired from a distance."

As the laughter faded, Rockford leaned slightly toward Hastings, his voice measured and polite. "Hastings, I was hoping we could discuss the recent developments at the clinic. I believe there are some matters we need to address."

Hastings met his gaze with a hint of defiance. "Of course, Rockford. What seems to be the issue?"

Rockford spoke calmly, but his words held a hint of concern. "I've received reports of unorthodox methods being used to secure funding. I appreciate the ambition, but we must ensure our actions uphold the clinic's integrity and reputation. The trust of the community and the long-term success of our efforts depend on it."

Hastings' expression hardened, but he maintained his composure. "I assure you, my actions are in the clinic's best interest. Sometimes, decisive measures are necessary for success."

"At what cost?" Rockford's voice was soft but firm. "Integrity is the foundation of our work. Without it, everything we've built could fall apart and lose the community's trust."

Hastings leaned in slightly, a knowing glint in his eye. "You should know, Rockford, that sometimes a little risk is necessary. After all, we both have left things behind in London that we'd rather forget."

Rockford met his gaze steadily, a knowing smile playing on his lips. "It's interesting you have time for tea, Hastings. One would think you'd be more occupied dealing with your... financial troubles."

Hastings' expression faltered for a moment, a flicker of unease crossing his features. He recovered quickly, but the seed of doubt had been planted, and Rockford knew he had struck a nerve.

LATER THAT EVENING, across town, Hastings brooded in his modest rooms in the Stonefield Inn. Though better than his London accommodations, they were a far cry from the opulence he craved, it was rather a stark reminder of his current...limitations. He glanced at the faded wallpaper. It bore the marks of time and countless previous occupants. The single window offered a view of the winding road leading into town. Its only saving grace was his glimpse over the rooftops of the sea on the horizon.

The room had a faint scent of beeswax and linseed oil hinting at the innkeeper's pride in maintaining a clean establishment. Yet, despite the room's adequacy, it fell short of the luxury he longed for. Hastings yearned for polished mahogany furniture, silk drapes, and a grand view from a manor's lofty window. He wanted the intricate tapestries that whispered tales of nobility and the warmth of a fireplace glowing with ornate ironwork. His rooms were sufficient for now, but it was a reminder that the lifestyle he craved was beyond his reach.

He insisted on a semblance of order and purpose in the space. Copies of Adam Smith's, 'The Wealth of Nations' and David Ricardo's, 'Principles of Political Economy and Taxation,' were on one corner of the desk. An orderly pile of his correspondence was alongside.

His gaze drifted out the window, where he caught a glimpse of a carriage. As it turned onto the road, he saw an elegant family crest on the door. It set his mind wandering.

The room seemed to fade away as memories of the small room he shared with his family came to mind. "You can rise above this," his father said as his mother brought dinner to the table. "You're smart. With determination and hard work, you can achieve anything."

His mind wandered from the family table to a friendly tavern and the day he found that hard work wasn't enough to achieve anything, much less success. He saw himself with a pint of ale at a remote tavern. It ached to remember that day. It had been an utter failure. But he would never forget it. His latest job had ended abruptly after he was caught tampering with the company's petty cash box, skimming off small amounts over time. The employer's stern words still rang in his ears.

He stared into the golden liquid. He had been on the edge of success, or so he thought. He took a gulp. He was worth more than the pittance he was being paid. Every coin he took had been a small correction, a way of balancing the scales. He worked harder than anyone else, and if the company couldn't see his value, then he would just have to take it for himself.

"It's not stealing," he muttered under his breath. "It's taking what I'm owed."

The man next to him chuckled, a knowing look in his eyes. "It sounds like you've been through quite a bit. Sometimes, frustrations can lead to unexpected paths."

Hastings stiffened, caught off guard by the stranger's words. "What do you mean by that?"

The man shrugged nonchalantly. "Look around you. Do you think everyone here got to where they are by always following the rules? The world isn't so clear-cut. Those who can see a way to get what they want and understand how to navigate the grey areas are those who really get ahead."

Hastings hesitated, the man's words so opposite of his father's. Yet, a part of him couldn't deny the truth in what he said. "You think I should just…take liberties?"

"Call it what you will," the man replied with a smirk. "But sometimes, a little audacity and cleverness can go a long way."

Hastings looked at him, intrigued. The idea of bending the rules to his advantage rather than being constrained by them appealed to him. Perhaps success, indeed, required a touch of audacity and cunning. Hastings found the idea both enticing and unsettling. "I'm not sure I understand."

The man chuckled again, clapping Hastings on the shoulder. "There's a fellow I know, a man of integrity." The man wrote a name and address on a scrap of paper and handed it to him. "He's helped many find their path. Show him your potential, and he might offer you the opportunity you need."

Hastings took the paper, the words swimming before his eyes as the importance of the moment settled on him. This chance meeting in a dimly lit tavern with this stranger felt like a turning point. A departure from the path his father had expected him to follow.

"Follow his instructions," the stranger pointed at the paper. "I wish I had."

"Thanks," Hastings said, slipping the paper into his pocket. "I appreciate it."

"Sometimes, all we need is a little push in the right direction."

"Will I see you again?"

"No, my friend." He stood and put a coin down on the table. "I'm off to France to fight for… Well, to fight." The man raised his glass in a toast. "To the journey ahead." Then he slipped into the night.

Hastings watched him leave. He couldn't help but wonder what this new direction would bring. He found himself available at the moment with nothing to lose.

To the journey ahead. Hastings took those words to heart, dreaming of a future where he had everything he wanted.

He was fortunate, indeed. The next day, Hastings found himself outside a stately home. He took a deep breath and knocked on the door, ready to embrace whatever opportunity awaited him. The door swung open, revealing a tall man with a stern yet welcoming expression. His imposing frame was softened by a neatly trimmed beard and a pair of sharp, intelligent eyes. His attire was refined and casual, hinting at a man of means who valued substance over show.

"Mr. Thompson, I presume?" Hastings asked.

"Indeed," the man replied.

Over the course of three short months, Hastings came to deeply respect and trust the man. He understood what the stranger had meant when he said he should have followed Mr. Thompson's advice. So, Hastings listened and learned, valuing his guide and advisor's wisdom.

"Charles, you have the potential to do great things," Mr. Thompson had said. "But remember, true success requires integrity. Never lose sight of who you are."

"Another young man is joining us today," Mr. Thompson continued, "His father, may he rest in peace, was a good friend of mine. He's in the drawing room."

Together, they entered the drawing room.

Reid, Viscount Lonsdale, stood tall with an air of confidence that came from a lifetime of privilege. His presence was commanding, not because of his physical appearance but because of his grace and integrity. His eyes, sharp and intelligent, seemed always to be observing and understanding those around him. He was the kind of man who listened intently, spoke thoughtfully, and made those around him feel valued.

The two men quickly formed a strong bond, their camaraderie rooted in mutual respect. Hastings adhered strictly to the rules, determined to prove his worth through hard work and dedication.

Their friendship shifted when Hastings and Lonsdale found themselves competing for a prestigious scholarship. It had been a bright summer morning when the announcement was made.

Hastings stood among the other candidates, his heart pounding in his chest. When Lonsdale's name was called, a wave of frustration and bitterness crashed over him. He forced himself to shake Reid's hand. *'You gave it your best. Don't lose hope.'* But inwardly, Hastings seethed. He believed that bending the rules could have secured him the scholarship.

"I know you are disappointed." Mr. Thompson said gently, his face etched with concern. "But integrity matters. True success isn't just measured by what you achieve, but by how you achieve it. The choices you make define who you are."

Hastings listened, his expression neutral, but nothing could dull his resentment. Reid's triumph was a stinging reminder of everything Hastings had been denied. That day, he made a decision, he would never let integrity stand in the way of ambition again.

Now, sitting in his rented room, Hastings reflected on that vow. The world didn't favor those who played fair, it rewarded those willing to seize what they wanted. And so, he had embraced ambition, no matter the cost.

He returned his attention to the documents before him. The clinic was his means to an end, a carefully crafted stepping stone to elevate his standing. It wasn't about proving he was as good as the others. It was about surpassing them and securing the influence he craved. Manipulation, deceit, and bribes were merely tools in his arsenal.

But Lora's words from their last encounter echoed in his mind. She had spoken of integrity, trust, and the value of honorable actions. Her conviction had struck a chord, one he had long buried beneath layers of his ambition.

His hand slammed onto the desk, scattering papers to the floor. He couldn't afford to waver now, not with success so close. Sentiment was a luxury for those who had nothing to lose, and Hastings intended to take it all.

Chapter Thirteen

8 October 1822
Afternoon

A T 3:30 IN the afternoon, carriages entered the drive at Fallsmith Manor. Lady Beatrice, Lady Harriet, and Mrs. Bainbridge had come for tea, as did Lord Davenport, Mr. Hastings, and Rockford. All were greeted with the aromas of strong black tea and Mrs. Kelly's freshly made lemon bars, scones, and sumptuous trifle.

The guests gathered in the drawing room, where the afternoon sun filtered through the lace curtains, brightening the room. Lora moved gracefully among her guests, ensuring each was comfortably seated with a cup of tea. The room buzzed with conversation ranging from the latest London gossip to passionate debates about art and culture.

"Have you all heard the latest scandal in London?" Hastings announced with a sly grin, his eyes locked onto Rockford's. "A certain prominent Member of Parliament has found himself in quite the financial debacle. It seems he's been creative with the books at the investment firm where he serves as a board member, and now the entire firm is under investigation." His words hung in the air, a provocative challenge clearly intended for Rockford.

Lady Beatrice leaned in with interest, momentarily distracted from recounting her recent travels. "Oh, do tell more, Mr. Hastings. Scandals always make for the most riveting tales."

Hastings smirked, taking a leisurely sip of his tea. "Indeed,

Lady Beatrice. It appears this gentleman's house of cards is tumbling down, and I wouldn't be surprised to see more heads roll. London society is abuzz with speculation."

Rockford maintained his composure, a cool smile playing on his lips. "It's curious, Hastings, how those who manipulate their way to the top are always the first to point fingers. I trust your own ventures are as… transparent as they should be. Do give my regards to Lady Warburton. I've always admired her diamond and ruby necklace."

Hastings' smirk faltered for a moment, a flicker of unease crossing his features. He recovered quickly, but the seed of doubt had been planted, and Rockford knew he had struck a nerve.

Before the tension could escalate further, Mrs. Bainbridge interjected, "On a brighter note, my recent travels to Brighton were most delightful. The waters truly are rejuvenating, and the architecture… simply splendid!"

"Speaking of splendid," Lord Davenport added, seizing the opportunity to change the subject, "I recently visited Crispin Montgomery's gallery. He has an exquisite John Constable on display. The brushwork is superb, capturing the English country-side with such vividness. I believe it would be a highlight at any gathering."

The conversation flowed naturally, the tension eased as the guests moved to lighter topics. Laughter and the clinking of porcelain filled the room.

By 4:30 p.m. Lady Beatrice and Lord Davenport said their farewells and left to call on Lady Dorset. Lady Harriet, Mr. Hastings, and Duke Rockford remained.

"More tea, Mr. Hastings?" Lora asked, holding the teapot poised to pour.

"No, thank you." Hastings' smile was polite but didn't quite reach his eyes.

Turning to Mrs. Bainbridge, Lora offered a warm smile. "And for you, Mrs. Bainbridge?"

Mrs. Bainbridge raised her cup with a gentle nod. "Yes,

please. Just a bit more."

"I'm so glad you stopped by today," Lora said as she poured the tea. "It's always lovely to see you." She set the teapot down gently. Lora had fond memories of Mrs. Bainbridge's female seminary, where she had met her dear friend Harriet.

Mrs. Bainbridge's eyes twinkled with warmth. "The pleasure is mine, Lora. How are the plans for the clinic's expansion coming along?"

Lora hesitated, glancing briefly at Hastings, then back to Mrs. Bainbridge. "It's quite an undertaking. There are many perspectives and interests to balance, and I worry about ensuring everyone's intentions align with the clinic's mission."

Mrs. Bainbridge nodded. "Yes, I am aware. Gossip travels quickly, I'm afraid." She sipped her tea.

"The clinic's expansion means so much to the community." Lora stirred her tea. "We must safeguard its purpose and ensure it remains a place of trust and integrity."

Mrs. Bainbridge reached out, patting Lora's hand. "I know you will, Lora. Your dedication is your strength. Trust your instincts."

Harriet, who had been listening quietly, added, "Lora, you have a wise head on your shoulders. Stay true to your principles and follow your heart."

The door opened, and Mr. Axbridge entered carrying a vase filled with fresh lavender and other blooms, a gift from Rockford to Lora. Lora's eyes lit up as he placed the vase on a nearby table. She gently touched the petals, bringing the vase closer to admire the flowers, and inhaled their soothing fragrance with a smile.

"How thoughtful, Your Grace. Lavender is my favorite," she exclaimed, clearly pleased. "This is just what the room needed! The scent is so calming." She raised an eyebrow in a playful, knowing gesture only Rockford could see.

"I should be going." Hastings stood and nodded to the others. "Thank you for the tea, Lady Lora."

"Of course, Mr. Hastings. Thank you for coming," Lora replied with a warm smile.

As Hastings departed, Lora adjusted the vase and inhaled the fragrant blooms, the calming scent steadying her thoughts. Rockford approached, his presence warm and reassuring.

"I'm glad you like them," Rockford said softly.

She opened her eyes and glanced at him. "They're beautiful."

She hesitated for a moment, then asked. "What made you so riled up with Mr. Hastings? I couldn't help but notice the tension between you two."

Rockford raised an eyebrow, surprised. "What makes you think I'm angry at Hastings?"

Lora chuckled lightly. "I've known you long enough to recognize that tone. You may fool others, but not me. And what about Lady Warburton's necklace? It's been in her family for generations."

Rockford sighed, running a hand through his hair. "It's just… differences in our approach to managing the clinic expansion finances. He has been speaking with the clinic board, and I fear his methods may lead to difficulty."

Lora's eyes softened with concern. That didn't answer her question, but she didn't pursue it. "If there's anything I can do to help, please let me know."

Rockford's expression shifted to a mischievous smile. "You said you know me. Do you know me as well as you did when I was untying the knots in my breeches at the lake?"

Lora couldn't help but laugh, the memory of that day bringing a picture to mind. "Oh, I remember that day well! You were so furious, and I couldn't stop laughing."

Rockford's smile widened, the tension easing. "You've always had a knack for getting under my skin." He leaned close so only she would hear, "Lora."

She shook her head, still smiling. "And you've always had a way of making everything seem less serious."

For a moment, they stood together, the air thick with unspoken memories and a deep, shared understanding. In that brief silence, the rest of the world seemed to fade away.

Rockford's eyes grew serious as he searched hers. "Lora, these past weeks have opened my eyes. You mean more to me than I ever realized. It's not just friendship anymore. It's something much deeper. You've become a part of me, and I can't imagine my days without you."

Lora's breath caught, and her heart pounded. His words echoed in her head, stirring a whirlwind of emotions, fear of risking their friendship, hope for a deeper connection, and the uncertainty that came with stepping into the unknown. The shift in their relationship, the deepening of their connection, it wasn't her imagination. Could she risk their friendship for the possibility of something more?

She looked into his eyes, seeing vulnerability and passion in his gaze. At that moment, she couldn't keep her feelings to herself any longer. Lora took a step closer, her hand reaching out to touch his. "I feel that way, too. You've always held a special place in my heart, but now it's different. It's stronger."

She took a step closer. "I've been afraid to say it, fearing it might change everything between us. But hearing you now... it fills me with hope."

Rockford gently took her hand, his touch warm and reassuring. "Then let's not waste any more time. I'm ready to see where this takes us."

Tears of relief and joy welled in Lora's eyes, and she nodded, unable to find the words.

She squeezed his hand, her voice filled with emotion. "I don't know what to say."

Before Rockford could respond, the fragile stillness between them was interrupted by a sharp laugh, grounding them back in the bustling reality of the room. The abrupt sound shattered the intimate moment.

Mrs. Bainbridge had just told a particularly amusing anecdote, and Harriet was doubled over in laughter, her eyes sparkling with amusement.

Mrs. Bainbridge, noticing the subtle shift in the atmosphere. She turned to Rockford with a charming smile. "Your Grace, I've been meaning to discuss the upcoming charity ball with you. I hear your experience with such events is unparalleled, and I could use some advice on hosting something equally splendid."

Rockford nodded graciously. "I would be delighted to assist, Mrs. Bainbridge."

Mrs. Bainbridge beamed. "Wonderful! Perhaps we could discuss it here for a moment?" She gestured to a nearby chair, inviting Rockford to join her.

"I'll leave you both to your discussion." Harriet rose and walked over to Lora. Harriet's eyes sparkled with curiosity.

Harriet admired the vase of flowers. "Mr. Hastings is ambitious, no doubt. He is jealous of the attention that Rockford gives you. Would you be interested in Mr. Hastings if he wasn't dangling the clinic in front of you?"

Lora sighed, her thoughts still tangled with concerns about the clinic. "I have a great deal to sort out."

Harriet patted her hand reassuringly. "Love is a mysterious thing, Lora. Sometimes, it appears when you least expect it."

⇶✕⇷

OUTSIDE THE ESTATE, the town was abuzz with whispers of the recent events. The tension between Rockford and Hastings had not gone unnoticed, and the community kept a close watch.

As he made his way back to the Stonehill Inn, a sly smile lit Hastings' face. Cordial and polite. Weak, that's what Lady Lora is. He could easily lead her and make Lady Lora his pawn to further his ambition. As for Rockford, he couldn't wait to crush him.

When he reached the inn, Hastings bypassed the tavern's noisy revelry, retreating to his room to review the documents he had 'fixed' yet again. He removed his jacket, poured himself a glass of port, and sat at the table. As he read the documents,

Lora's words echoed in his mind. She had spoken of integrity, of trust, and the value of honorable actions. Her conviction had struck a chord, one he had long buried beneath layers of ambition.

With the documents he had, even the King of England would listen to him. That kind of power was bigger than he'd ever dreamed as a boy scraping by. Yet her words made him pause. Was it enough to just be heard, or did he want more than just power? Respect? For the first time in a long while, his father's voice echoed in his head. And with it, came a sense of guilt.

His thoughts drifted back to a dimly lit warehouse by the waterfront in London, where he met a man who had the power to change his life.

The flickering lantern cast long shadows on the stone walls, creating an atmosphere thick with secrecy. He straightened his coat, masking his apprehension with a veneer of confidence.

A voice emerged from the shadows, smooth and controlled. "Mr. Hastings, your punctuality is appreciated."

Hastings kept his gaze steady, staring into the darkness. "I believe in seizing opportunities, and this meeting promises to be quite beneficial."

"It has been some time since we've last met."

Silence. What was he supposed to do? Say? He took a steadying breath and said nothing.

Out of the darkness came a soft chuckle. "Perhaps you have learned after all. We have heard of your ambitions," the voice continued, unwavering. "The clinic is your path to redemption. After the debacle in France, you need to prove your worth. But don't be fooled. This is your last chance."

A shiver ran down Hastings' spine, though he maintained his position. "I won't fail."

The voice grew colder. "You better not. I've gone to great lengths to get you a second chance. Fail us, and there is no coming back."

Hastings' heart pounded beneath his composed exterior. "What do you need from me?"

"Information and influence," the voice replied. "Use your clinic to gather intelligence. Identify key people in the town who can be swayed or eliminated. Ensure our interests are protected and advanced."

"Consider it done," Hastings nodded, determination flaring in his eyes. "Remember, trust is a two-way street. I'll expect you to hold up your end of the bargain."

The voice responded with an air of finality. "We will be watching, Mr. Hastings. Do not disappoint us."

Silence. Alone at last, he allowed himself a moment to breathe. The path he had chosen was dangerous, but the rewards outweighed the risks. He would never return to the streets of London. He would rather die first.

Hastings returned to the present, the memory of that fateful meeting a constant reminder of the high stakes. Failure was not an option, not when everything he craved was within reach and the price of defeat was unimaginable.

Chapter Fourteen

10 October 1822
Early Morning

ROCKFORD SAT AT his desk, the soft scratch of his pen moving across parchment as he finished penning a letter. He paused. His thoughts wandered to the not-so-subtle attack from Hastings at tea with its undercurrents of tension. He dusted and blotted the letter, then put it into his folio.

Hastings sauntered into Rockford's library, his eyes flitting briefly to Rockford's before darting away, unable to withstand the force of Rockford's gaze.

Close behind him, the butler, Mr. Turner, followed, his face flushed with concern. "I apologize for the intrusion, Your Grace," Mr. Turner began, his voice steady but touched with unease. "Mr. Hastings insisted on speaking with you immediately. I attempted to dissuade him, but he would not be deterred."

Rockford's expression hardened, but he maintained his composure. "Thank you, Turner. That will be all." The butler nodded and retreated from the room, closing the door quietly behind him.

Rockford leaned back in his chair, his eyes boring into Hastings with a steely intensity that spoke of barely contained disdain. "To what do I owe this unexpected visit, Hastings?"

Hastings shifted uncomfortably, his earlier bravado faltering under Rockford's unyielding stare. He cast a dismissive glance at the bookshelves and maps as if trying to regain his composure. "I find the stillness of night conducive to meaningful conversations. Besides, Your Grace, we seem to have much to discuss." He attempted to sound nonchalant but failed to conceal the underlying tension in his voice.

Rockford arched an eyebrow. His gaze remained steady. The flickering candlelight cast sharp shadows over the chiseled features of his face, giving him an almost otherworldly presence with eyes that glinted and pinned a man in his place. "A private discussion, indeed? I can hardly imagine what matter could be so urgent that it necessitates barging into my home uninvited."

The atmosphere grew taut as Rockford waited for Hastings to explain himself, the power dynamic clearly established in the room.

Hastings forced a faint smile, stepping further into the room with deliberate slowness. His fingers brushed the spines of the books, a subtle gesture of disdain. "Come now, we've known each other long enough to dispense with formalities. I couldn't help but notice you've settled comfortably here in Sommer-by-the-Sea." His eyes flickered nervously before locking with Rockford's steely gaze.

"I wasn't aware my whereabouts were of interest to you," Rockford barely glanced up as he returned to reading the document on his desk.

"On the contrary." Hastings paused to examine the maps on the wall. The too-quick flicker of his gaze betrayed the tension beneath his composed demeanor. "I'm always intrigued by the movements of influential figures, especially those with whom I share a history."

Rockford didn't look up from his document. "A history? Our acquaintance has been... peripheral at best." His tone was as dismissive as a wave of the hand.

"Perhaps." Hastings turned, stepped toward the desk, and absentmindedly picked up a small nautical compass. "But sometimes paths cross in the most fascinating ways. Take, for instance, our time in France."

Rockford continued to read the document. "France was a complex time for many of us." His tone gave nothing away.

"Indeed," Hastings agreed, setting the compass back in its place. "So many stories left untold. Heroes and villains trading places in the blink of an eye."

"War has a way of blurring those lines." Rockford raised his quill and signed, sanded, and blotted the document.

"True," Hastings replied. "Yet, I recently came across some military records. They were quite fascinating, really, the names of those no longer with us. I found acquaintances and old friends among them. Nasty thing, war." He paused.

Rockford's heart skipped a beat, but his impassive expression never faltered.

"Ah, but the names of those brave men who are missing in action." Hastings' voice took on a sharp edge. "They conjure up ideas of what could have happened to them."

An invisible hand clutched Rockford's heart. Each beat echoed with unspoken fears and buried secrets. But he kept his expression neutral. "War is riddled with unfortunate losses."

"Unfortunate, yes," Hastings said, placing the paperweight back down. "But sometimes, one can't help but wonder about the circumstances. Disappearances without a trace can spark... curiosity."

Rockford's fingers drummed lightly on the desk in a steady, controlled rhythm. He let out a sigh. "Curiosity can be dangerous, Hastings. Digging into the past might unearth things best left buried."

Hastings smiled thinly and stepped closer to the desk. "Perhaps. But secrets have a way of surfacing. It's interesting how some men go missing while others are unscathed."

"Spoken like a person who's never served. War takes its toll on everyone, one way or another. Is there a point to this visit?" His voice edged with a quiet authority. His patience was wearing thin.

"Simply a friendly observation," Hastings said lightly. "And perhaps a reminder that our actions can have unexpected echoes."

"I appreciate your concern." Rockford's fingers still drumming, then ceased abruptly as he fixed Hastings with a pointed gaze. "Now, if there's nothing else—"

Hastings inclined his head. "Of course. I won't keep you any longer. Good evening, Your Grace."

As Hastings turned to leave, he paused at the door. "Oh, and do give Lady Lora my regards. She's quite the captivating hostess."

Rockford's eyes flickered for the briefest moment, but he held his composure. "I'll be sure to pass them along."

Hastings lingered for a moment longer, his voice dropping to a conspiratorial whisper. "And do consider our time in France, Your Grace. I may not have served, but I find the fate of men like Captain Edward Langley to be intriguing."

With a final, knowing look, Hastings exited the study.

As the door clicked shut, Rockford allowed the mask to slip momentarily, a frown creasing his brow. Rockford recognized the veiled threat, each word from Hastings striking a nerve. The mention of Langley stirred buried guilt and fears he had fought to suppress. If Hastings had unearthed the truth, it could unravel everything he had worked to protect.

He moved to the window, gazing out at the moonlit grounds. There was a possibility that Hastings was bluffing, using whatever scraps of information he could find to unsettle him. After all, the official records only stated that Langley was missing in action, a fate not uncommon in the chaos of war. Yet, the fear remained that Hastings might dig deeper or, worse, fabricate details to serve his own agenda.

He couldn't allow Hastings to use Langley or Lora as pawns in whatever game he was playing.

Rockford had to uncover Hastings' true intentions and the depth of his organization and stay one step ahead. The stakes were rising, and he needed to be prepared for whatever moves

Hastings would make next. He'd discreetly consult with Barrington. Langley's name is listed with those missing in action. Moreover, he needed to protect Lora. Hastings' interest in her could be innocent flirtation, but Rockford couldn't take any chances given his propensity for manipulation.

Rockford moved away from the window. The flickering firelight cast shadows across the room, mirroring the storm of emotions that raged in his heart. He sank into a nearby chair. The image of Lora's radiant smile filled his mind, the way her eyes sparkled with warmth and trust when she looked at him.

Protecting Lora was all that mattered now, even if it meant condemning himself to a life without her. He raked his hand through his hair. He needed time to think.

MEANWHILE, AT FALLSMITH Hall, the first light of dawn filtered into Lora's bedroom. Sleep had been elusive, retreating like the ocean's tide, leaving her adrift in a sea of tangled thoughts. She sat upright in her bed, the crisp linen sheets pooled around her waist, fingers clenched tightly around a book she had long abandoned.

Her mind returned, uninvited, to that moment with Rockford, the warmth of his lips against hers, the unexpected tenderness in his eyes. The memory should have brought a smile to her face, yet frustration simmered beneath the surface. How dare he kiss her so profoundly, declare his feelings, stirring emotions she had carefully guarded, only to vanish without an explanation? For two days, he hadn't come to call, nor did he send a note, not a whisper from him. Her pride bristled at the thought of being dismissed so casually.

"Am I to be treated as a passing fancy?" she whispered to the empty room, her voice touched with indignation. Rising swiftly, she crossed to the window, pushing it open to let the cool morning air wash over her. The distant cries of gulls and the rhythmic hush of waves did little to soothe the brewing tempest.

Her gaze drifted toward the horizon, where the sky met the sea in a blush of pink and gold. Somewhere out there, perhaps, was an explanation for Rockford's sudden disappearance. But waiting patiently was not in her nature. He was gravely mistaken if he thought she would accept his silence.

Drawing a deep breath, Lora steadied herself. "I won't be ignored," she declared, more determined than ever. She would seek him out and demand the truth.

"Enough," she declared, straightening her shoulders. It was mid-morning. She would not sit idly by. If Rockford thought he could dismiss her so easily, he was mistaken.

Lora dressed in a deep blue velvet walking gown, instructed Anna, her maid, to ask the groom to bring the carriage around.

She stepped onto the front steps and let the crisp sea air fill her lungs. The footman helped her into the carriage. As the groomsman drove toward Rockford's estate, she began to have second thoughts. Perhaps he had a reasonable explanation. Her hand went to her stuttering heart. What if he had been injured or was unwell? But why hadn't he sent word?

The carriage slowed as the groom stopped at Rockford Manor and handed her down. She straightened her skirt, took a deep breath, and marched up to the grand entrance.

"Good morning, Lady Lora," Turner said with a polite bow. "How may I assist you today?"

"Good morning, Mr. Turner. Is His Grace at home?" Lora asked, striving for a casual tone as she prepared to remove her gloves.

Turner hesitated almost imperceptibly. "His Grace is currently engaged, my lady."

She stopped fussing with her hands. Lora's brow furrowed. "Engaged? Might I wait to see him?"

"I'm afraid that may not be possible," he replied, his expression apologetic. "His Grace has left instructions not to be disturbed."

A flicker of hurt crossed her face. "I see. Do you know when he might be available?"

"I cannot say with certainty, my lady. Perhaps later in the week," Turner offered.

Before she could respond, a familiar voice sounded from behind the butler.

"Lady Lora! What a pleasant surprise."

Hastings stepped into the foyer, a sly smile on his lips.

"Mr. Hastings," Her tone was cooler. "I wasn't aware you were acquainted with His Grace."

"Oh, we have... mutual interests," Hastings said smoothly. "Are you here to see him as well?"

"I was, but it seems he is unavailable." She was disappointed that she could not keep the edge from her voice.

"Ah, that's unfortunate." Even in her current twist, she was aware that Hastings' smile didn't reach his eyes. "He's been quite preoccupied lately."

Lora straightened her back, her chin lifting in a subtle display of defiance. "Thank you for your... concern, Mr. Hastings," she replied, her voice steady but edged with a controlled ire. "With what might His Grace be preoccupied?"

Hastings took a step closer, his presence invasive. "Matters of importance, I'm sure. Though one might wonder what could be more pressing than attending to certain social obligations."

Lora, her back straight, lifted her chin slightly. "I find it curious that you seem so well-informed about His Grace's affairs. Can you elaborate?" She kept her voice steady, but it was laced with controlled anger.

He chuckled softly as he played with the brim of his hat in his hands. "I merely find it interesting that His Grace seems to be... otherwise occupied, especially after making certain affections apparent. It would be a shame if his attentions were fickle."

"Your insights are always... interesting, Mr. Hastings. Though I must admit, I find trust to be a commodity earned through actions rather than words."

Hastings' smile faltered for a brief moment, his eyes narrowing slightly as he processed her words. He recovered quickly, though, his tone remaining light but with an edge of mock politeness. "Ah, Lady Lora, your candor is as refreshing as ever. One can only aspire to meet such high standards. I do hope to prove my worth in time."

"Good day, Mr. Hastings." Lora turned sharply, signaling the end of the conversation.

He inclined his head slightly, a gesture that was more mocking than respectful. "Until then, Lady Lora. I suspect our paths will cross again soon, perhaps under more... intriguing circumstances."

Chapter Fifteen

As Lora returned to the carriage, a knot of doubt tightened in her chest. She climbed inside, and the coachman turned for her instructions.

"Home, my lady?" he asked.

Lora hesitated, her gaze distant as she stared unseeing at the road ahead. Return home? Alone with her turbulent thoughts and the silent rooms echoing with questions she couldn't answer? The walls would close in, magnifying her uncertainty.

She needed clarity, some help to pull her from the confusion. Harriet's steadfast friendship and keen intuition were that beacon.

Taking a breath, she met the coachman's gaze. "No, take me to Lady Harriet's," her voice steadier than she felt.

As the carriage drove on, the rhythmic clatter of wheels matched the anxious cadence of her heart. Rockford's silence, the butler's curt dismissal, and Hastings' smug insinuations churned in her mind, an endless storm.

At Harriet's home. Lora scarcely waited for the footman to open the door before alighting. The familiar scent of sandalwood and old books greeted her, a brief comfort against her inner turmoil.

Harriet looked up from her embroidery as Lora entered the drawing room. A warm smile spread across her face, but it quickly faded as she saw Lora's strained expression.

"Lora, dear, what brings you by at this hour?" Harriet set aside her hoop and hurried to her friend.

"Harriet," Lora began, her voice scarcely above a whisper. The words caught in her throat as she struggled to swallow a lump of emotion. Her carefully maintained composure was fracturing, her vulnerability threatening to surface.

Harriet gently took Lora's hands. "Come, let's sit. Whatever it is, you can share it with me."

They settled on the plush settee near the hearth, the crackle of the fire filling the silence. Harriet waited patiently, her steady presence a comfort to Lora's frayed nerves.

"It's Rockford," Lora finally managed, her gaze fixed on the carpet's intricate pattern. "I haven't heard from him in two days. When I called today, I was turned away. And..." She paused, her hands clenched in her lap. "Hastings was there. He implied things, suggested that Rockford might be... neglecting certain obligations."

Harriet inhaled thoughtfully. "That doesn't sound like Rockford at all," she said softly. "What exactly did Hastings say?"

"It's not just what he said, but how he said it," Lora replied, frustration and hurt mingling in her chest. "With that smirk, as if he knows something I don't. I pride myself on not being swayed by idle gossip, but his words..." She paused. "They're difficult to ignore."

"Hastings has a way of twisting words, doesn't he?" Harriet placed a comforting hand over Lora's. "Always looking to stir the pot and leave a trail of doubt."

"I know." Lora nodded, her voice quavering slightly. "But I can't help feeling that there's truth lurking beneath his insinuations. Why else would Rockford avoid me? Especially after..." She flushed, the memory of their shared kiss rising unbidden.

"After what, Lora?" Harriet prompted gently.

Steeling herself, Lora met Harriet's gaze. "We shared a moment, a... a kiss. It felt significant, as though we acknowledged what was growing between us. And at tea, he spoke of his feelings. But now...I'm left questioning if it meant anything to him at all."

"Oh, Lora," Harriet murmured, squeezing her hands gently. "Matters of the heart are seldom straightforward. But Rockford doesn't appear to me as a man who takes such things lightly."

"Then why his silence?" Lora's composure slipped further. "Why distance himself now? It feels as though he's built a wall between us overnight, and I don't understand what I've done wrong."

"You may have done nothing wrong," Harriet assured her. "Men often grapple with their own battles, internal and otherwise, and believe they must do so alone."

Lora's eyes flashed with frustration. "But I am not some fragile creature to be protected from the world's harshness. I thought he saw me as an equal, a partner. How can we build anything lasting if he shuts me out at the first sign of difficulty?"

"Your feelings are valid. But patience might serve you here. Give him a little time. He may come to you when he's ready."

"Patience has never been my virtue," Lora muttered, a wry smile tugging at her lips.

"I am well aware," Harriet replied with a soft laugh. "But consider this. Acting in haste might push him further away. If you confront him now, while emotions are high, it could lead to misunderstandings that are difficult to mend."

Lora leaned back, closing her eyes briefly. The logical part of her recognized Harriet's wisdom, but her heart ached with the need for an immediate resolution. "Perhaps you're right," she conceded quietly. "But what am I to do in the meantime?"

"Focus on the things in your control," Harriet suggested. "Isn't the gala approaching? Pour your energy into ensuring its success."

"The gala," Lora echoed, the thought distant. "Yes, there's still much to be done."

"And remember, I'm here whenever you need me." Harriet gave her an encouraging smile.

"Thank you, Harriet. Your friendship means more to me than I can say."

"Nonsense," Harriet put her arm around her and drew her close. "That's what friends are for."

They sat in companionable silence for a few moments, the warmth of the fire seeping into their bones. Lora felt a measure of peace returning, the chaos settling ever so slightly. While the path ahead remained uncertain, she took comfort in knowing she didn't have to navigate it alone.

As she prepared to leave, Harriet walked her to the door. "Promise me you'll be kind to yourself," Harriet said, her eyes earnest.

"I'll try," Lora replied, mustering a small smile.

"And if you decide that patience isn't the way," Harriet added with a teasing glint, "just make sure you're prepared for whatever you might uncover."

Lora nodded, a determined light reigniting in her gaze. "I won't shy away from the truth, whatever it may be."

"That's the Lora I know." Harriet pulled her into a brief hug.

Lora drew a deep breath as she stepped out into the fading midday light. The air was crisp, carrying the briny scent of the North Sea and a hint of unknown possibilities. Her emotions still swirled, but they were tempered now by a renewed determination. Whether through patience or action, she would find her way forward.

LORA'S IMPATIENCE GREW as the day waned, her mind swirling with unanswered questions and the growing fear that something was deeply amiss. Every moment of silence chipped away at her composure, leaving her restless and uneasy. *Harriet means well.* She paced the length of the drawing room. *But she doesn't feel this suffocating uncertainty. I can't just sit here and wait while everything feels like it's slipping away.* Her stubbornness refused to let the matter rest. She needed to take matters into her own hands.

But where to begin? The memory of Rockford's kiss lingered like a bittersweet echo, stirring vulnerability she had long guarded against. Opening her heart had been a risk, and now the silence made her question if it had been worth it. Her fingertips grazed her bottom lip absentmindedly, recalling the warmth and tenderness of his kiss. It had stirred something deep within her, a vulnerability she rarely allowed herself to feel. Opening her heart had always been her greatest fear, and now, that fear threatened to consume her.

"How could he…" she whispered, her voice barely audible in the vastness of the room. A surge of frustration welled up and mingled with the lingering ache of disappointment. She had let down her guard and shared a piece of herself she had kept hidden from the world, and now he had retreated into silence.

"Enough," she declared aloud, the word echoing off the ornate plasterwork of the ceiling. The determined tone startled her but ignited a spark of conviction in her chest. She would not be left in the dark nor allow her emotions to make her powerless.

Crossing swiftly to her writing desk, she pulled out a sheet of fine stationery. The familiar scent of parchment and ink offered a small comfort. She sat, the delicate chair creaking softly beneath her, and took up her quill. Her hand hovered over the page for a moment, her thoughts racing. Should she express the depth of her confusion? The hurt? No—her pride bristled at the thought. No, something neutral. Perhaps it would be best to address him under the guise of their shared responsibility. The gala. It was reasonable to contact him without revealing her inner turmoil.

She penned a concise note:

Dear Lord Rockford,

I hope this letter finds you well. As the date of the gala draws near, there are several pressing matters that require your attention. Your guidance is essential to ensure the event's success. Might we arrange a time at your earliest convenience to discuss the details?

Warm regards,
Lora

She read over the note, satisfied that it conveyed urgency without giving way to her personal frustrations. It was formal yet personal enough to prompt a reply.

Sealing the envelope with her signet, she summoned a footman.

"Please ensure this letter is delivered to His Grace immediately," she instructed. "It is important that he receives it as soon as possible."

"At once, my lady," he replied, taking the letter with careful hands before departing swiftly.

As the door closed behind him, Lora let out a slow breath she hadn't realized she'd been holding. She hoped that invoking the gala would prompt Rockford to respond. After all, they had committed to working on it together, and the approaching date necessitated collaboration.

Hours slipped by with no reply. She attempted to occupy herself reviewing guest lists, and coordinating the vendors, but her mind kept drifting back to him. The silence was maddening, each passing moment amplifying her concern.

The day waned, and twilight shadows crept across the room. Lora stood by the window, staring at nothing in particular. The sky blazed with hues of amber and crimson, but the beauty did little to soothe her restlessness.

The sky outside darkened, she lit a few candles, their flickering light cast long shadows that danced on the walls. She reviewed the inventory list Harriet had given her to identify what her household could provide. She glanced at the clock again, her heart sinking with each passing minute.

She added the responses that arrived in the day's mail to the guest list, scanning its contents without really reading it, her mind too preoccupied with thoughts of Rockford. The silence was maddening, a constant reminder of her growing anxiety. Every creak of the house, every rustle of the curtains stirred by the evening breeze, made her heart jump.

No matter how she tried to occupy herself, Lora kept returning to the window, staring into the darkness. Each moment of silence deepened her unease.

As the hours slipped by and Rockford's silence stretched unbroken, a thought pierced her mind—a man of his word would not ignore something so important. Something was wrong. Her impatience sharpened into steely conviction. "If he refuses to respond, then I'll find the truth myself," she resolved, her reflection in the glass hardening with purpose. Her stubbornness refused to let the matter rest. She would seek answers, even if it meant stepping beyond the bounds of propriety.

She rang for Anna.

"Please have my riding habit available early in the morning and ask the stable master to have Astra ready at first light," Lora instructed, her voice calm but resolute. This was not a decision she made lightly, but one born of necessity and an unwavering determination to confront the unknown. "Tomorrow I shall be riding early."

Anna looked up, a hint of surprise flickering across her features. It was uncommon for Lora to request her riding attire at such an hour. "Very good, my lady," she replied, curtsying slightly.

"I'll need a small satchel as well."

"Of course," Anna said, though curiosity lingered in her gaze. "Will there be anything else?"

"That will be all for tonight. Thank you, Anna," Lora offered a reassuring smile, hoping to quell any unspoken questions.

As Anna left the room, Lora released a slow breath. She turned back to the window as the stars grew brighter against the velvet sky. The silver glow of the crescent moon cast gentle shadows across the estate grounds. The tranquil estate seemed to mock her turmoil. Its serene beauty contrasted sharply with the storm of emotions within her, each shadow outside reflecting the unanswered questions that haunted her.

"Whatever you're hiding, Rockford," she vowed, her gaze fixed on the crescent moon. "I'll uncover the truth, no matter the cost."

Chapter Sixteen

11 October 1822

For Lora, the night passed fitfully. Sleep came in pieces, her dreams a tangle of fragmented images, a waltz under shimmering chandeliers, whispers in shadowed corridors, the echo of Rockford's voice calling her name. She awoke before dawn, the faint blush of sunrise just beginning to lighten the horizon.

Lora dressed quickly, with practiced efficiency. The deep green riding habit fit her perfectly. The tailored lines accentuated her form. She pulled on her polished boots and fastened the silver buttons of her fitted jacket. Standing before the mirror, she pinned her hair neatly beneath a simple velvet hat, allowing a few tendrils to escape and frame her face.

Her reflection gazed back with a steadfast expression. There was no room for hesitation now. She retrieved the small satchel Anna had prepared, ensuring she had all she might need for the journey: a map, a small pouch of coins, and her papers for the events.

Quietly descending the grand staircase, Lora moved through the silent house. The staff would not expect her this early, and she preferred to leave without their attention. As she stepped outside, the cool morning air embraced her, carrying the fresh scent of dew-kissed grass and blooming heather.

Her mare, Astra, awaited her alert and ready, just as Lora had instructed. The chestnut coat gleamed in the soft light, and Astra nickered softly at Lora's approach.

"Good morning, girl," Lora whispered, stroking Astra's sleek neck. "We've a journey ahead of us."

She secured her satchel and mounted gracefully, settling into the saddle with ease. With a gentle nudge, they set off down the drive, hooves muffled against the earth.

The world was awash with the colors of dawn, rosy pinks fading into golden yellows as the sun began to rise. The countryside stretched before her, a patchwork of rolling hills, lush green fields, and hedgerows still cloaked in the remnants of morning mist.

As they rode, Lora's thoughts churned as she recalled how Rockford often sought solitude at his family's hunting lodge near Briarcliff Woods. If he was anywhere, her instincts told her she would find him there.

The journey was not a short one, but Lora was an accomplished rider, and Astra's stamina and steady pace ate up the miles with ease. The crisp air sharpened her focus as each stride brought her closer to the answers she sought.

They followed the River Sommer for an hour and a half until she reached Stonefield's Crossing, the halfway point. Lora stretched her legs and watched as Astra drank from the cool river. Lora glanced westward. The old road would take her past the old Stonefield farm and Royston Mills beyond. But she was bound north to the woods.

What would she say when he opened the door? Should she be nonchalant? Concerned? Angry?

She glanced south. This was a fool's mission.

Astra raised and shook her head. "Had enough? Then we best be on our way."

She should go home. Lora took the reins draped over her saddle, mounted Astra, and headed north, admitting to herself, at least, that she was the fool.

Thirty minutes later, she approached the fringes of the forest, where the trees were denser and their branches intertwined overhead, forming a canopy. The path narrowed, winding through the ancient woodland as shafts of sunlight danced through the foliage, lighting patches of wildflowers that dotted the underbrush.

They rode on another hour before the lodge came into view. It was a stately yet rustic timber and stone structure blending into its surroundings. Smoke curled lightly from the chimney. Someone was there.

Lora brought Astra to the hitching post, dismounted, and removed her satchel. Her boots crunched softly on the gravel path. She took a moment to steady herself, smoothing her skirt and taking a deep breath. The lodge was well situated, but she didn't hear the soft song of the birds or the gentle rustling of leaves that filled the air. Her nerves fluttered. She closed her eyes. "Foolish girl," she muttered.

With her satchel in hand, she approached the heavy oak door and hesitated. Finally, she lifted the brass knocker and let it drop.

⟫⟫⟩✕⟨⟪⟪

ROCKFORD SAT BY the hearth, the warmth of the fire doing little to ease the chill of his troubled thoughts. He turned the letter from Barrington over in his hands. The mission was becoming increasingly complex. Being close to Lora was supposed to be a means to an end, to gather information on Hastings. But now, emotions had entangled that plan.

He rubbed his temples, closing his eyes. "What am I doing?" he muttered. The lines between duty and desire were blurred. The king was arriving in ten days, and time was running short. Yet, the thought of deceiving Lora any further was unbearable.

A fall of the brass knocker at the door pulled him from his reverie. His brow furrowed. He wasn't expecting anyone. Rising cautiously, he crossed the room and opened the door.

"Lora?"

She stood before him, determination and vulnerability flashed in her eyes. "Good morning, Rockford," she said evenly. "I hope I'm not intruding."

For a moment, words escaped him. Part of him had feared this moment, while another part had longed for it. "Please, come in." He stepped aside.

As she entered and placed her satchel by the door, he couldn't help but feel a surge of conflicting emotions. Had she discovered his true intentions? Was this the moment everything unraveled?

"Are you planning to stay long?" He stared at her, then at her satchel, his smile inviting and suggestive.

Her gaze met his with defiance, snuffing out his implied question. "You're not the only one who can run away."

They stood gazing at each other for several long heartbeats.

"How did you find me?" he finally asked, attempting a casual tone.

She offered a faint smile. "It seemed a logical place to look when you vanished without a word. Besides, you invited me."

He nodded slowly, closing the door behind her. "I suppose I underestimated your ability to find me."

She faced him directly, her chest heaving at his words. "So, you have been avoiding me. I deserve to know why. Especially after..." She hesitated, the memory of their kiss a bittersweet reminder of what had been left unsaid.

He grasped her shoulders. "No, not because of you. Never." He took a deep breath wrestling internally. Could he confide in her without jeopardizing the mission? Without putting her in danger? His feelings for her warred with his sense of duty.

"Lora, there are things you don't know, things I can't fully explain right now."

She stepped closer, her gaze unwavering. "Then trust me enough to understand," she implored, her voice soft yet resolute.

He hesitated, the impact of his decision bearing down on him. Would revealing just enough keep her safe or push her further into harm's way? He looked into her eyes, seeing the sincerity and strength that had drawn him to her from the start. Perhaps he owed her the truth or at least part of it.

"Come, you must be cold. We'll sit by the fire." As Rockford and Lora sat in the warmth of the lodge, Lora's gaze reflected the hurt he had caused. He took a deep breath and began to explain.

"I've been avoiding you because of my misstep," he admitted, his tone heavy with regret. "It's led to insinuations, and I didn't want you caught in Hastings' schemes." He paused. If he told her anymore, she wouldn't be in the fray. She'd be in the fire.

"Hastings," she said with conviction.

He felt the blood drain from his face.

Lora placed a hand on his arm. "Hastings has made similar insinuations to me."

"I had no intentions of compromising you. Hasting wants to be something he is not, an aristocrat with all that he thinks goes with it. Money, position, and a title. He'd be willing to marry as long as it was a profitable arrangement."

"My trust."

His eyes widened.

"Please, don't be surprised. Harriet already told me he was questioning my trust. He thinks he will..." She stopped and looked at him. "You know that already."

"Yes. It wasn't until recently that I realized Hastings was rooting around in other people's finances besides mine. He has been making moves to undermine the new reforms, organizing some of the most influential and wealthiest men to stop workers from banding together. They are particularly against the expansion of the clinic."

Lora listened attentively, her eyes fixed upon his. "Why didn't you tell me sooner?" she inquired softly.

"Matters have grown more intricate. Hastings and his accomplice are determined to halt progress at any cost, and their actions pose a significant threat to us all. I have been gathering intelligence, keeping watch over their activities, and seeking a means to stop them without drawing undue attention. But it is perilous work. If you were not involved, there was no need to put you in harm's way."

Her expression softened, but she didn't offer him immediate relief. "I am involved. Why is he looking into your finances?"

"He is searching for something to use as leverage to have me do his bidding. He operates on the assumption that everyone has something to hide. That is his preferred currency."

Lora leaned in, her voice barely a whisper. "What is he hoping to find, Rockford? What are you hiding?"

His jaw muscle visibly tensed as he weighed his options. The scandal in London was a convenient decoy, but it was far from the whole truth. Could he keep her safe while keeping her in the dark? Every moment spent in silence felt like an eternity as he wrestled with the dilemma. The mission is paramount.

"There was a scandal in London," Rockford said, his voice firm. "I was accused of indiscretion, and though the accusations were unfounded, the stain on my reputation remains. Hastings knows this and seeks to use it against me. But you must believe me, Lora, my intentions toward you are sincere."

"We'll turn this to our advantage," she said firmly. "Together, we'll outmaneuver Hastings, quietly, but decisively."

The muscle along his jawline pulsed as he stared at her. When he looked into her eyes, he saw unwavering determination and strength. And something shifted inside him.

It was as if a tight knot in his chest suddenly gave way, and he was flooded with clarity he hadn't felt before. He would sacrifice the mission if it meant keeping her safe. She was more than a part of his life now; she was the very center of it. The mission and its secrets paled beside her safety. He would face any danger to ensure she remained unharmed. Losing her was unthinkable.

"Do you want to tell Barrington, or shall I?" Rockford's smile softened, a rare warmth in his voice. "That you're part of Barrington's Brigade."

Barrington was in for a surprise. Lora was smarter than he thought, and, more importantly, she was up to the challenge.

The conversation, heavy with unspoken truths, was interrupted by a firm knock at the door. Rockford's eyes widened, a flicker of concern crossing his face. "Wait here," he said quietly, rising to his feet.

He opened the door, "Barrington," he paused more from relief than surprise. "This is unexpected. It seems to be a day filled with surprises."

"Rockford, may I come in? There's an urgent matter we need to discuss."

Rockford stepped aside. "Of course." He stepped aside.

Barrington entered, his gaze falling first on Lora by the hearth, her satchel at her feet. Surprise flickered across his face before disapproval settled in his eyes. Rockford braced himself.

"I was preparing to return to Rockford Manor when Lora arrived."

Barrington straightened, his posture impeccably formal. "Lady Lora," he greeted with a slight bow. "I hadn't expected to find you here."

Rockford tensed when a flush rose to Lora's cheeks, but he knew he needn't have been concerned when Lora met Barrington's gaze with composure. "Lord Barrington," she titled her head. "I needed to discuss urgent gala matters with His Grace."

Barrington's expression softened slightly. "I see." He straightened his coat with a deliberate motion, then turned to Lora. "Forgive me, Lady Lora," he said before turning to Rockford. "May we speak privately?"

"Of course," Rockford replied, his stomach tightening at the urgency in Barrington's voice. Whatever the matter, it promised to test his already strained resolve.

Chapter Seventeen

"ROCKFORD, DO YOU realize the position you've put Lady Lora in? And if you believe for one minute that I consider that feminine satchel at her feet to be yours, you are mistaken." Barrington began, his voice firm but not unkind. "To play the rival for affection is one thing, but this is…not like you."

Rockford met his gaze steadily. "She came here unexpectedly. I did not plan, nor did I invite her here." He glanced at the door. "If anything, I came here to get away from her."

Barrington sighed, his brows knitting together. "Regardless, if discovered, an unchaperoned lady alone with a gentleman at a remote location could lead to ruinous gossip."

"I am well aware," Rockford replied, tension edging his voice. "I intend to escort her back promptly."

"Good." Barrington gave a firm nod. "I know you care for her. That's clear. But you must proceed with caution. The stakes are high, and not just regarding Hastings."

"I appreciate your counsel," He was sincere with Barrington as they walked toward Barrington's horse. "She's already entangled in this more than I'd like. It's time we involve her properly. Our original plan was for me to stay close to Lora to gather information about Hastings and become his rival for her attention."

"You're letting emotions cloud your judgment. You care for her—anyone can see that—but including her in this mission? That's a dangerous precedent."

"Hear me out. She has proven herself to be resourceful and trustworthy. I believe she should be included in what we're doing."

Barrington raised an eyebrow, considering Rockford's words. "You're that certain? This is not a decision to be taken lightly."

"I'm that certain. I wouldn't have suggested it if I hadn't thought it through." Rockford waited and watched Barrington tumble his words in his head. "She knows more than we give her credit for, and her insight could be invaluable. Besides, keeping her in the dark puts her at greater risk."

Barrington untied a rolled parchment from his saddle and then turned to Rockford. "Very well, then. We proceed together. We must ensure her safety and propriety. Now we best return."

Relieved, Rockford and Barrington started back to the lodge. They found Lora at the table, her pen and paper ready, her open satchel beside her. Her gaze met Rockford's. He nodded at her makeshift desk with a smile.

"Lady Lora."

She directed her attention to Barrington.

"To safeguard your reputation," he continued gently, "it would be best if His Grace escorted you back to Fallsmith Hall as soon as possible. In the meantime, perhaps we could briefly discuss the urgent matters pertaining to Hastings."

"Luckily, I came prepared." She gestured toward the table.

"I see." Barrington smiled. Rockford took it in for what it was, a smile of contrition.

Had he or Barrington thought for one minute she was there to… No, she was a bluestocking, but even she had her limits, although, to be with him…

The firelight cast flickering shadows across their faces, dancing in tandem with their thoughts. Barrington's fingers drummed on the table, his brow knit in thought. Lora, her hands clasped tightly in her lap, sat quietly, determined to move her musing to something more acceptable.

"Time is not on our side," Barrington began, his tone serious.

"We have nine days to capture the highwayman and find out who he works for. Every moment counts."

Lora listened as she absorbed the importance of what Barrington and Rockford discussed. But her mind was already turning over the possibilities and implications.

Barrington unrolled the parchment and carefully spread a detailed map on the table. He bent over it, examining the area around Sommer-by-the-Sea. "Timothy Wilkins is the royal courier who will be riding tomorrow. He will courier the pouch to the king in Royston Mills," he said, his eyes tracing the route. He straightened up and let out a breath. "It's only a half day's journey from here." He bent down, scrutinizing the map.

In the quiet moment, with Barrington reviewing the map, Lora whispered, "Thank you."

Rockford nodded slightly, his eyes conveying more than words ever could.

"Do you agree?" Barrington asked, still concentrating on the map.

"Timothy's usual route passes through these areas." Rockford traced a finger along the route. "Based on previous attacks, we've identified two prime locations where the highwayman is likely to strike."

Lora leaned in, her keen eyes scanning the details. She moved closer, her glance following the roads. "Those are two different roads," she observed, her voice thoughtful. She lifted her head and looked at Rockford. "They converge near the old Stonefield farm at the edge of town, at Stonefield Crossing. His son converted it into an inn. It's secluded, where the highwayman could plot and plan and not be disturbed."

Barrington's eyes widened as he took in her words. He quickly masked his surprise with a controlled expression, one he gave out sparingly. "Well done." His expression then shifted to one of genuine admiration. "That's a valuable observation, Lora. We can use that to our advantage."

"Peter Simms and Simon Watts arrived a few days ago. They

were joined by Thomas Greene, who has been working for me for the last six months," Barrington continued. "They will be instrumental in this operation. Simms, our master of concealment, will shadow the highwayman without detection. Watts, with his exceptional marksmanship and tactical expertise, stands ready to intercept and counter any threat. And Greene, with his expertise, in counterintelligence. In his case, undercover and in Hastings' employ."

Rockford leaned over the map, his gaze intense. He tapped the map at the two places near the farm. "We can position Simms and Watts at these two locations." He indicated a bend in the road on the north and another on the south approaches to the old Stonefield farm. "This way, we cover both possible routes and the area around the farm."

"Agreed," Barrington said, his tone decisive. "Tim departs tomorrow morning at ten o'clock. We must all be ready by then. He got to his feet. "There isn't much more we can do here."

Rockford folded the map carefully, glancing at his companions. "We'll use Rockford Manor as our headquarters."

Barrington nodded in agreement. "I'll take the south road. We'll cover every inch."

"And I'll take the north road," Rockford added. His gaze shifted to Lora. "Can you be at Rockford Manor by eight o'clock in the morning?"

Lora straightened, meeting his eyes. "By all means. What would you have me do?"

"I need your keen eyes to review the map and routes." Rockford's tone was determined, reflecting the gravity of their mission. "Identify any potential escape routes or contingency plans the highwayman could have. If you find anything, give the information to Jeffers. He will bring it to me immediately. You don't have to do this—"

"I know I don't, but I want to." Lora's determination and trepidation flared in her eyes.

Satisfied, Rockford placed a reassuring hand on her shoulder.

"You are the best person for this assignment."

Barrington addressed Lora. "I agree with Rockford. Your involvement is an asset and greatly appreciated, but we must prioritize your safety and reputation." He shook his head gently. "These are challenging times. We must all be cautious."

As they prepared to depart, Barrington spoke privately to Rockford once more.

"Make sure she's seen returning from a respectable direction. The last thing we need is unnecessary scrutiny," he advised. "Perhaps suggest that you encountered one another during an afternoon ride."

"You needn't be concerned," Rockford assured him.

Barrington clasped his shoulder briefly, then waved his good-bye to Lora. "Take care, my friends." He mounted his horse and turned back toward Sommer-by-the-Sea. As Rockford and Lora watched him disappear into the woods, the impact of the conversation settled over them.

⤖⤗

ROCKFORD AND LORA set out on horseback, the path winding through the woods. Silence settled between them, thick with unspoken words. Sunlight filtered through the trees, casting dappled shadows on the ground. Their only accompaniment was the rhythmic clopping of hooves and the distant rustle of leaves. After a while, he noticed Lora adjusting her gloves, a nervous habit she could not overcome.

She broke the silence. "I hadn't fully considered the implications when I came this morning." Her eyes remained fixed on the path ahead.

Rockford glanced at her. "You were seeking answers." He rubbed the back of his neck as he searched for the right words. "I should have been more mindful."

She shook her head gently, the motion causing a few loose

strands of hair to catch the sunlight. "We both hold some responsibility. What's important now is handling the situation as Barrington suggested, appropriately."

He nodded, the corner of his mouth lifting in a small, rueful smile. "Barrington suggested we create the impression we met by chance during a ride." He gave her a side glance, hoping for her agreement.

"That seems wise." Her voice was barely a whisper.

They rode silently for some time, the atmosphere thick with unspoken words. Rockford exhaled slowly, the sound mingling with the afternoon's quiet. His mind churned, grappling with the gravity of the direction the mission had taken. Each heartbeat pounded with the realization of what he stood to lose. When he and Barrington first derived the plan, he thought it would be good to spend time with Lora and if it bothered Hastings, all the more reason to do it. He never thought, God's Blood, how had this happened? But as he looked at her, riding beside him with quiet determination, the truth was undeniable. He had fallen in love with her.

He closed his eyes as the word seared into his brain. Love. Since he returned from France, he had made honesty, loyalty, and trustworthiness the bedrock of his identity. Yet here he was, entangled in a deceitful plan.

He glanced at Lora, her profile illuminated by the dappled sunlight. She had shown such courage and determination, qualities he admired deeply. He had always prided himself on being a man of honor, yet now he found himself violating the very principles he held dear. The mission demanded secrecy, but the cost was eroding his self-respect. He couldn't bear the thought of Lora seeing him as a liar and a fraud.

Finally, he spoke, his voice low and tired. "Lora, I want you to know, I never intended for you to become embroiled in all this.

She turned to look at him, her gaze steady and unwavering. "I chose to involve myself. And despite the… complexities, I don't regret seeking the truth."

The path gradually widened, leading them out of the dense woods and into open fields. The landscape was a patchwork of meadows and farmlands, bathed in the golden light of late afternoon. They reached Stonefield Crossing and turned south to follow the Sommer River.

Rockford's gaze flickered to Lora. "Lora, you don't have to take this on. Hastings is not a man to be underestimated."

Lora met his gaze with quiet determination. "I am aware of the risks, Rockford. But I cannot stand idly by. The clinic is vital. I cannot turn my back on the people it serves. I must see this through."

How had he not known about her valor? He laughed to himself. All he had seen was Adam's little sister in a beautiful woman's body. "Together, we will see it through." Silently, he made another vow. No matter what happened, if he had to put his own back to it, she would get the clinic expansion she was fighting so hard for.

As they approached the outskirts of her family estate, Fallsmith Manor came into view, its imposing silhouette softened by the waning light. Rockford guided Lora to the front door, reluctant that their journey was ending.

Before she dismounted, Rockford reached out, placing a gentle hand on her arm. "Promise me you'll be careful. We have a long road ahead, and I need to know you'll stay safe."

Lora nodded, her expression resolute. "I promise, Rockford."

He helped down. She shook out her skirt. The stable boy came out to take Astra. She looked around.

"Is something amiss?"

"My satchel," she looked up at Rockford, her face a mirror of distress. "I left it at the lodge."

"Not to worry. I'll have it for you in the morning."

As she disappeared into the house, Rockford lingered for a moment, watching the door close behind her. With a heavy heart, he turned his horse and began the ride back. The path ahead was uncertain, but his commitment to protect her was unwavering.

⧽⧽⧽⧼⧼⧼

LORA STOOD AT the threshold of her father's study, her heart pounding. She had heard the familiar sound of his voice mingling with the rustle of papers as she passed by the corridor. Taking a deep breath, she raised her hand and knocked softly on the door.

"Lora, my dear. Come in," her father called warmly from inside.

She pushed the door open and stepped inside, a smile on her face. "Welcome home, Father. How was Brighton?"

"It was delightful," he replied, setting his quill down and motioning for her to sit. "Your mother had quite a list of tasks for me, but we managed to get through them all. Adam sends his regards as well."

Lora nodded, feeling a moment of peace in the familiarity of their conversation. "I'm glad to hear that. It's good to have you back."

Her father studied her for a moment, then asked, "Do you have any plans for the next season?"

Lora was startled by the question, her heart skipping a beat. "Absolutely not."

Her father raised an eyebrow, a hint of disappointment in his eyes. "And Lady Harriet has not been successful in finding you a suitable match?"

A surge of anger welled up inside her. "Not for any lack of trying, Father."

"Well," he said, his tone firm, "what you and she cannot accomplish, I will."

Lora's curiosity got the better of her. "What do you mean? What are you doing?"

"I'm writing to the king," he replied matter-of-factly. "I am making the arrangements where you and Harriet have failed."

Her anger flared, her mind racing. "You can't be serious! You're deciding my future without my consent?"

"Don't worry," he said, dismissing her concern with a wave of his hand. "You'll love his garden."

Lora's breath caught in her throat. She opened her mouth to argue, but her father had already turned back to his writing, dismissing her as if she were a child. Fury and disbelief surged through her. Without another word, she spun on her heel and stormed out, her pulse hammering with outrage.

Chapter Eighteen

12 October 1822

LORA ARRIVED AT Rockford Manor at exactly eight o'clock. The air was crisp with the promise of a new day. She had no time to enjoy the gentle, golden glow and the early morning light casting long shadows across the manicured lawns. She dismounted, her heart racing with the anticipation of the day's events.

At the door, Rockford's valet greeted her with a respectful bow. "Good morning, Lady Lora. I'm Jeffers. This way, if you please." He stood to the side as she entered.

Lora nodded, offering a polite smile. "Thank you."

She followed the valet through the halls, her eyes catching glimpses of familiar family portraits and antique vases. Her concentration focused on the job ahead. She was eager to see Rockford and, if anything, wish him well on today's adventure.

Entering the study, she was struck by the masculine elegance of the room. Dark wood paneling covered the walls, and shelves lined with leather-bound books filled the air with the comforting scent of aged paper and polished mahogany. A large, carved desk dominated the space, its surface cleared except for a single rolled document.

Her gaze was drawn to a single riding glove draped over a satchel, her satchel by the foot of the desk.

"Would you care for some breakfast, Lady Lora?" Jeffers asked.

Lora shook her head gently. "A cup of tea will suffice, thank you."

Moments later, a footman entered the room and placed the tea service on the desk.

"Mr. Jeffers, will His Grace be joining me?"

"No, my lady. He has gone. He has left me instructions to assist you. You only need to engage the bell pull if you need me." He gestured to the velvet cord hanging against the desk wall.

"Thank you." Sitting at the desk, she poured her tea. This was Rockford's domain, a place where critical decisions were made. As she sipped her tea, she realized the gravity and importance of what she, Barrington, and Rockford were about to undertake were paramount in her mind.

She reached into her pocket for her handkerchief and felt the crinkle of paper. Puzzled, she pulled out a letter. Letting out a deep sigh, she closed her eyes. She closed her eyes at her father's letter to the king. It had been on the hall salver waiting to be delivered, a stark reminder of her predicament. In a moment of defiance, she swiftly snatched the letter and hid it within the folds of her dress.

Now, here it was, reminding her of the lengths she was willing to go to control her own fate. She stuffed it back into her pocket with a sigh, knowing she needed to focus on the task.

She set the half-full teacup down and spread the map across the desk, her fingers tracing the routes with focused precision. The quiet of the morning amplified the urgency in her heart, each detail on the map taking on heightened significance.

Lora pored over the map, reviewing the two identified routes in detail. She knew both well from riding in this area often. As the minutes ticked by, the soft chime of the mantel clock's rhythmic ticking was a constant reminder of the looming deadline.

Her fingers moved slowly, almost methodically, over the map, her mind racing to search out anything they had overlooked. The early morning light shifted, casting different shadows on the map as the minutes turned into an hour, then an hour and a quarter. The soft hum of activity in the manor outside the study seemed distant, her focus entirely on the task at hand.

Her gaze locked onto an area near Stonefield Farm, and her heart quickened. The old private road wasn't marked—it had been forgotten, overgrown after years of disuse. A jolt of realization struck her. A third route. The highwayman's escape path.

She grabbed the bellpull behind her and gave it a hard tub. "Jeffers," she called out as she marked the place on the map and began to roll it up.

The valet hurried in. "Yes, my lady?"

"Jeffers, I found another route, Rockford needs to know immediately." She put it in a long leather cylinder. "It's critical Rockford knows about this immediately. He's the closest to the route."

Jeffers nodded as he took the cylinder. "Leave it to me. I'll get this information to him."

The valet had barely ridden off when Lora began to worry. She absentmindedly picked up Rockford's glove and paced the study. Her eyes flicked to the mantel clock with increasing anxiety. Every tick seemed louder, a relentless reminder of the precious minutes slipping away.

"Rockford won't reach the private roadway in time, especially if he doesn't even know it exists. If she didn't act now, it might be too late," she muttered as she paced, her mind racing for solutions but at each turn facing imminent failure. Another glance at the blasted clock only heightened her anxiety.

She threw the glove onto the desk and hurried out of the study, bumping into James, the footman. Her footsteps echoed softly against the marble floors as she rushed down the hall. Her heart pounded with each step as she left the house, fear and fierce determination driving her forward.

She reached the horse barn and scanned the area for Astra. Her horse nickered and tossed her head. The mare sensed she was anxious.

"Easy girl," the groom said, trying to calm her as Lora approached. The groom turned toward her. "Can I help you, my lady?" a young girl stood ready to help her.

Lora stared in disbelief. "Are you the groom?" The young girl, about her size, nodded.

"Yes, my lady. I'm Amy Burn, milady."

"You certainly may help me." Lora allowed herself a brief smile for the first time in the last hour and a half.

Moments later, Lora rode Astra out of the barn, the borrowed groom's clothes making her nearly unrecognizable. She leaned forward, determination hardening her gaze. Astra, sensing the urgency, pinned her ears and surged forward the moment they cleared the manor gates. The world blurred into streaks of green and gold as they raced toward the woods. Astra's hooves pounded in rhythm with Lora's racing pulse, closing the distance to the woods.

They cut across open fields, the tall grasses whispering against Astra's legs. Dew sprayed up, but Lora didn't have time to savor the coolness. She had to get to the private road.

Reaching the stream that fed Sommer River, she guided Astra across without hesitation. The mare plunged into the shallow water, the chill splashing up and dampening Lora's legs. The current tugged at her mount, but Astra's stride remained strong and sure as they went downstream, cutting more time off their mission.

Climbing out of the river on the far bank, they pressed onward. The countryside stretched in front of them in a patchwork of rolling hills and meadows, but Lora's gaze remained fixed ahead. Time was slipping through her fingers like sand, and every moment counted.

Lora gently squeezed her legs, asking for more speed. Astra responded to her rider's request, her muscles bunching and stretching with each powerful stride. Every jolt, every shift in Astra's gait, was felt keenly by Lora, her connection to the horse as strong as ever.

Ahead, a series of fences and low walls dotted the landscape, the remnant of old boundaries that had challenged them in the past. Lora's throat tightened as apprehension welled up. She could feel the horse's muscles tensing beneath her, picking up on her unease.

"Steady, Astra. We've done this before," she murmured, leaning forward slightly, her fingers threading through Astra's mane for reassurance.

Astra's ears swiveled back, listening. The mare surged forward, her stride lengthening as they approached the first fence. Lora rose slightly in the stirrups, her body moving in harmony with the horse's motion.

They sailed over the fence with graceful ease, the wind rushing past them. Lora's heart soared, and a triumphant smile spread across her face.

A laugh of pure exhilaration escaped her. "Brilliantly done, my girl!" Lora's gloved hand patted Astra's neck. But the path ahead still stretched long and uncertain. There was no time to linger in their success.

As they galloped onward, the familiar silhouette of the old stone fence emerged from the mist. Memories of past attempts flickered in Lora's mind, the hesitation, the stumble. Now, there was no room for doubt.

Lora's grip on the reins tightened ever so slightly. She could feel Astra's heartbeat, fast and strong, mirroring her own. "We're going to soar like birds over the wall," she whispered.

As they drew nearer, the world seemed to narrow until only the wall and their path to it remained. The sounds around them faded, replaced by the thunderous rhythm of hooves and the rush of blood in Lora's ears.

The wall loomed in front of them as they rushed toward it. Lora adjusted her seat. Astra appeared to be instinctively aware of when to jump. Astra ran faster without the need for further urging, her powerful legs eating up the ground. Lora lowered herself closer to the mare's neck, the coarse hairs of the mane brushing against her cheek. They moved as one creature, their wills united.

Lora stared ahead at the rapidly moving ground and visualized the spot where Astra needed to begin the jump. This wall was high and wide. If they were going to get past this obstacle, starting the jump too soon or too late would be disastrous.

Astra ran faster still, her powerful legs devouring the ground beneath them. "Steady. Wait. Just. A. Bit. Longer." Her voice could barely be heard above the rush of wind.

"Now!"

Astra launched herself into the air. For a breathless instant, they soared, suspended between the earth and sky. The world seemed to hold its breath as it passed beneath them. Time stretched, the sensation of flight exhilarating and terrifying all at once.

Gravity reclaimed them. Astra landed firmly, her hooves striking the earth with a solid thud, vibrating up through Lora's legs. Astra immediately found her stride without so much as a stumble, and they continued on.

HIDDEN IN THE thicket near the abandoned roadway, the highwayman surveyed his surroundings with practiced ease. His eyes flickered to the north road, where he expected the courier to appear. The plan was simple, intercept the courier, secure the documents, and disappear without a trace.

He adjusted his mask and checked his gear, ensuring everything was in place for a swift operation. He settled deeper into the shadows, the dense foliage providing ample cover. His breathing slowed as he waited for the perfect moment to strike.

As LORA AND Astra approached Briarcliff Woods, the cool air

beneath the foliage carried the scent of pine and damp leaves surrounding them. Lora slowed Astra to a canter, then a careful trot.

"Easy now," she murmured, her gaze sweeping the surroundings. The woods were quiet, save for the occasional rustle of leaves and the melodic bird. Beams of sunlight pierced through the branches, illuminating specks of dust that danced in the air.

She dismounted, her boots sinking slightly into the soft underbrush. Astra nickered softly, her ears twitching as she surveyed the area. Lora led her to a secluded spot among the trees, a thicket of bramble and fern where they wouldn't be seen. She stroked the mare's muzzle. "We've made it. Now, we rest and wait, my friend."

Minutes ticked by, each one feeling longer than the last. Lora's thoughts swirled. Had she arrived in time? Had Jeffers reached Rockford? Doubt threatened to creep in, but she firmly pushed it aside. No use fretting now. She'd done all she could. She sat at the base of the old hollow tree and waited.

As she rested, she recalled she had her father's letter to the king, which she had placed in her pocket when she changed clothes with Amy Burn. Angry at her father and needing to distance herself from the letter, she stood to tuck the letter into her saddlebag. However, as she turned towards Astra, she noticed the tree and smiled. Her fingers traced the familiar knot in the tree's bark. With one last glance at the letter, she pressed it into the hollow. A quiet resolve settled over her, this was one secret she would keep safe, no matter what came next.

As Lora waited in the shadows of the dense woodland, the stillness of Briarcliff Woods surrounded her. The soft rustling of leaves overhead was the only sound. She strained her ears, hoping to catch any hint of Timothy or perhaps Rockford approaching. Time seemed to crawl, each passing minute magnifying her anxiety.

She froze. Footsteps? Her heart hammered as she held her breath, straining to listen. A rustle, then a small hare darted from the underbrush. She exhaled sharply, forcing her pulse to steady. But the unease remained. If Rockford didn't arrive soon, she would have to act alone.

Chapter Nineteen

HOOFBEATS THUNDERED IN the distance, growing louder. Lora's heart leaped, but something was wrong. The rhythm was erratic, frantic. She peered through the foliage and froze. A horse galloped wildly down the path, its reins flapping. There was no rider.

A chill ran down her spine. Whose horse was it? Emerging from her hiding place, she stepped onto the path.

"Whoa there," she called softly, holding out her hands. The horse slowed, its sides heaving as it approached her cautiously.

Just as she reached for the bridle, a shadow shifted at the edge of her vision. Before she could react, a gloved hand clamped firmly over her mouth and stifled her startled gasp.

The highwayman's grip on her mouth remained firm as he leaned closer. "Not a sound." His voice was a low growl.

Lora's heart pounded, but she forced herself to stay calm. After a tense moment, he slowly removed his hand from her mouth but remained intimidatingly close.

"Now, listen carefully." His tone was muffled but command-ing. "You will do exactly as I say, or there will be consequences. Understand?"

She nodded and caught a glimpse of her assailant. He was a tall figure cloaked in black, a mask concealing his features. The highwayman.

"Why are you doing this? What are you after?" Her questions were real, but they were also a delay tactic.

"State secrets can be valuable to so many people. As for royal correspondence, you would be surprised what you can find out and use to your advantage."

He leaned in, his tone cold and devoid of emotion. "Enough questions. If you wish to remain unharmed."

She nodded slowly, her mind whirling. How did he approach so silently?

"Mount your horse," he commanded, gesturing toward Astra.

Swallowing her fear, Lora adjusted her cap, hoping he wouldn't realize her identity. She mounted Astra, the highwayman mounted his horse. Lora took Astra's reins. They set off and went deeper into the woods.

They rode in an oppressive silence as the canopy above thickened, casting the surroundings into a dim twilight despite the morning hours. Lora was well aware that the deeper they ventured into the wilderness, the farther she was from the safety of the main path. Lora tried to memorize landmarks, a gnarled oak here, a rocky outcrop there, but the unfamiliar terrain soon became a labyrinth.

After what felt like an eternity, they arrived at an old hunting lodge set among towering pines. The structure was weathered but sturdy, its stone walls covered with ivy. He dismounted and then signaled for her to get down from her horse.

They walked up to the lodge. "Inside," he ordered, holding the door open. She hesitated briefly but decided compliance was her best option for now. The interior was dim, too dim to take note of any furnishings. The air was filled with the rich scents of aged wood, damp stone, tart citrus, and a smoky aroma. The floorboards creaked underfoot.

"Through there," he pointed toward a door at the back. She stepped forward, her senses alert. As she entered the small room, she noticed only a simple bed and a window with shutters that were nailed shut, letting in a faint sliver of light that cast eerie shadows on the wall.

He started to close the door.

"Why are you doing this?" She kept her voice steady.

He paused for a moment, his eyes unreadable beneath the mask. "Let's just say you're an unexpected complication."

The villain stood at the doorway. With the light from behind him, all she could see was his menacing silhouette. Slowly, he walked in front of her. "You must be wondering what happens next." His voice was harsh. His gaze lingered on her, as if reassessing something. Then, with a swift tug, he yanked off her cap. Her breath hitched as her hair tumbled free, cascading down her back. A slow smirk curled his lips. "Well, well."

"Perhaps you're hoping for a swift rescue. A valiant duke, perhaps. So brave and trustworthy. Ha, if only you knew the truth. But until then, you'll have to make do with your surroundings."

He stepped closer, his eyes glinting with cruel amusement. "That bed," he gestured with a nod, "might seem like a place of rest. But it can easily become a place where your worst fears come to life, should you choose not to cooperate."

Lora's breath hitched, the insinuation clear and terrifying. He wouldn't dare. She didn't trust herself to speak. Instead, she lifted her chin and locked eyes with an unwavering, hard glint. She ignored the chill that ran down her spine and commanded her heart to stop pounding. Her thoughts raced, searching for a way out, a strategy to survive.

She could almost hear Rockford's voice. *Fear clouds judgment.* Rockford faced danger countless times and remained calm, and so would she. *Concentrate on finding the solution rather than dwelling on the obstacle* was his strategy. If he could remain composed and fearless, so could she. Lora pushed back the fear that threatened to take over.

The villain chuckled, the sound unsettling. "Rest well, my lady. You'll need your strength. I enjoy a challenge."

Before she could respond, he closed the door, the lock clicking into place with an unnerving finality. The room shrank around her, and for a moment, she could only hear the frantic rhythm of her heartbeat.

Left alone, she took a deep breath, allowing herself a moment to calm down amid the dust and moldy smell of the room. One breath, then another. Her heart was finally settling into its regular rhythm. That was when she noticed a faint scent, sharp citrus intertwined with a smoky undertone, drifting in the room, defying the stale air.

She blinked several times, adjusting her eyes to the dim light filtering through the shutters. Slowly, she turned, taking in her surroundings, and searched for a way out. The walls were solid logs. With the shutters nailed shut, the only exit was the locked door. Her gaze darted around the small chamber, noting the sparse furnishings—a simple bed draped with a worn woolen blanket.

Lora knelt and peered underneath the bed. Amidst the dust and cobwebs, she spotted a dangling slat. *I enjoy a challenge.* The words echoed in her head. Her stomach churned at the thought of touching the bed, but she forced herself to reach and grasp the piece of wood. The slat was rough and brittle in her hands. She wiggled it back and forth until it came free.

She stood up with the slat and brought it close to the shuttered window to examine it. A wide smile bloomed as she discovered two rusted nails protruding from the end. It was a small victory, but a victory, nonetheless.

Hefting her weapon, she found it light enough to wield swiftly and sturdy enough to deliver a decent blow if necessary. She wouldn't be afraid to use it.

She turned her attention to the window. It was tightly nailed closed. She pressed her ear against the wooden shutter, listening intently. The outside world was muffled, a whisper of wind through leaves, the distant caw of a crow, but no voices or footsteps.

A sudden creak from beyond the door made her freeze. Muffled voices drifted in from the room beyond, heated, urgent tones. She pressed her ear against the door, straining to make sense of the indistinct words. The agitation was clear, even if the words weren't. How many of them are there? she wondered. And what are they planning? She tried again, but the muffled voices remained unclear. Suddenly, a deep, throaty cough cut through the murmur. It was on the other side of the door.

She stepped to the far side of the room, clutching her weapon, her heart pounding. If an opportunity arose, she would not be defenseless. She waited.

Minutes stretched on, the voices in the other room rising and falling. Suddenly, the sound of hurried footsteps, boots against wooden floors. Another set, their rhythm uneven, creating a syncopated pattern that set her nerves on edge. Doors slammed, and the voices faded one by one until there was silence.

Lora pressed her ear to the door again, straining to detect any movement. Then, the creak of a floorboard nearby sent her heart into her throat. The hairs on the back of her neck rose. Someone was still there.

The unmistakable sound of a key turning in the lock reached her ears. She stepped back as the door handle slowly turned. She held her weapon behind her back and composed herself just as the door's lock clicked.

She braced herself, every muscle tense, ready for whatever came next.

The door swung open, the burst of light blinded her. Instinctively, she shielded her eyes, blinking rapidly to adjust. As her vision cleared, she saw a silhouetted figure step inside, his features becoming clearer as he moved closer.

"Lora?" The whisper was filled with urgency and disbelief.

Her eyes widened. "Rockford!" She dropped the makeshift weapon and rushed into his arms, the fear and tension melting away in his embrace. The warmth of his body, the solidity of his presence, grounded her in a way she desperately needed. Without thinking, she tilted her face up, and their lips met in a desperate, fervent kiss.

When they finally parted, Lora rested her head against his

chest, listening to his strong, steady heartbeat. Rockford gently cupped her face, his eyes searching hers, silently asking questions.

"I'm fine," she said, answering his silent question.

He smiled briefly, the hard lines around his eyes softened.

"We can't stay here." She looked past him into the main room. "The highwayman, the others, they might return any moment."

He gave a tight nod. "I doubt they will stay close by. Barrington and the others are searching the area."

As they emerged from the lodge, the cool night air hit her like a wave, refreshing yet chilling. They headed toward his horse concealed among the trees. Rockford turned to her, his eyes filled with concern. "Were you hurt?"

"No," she replied, her voice steady, though her mind was anything but calm. The villain's words, *I enjoy a challenge*, echoed in her head, a shadow that refused to lift. The fear she had managed to keep at bay resurfaced, gnawing at her.

She took a deep breath, trying to push the haunting memories aside. *Fear clouds judgment.* She glanced at Rockford. His presence was a lifeline, grounding her, but the anxiety clung to her like a stubborn fog.

"The highwayman knew someone would be along this route, but I don't think he realized who I was." Rockford reached for her hand. "Not until...I owe your Amy a new cap,"

Rockford's hands tightened on hers. His eyes were blazing with anger. "He could have stolen you away, vanished into the night—and I'd have spent the rest of my life searching." His voice was raw, his grip tightening as if anchoring himself to reality. "I can't lose you, Lora."

Lora's eyes widened. She should have known he would put the pieces together.

He pulled her into his arms, holding her tightly to comfort her and reassure himself that she was truly safe. "Do you have any idea what could have happened to you?" His voice was muffled against her hair. "You could have been lost to me... to us forever!"

Lora gazed at him, surprised by the intensity in his eyes. "Rockford, I couldn't just sit by and do nothing. I had to act."

He shook his head sharply. "Act? By recklessly endangering yourself? Riding out alone, unprotected, what were you thinking?"

She pulled away from him, a spark of defiance flashing in her gaze. "I didn't act impulsively. *Concentrate on finding the solution rather than dwelling on the obstacle.* Jeffers was on his way to you, but time was of the essence. My solution was to delay the highwayman until you or Barrington arrived. It was a good plan."

Rockford's expression softened slightly at her words, but his frustration remained. "I appreciate your courage, but this was foolhardy. You should have waited—trusted that we would arrive in time."

Her jaw set stubbornly. "But you didn't arrive in time."

His eyes widened, and he drew her closer, searching hers intently. "And what if he had harmed you? Taken you away where I'd never find you? Did you consider what that would do to—" He broke off, his voice strained. "To all of us," he finished weakly, though his eyes betrayed more.

She sighed softly. "I couldn't bear the thought of you, or anyone else, being hurt, especially not when I could help prevent it."

He exhaled slowly, the tension in his shoulders easing slightly. "Lora, your bravery is unquestionable, but please understand. The thought of you in danger... it terrifies me."

Her eyes softened. "I didn't mean to cause you pain."

He ran a hand through his hair, the gesture betraying his inner turmoil. "Lora, your bravery is commendable, but you underestimated the risk. You didn't account for your own safety in the plan. A good strategy includes ensuring that those executing it are safe. That's why we work in teams and use caution to ensure everyone's well-being. Just promise me you'll think twice before putting yourself at risk again."

She nodded, unable to speak. When had it begun? The admiration, the gratitude, the quiet pull toward him? It had always been there, growing unnoticed, waiting for her to acknowledge it. And now, as she met his gaze, the truth struck her. She loved him. Not just for his courage, but for his kindness, his fierce protectiveness, the way he understood her without words. The realization crashed over her like a wave, undeniable, overwhelming. She loved him deeply, truly, irrevocably.

Rockford helped her mount Astra. They began their journey back, but Lora's thoughts swirled with the events of the past hours. The warmth of Rockford's touch lingered on her skin, a reassuring anchor in the sea of chaos.

As they rode in comfortable silence through the familiar landscape, the sense of normalcy was almost jarring. The rhythmic clatter of hooves and the gentle rustling of leaves created a serene backdrop, yet Lora's mind was anything but calm. Despite her relief, her thoughts kept returning to the highwayman's words. *Unexpected complication.* It implied something bigger, something more dangerous afoot. She felt a surge of determination. She couldn't let this mystery go unsolved. She owed it to herself and to Rockford to uncover the truth.

As they emerged onto the main road, she glanced over at Rockford. "Thank you for finding me," she said softly.

"Always," he replied without hesitation, his gaze holding hers.

There was a vulnerability in his eyes that she hadn't seen before, offering her a glimpse into the depth of his feelings. A gentle warmth spread through her. "I suppose we make quite the pair."

He smiled faintly. "A matched set of stubborn souls."

They rode on silently, Fallsmith Manor coming into view. They rode down the drive and stopped at the front door.

Rockford swung down from his saddle and stood beside her, his presence comforting as he helped her dismount.

Lora offered him a tired smile. "Thank you, Rockford."

He cupped her face gently, his eyes searching hers for any sign of lingering fear. "I'll wait here until you're inside. Rest. I'll call on you later." He left no room for argument.

Lora turned and walked up the steps. Mr. Axbridge opened the door. She paused for a moment, looking back at him. Their eyes met, and a silent promise passed between them in that brief moment. He nodded, then she stepped inside. The door closed softly behind her.

Rockford mounted his horse and began the ride back. The memory of Lora's fear-stricken face and the relief in her eyes when he rescued her was etched deeply in his mind. He tightened his grip on the reins. He would face any challenge, endure any hardship, and conquer any foe. She was worth every sacrifice, and he vowed never to fail her. With each pounding hoofbeat, his determination solidified. He would face any danger, tear through any obstacle. Nothing, no enemy, no force on earth, would take Lora from him again.

Chapter Twenty

13 October 1822

LORA PERCHED ON the edge of the drawing room chaise, her hands knotted in her lap. The late afternoon light slanted through the windows, casting golden patterns on the Aubusson carpet. She traced its swirling designs with her gaze, willing the chaos in her mind to settle. Her fingers tightened, twisting a loose thread in the fabric of her gown. The delicate china clock on the mantel ticked steadily, each movement of its gilded hands marking a moment she wished would pass more quickly.

"Lady Lora," She flinched, her hand flying to her chest. "Forgive me, my lady. I didn't mean to startle you. Would you care for more tea?" Mrs. Kelly hovered near the untouched tea service with its gleaming teapot and unused porcelain cups.

Lora glanced up, her eyes momentarily unfocused. "Oh, no, thank you, Mrs. Kelly. I'm quite all right."

The housekeeper hesitated, worry lines etched on her face. "Very well, my lady."

The housekeeper left the room, passing Harriet, who glided through in a swirl of autumn color muslin and reserved anxiety. Her concern for her dear friend was obvious by the set of her mouth and look in her eyes.

"There you are! I was beginning to think you'd hidden yourself away." Harriet crossed the room with grace, then settled beside Lora. "I was here earlier but was told you weren't receiving callers. Really, Lora, did your morning not go as you planned?"

Lora's fingers tightened around the embroidered handkerchief. Its delicate fabric crumpled slightly under her grip. Planned? All she wanted to do was ensure the highwayman was delayed until Rockford arrived, not... "My morning ride was... more eventful than I anticipated."

Harriet tilted her head. "Eventful? I don't know if I should be concerned or delighted. Now you must tell me what happened. Did you encounter a dashing stranger on your ride?" She winked conspiratorially.

A flicker of something, fear, perhaps, flashed in Lora's eyes before she masked it with a practiced smile. "Nothing of the sort. I merely lost track of time while riding and found myself farther from home than intended."

Harriet studied her, the teasing glimmer in her eyes dimming. She let out a small sigh and took Lora's hand gently. "Lora, forgive me. I was only trying to bring back your smile." A pause. Then, more softly, "Mrs. Kelly mentioned you were out of sorts."

Lora opened her mouth to respond, but the words caught in her throat. How could she possibly convey the whirlwind of emotions in her head, the lingering dread, the relief, the confusion? She glanced toward the window to avoid Harriet reading more of her inner thoughts than she wanted.

"I'm just a bit tired," she finally managed. "Perhaps planning the gala has been more difficult than I thought. I don't know what I would do if you hadn't agreed to help."

Harriet's gaze softened. She reached out, placing a gentle hand over Lora's. "Then it's settled. If you're indebted to me, I demand we have fresh tea and not talk of tiring rides."

Before Lora could protest, Harriet tugged on the bell pull. Mrs. Kelly reappeared as if summoned by intuition.

"Would you please bring a fresh pot of chamomile tea, Mrs. Kelly? And perhaps some of those lovely lemon biscuits?" Harriet requested with a warm smile.

"Of course, Lady Harriet." The housekeeper's glance flickered briefly to Lora with quiet understanding and relief.

As Harriet turned her attention back to Lora, she began chatting about the upcoming gala, her words a soothing hum that required little in the way of response. Lora appreciated the effort—Harriet's unspoken gift of companionship without obligation.

Yet, beneath the veneer of casual conversation, Lora's thoughts churned. *I enjoy a challenge.* The sound of the highwayman's voice, the flash of his eyes. The phantom sensations refused to fade, and the searing grip of his hand still burned on her arm. She resisted the urge to rub the spot, unwilling to draw Harriet's notice.

"…and Lady Weatherby simply insists on wearing that atrocious feathered hat, can you imagine?" Harriet chattered, her nose wrinkling delicately. "Honestly, someone ought to advise her otherwise."

Lora nodded absently. "It's certainly… distinctive."

Harriet observed her quietly for a moment. "You know, you don't have to pretend with me."

Lora's gaze snapped to Harriet's, a hint of apprehension in her eyes. "What do you mean?"

"I mean that if something is bothering you, you can tell me," Harriet replied softly. "You've been distant. It's unlike you. Is it Rockford? Has he said anything, done something?"

"Not at all!" Lora's eyes widened as she sharply shook her head. She hesitated, torn between the desire to confide and the instinct to protect herself, and perhaps Harriet, from the darkness of the day's events. She took a steadying breath. "It's just been a rather overwhelming day. That's all."

Before Harriet could press further, the drawing room door opened once more. Rockford stepped inside, his presence commanding yet welcome. Dressed impeccably, there was a subtle tension in his posture. His eyes immediately focused on Lora.

"LORD ROCKFORD." HARRIET stood and greeted him with a pleasant surprise. "What brings you to Fallsmith Manor this afternoon?"

He offered a polite bow. "Good afternoon, Lady Harriet. I hope I'm not intruding."

"Not at all," she assured him. "We were just about to enjoy some tea. Would you care to join us?"

His gaze flitted to Lora, then back to Harriet. "I wouldn't want to impose."

"Nonsense." Harriet turned to Lora. "I just remembered there's a matter I must speak to Mrs. Kelly about concerning the gala invitations. Please make yourself comfortable. Lora could use the company."

Before either could protest, Harriet excused herself with a subtle smile.

An awkward pause settled as the door closed behind her. Rockford took a tentative step forward, not knowing what he would face. "I hope you don't mind the intrusion."

Lora managed a small smile. "You're always welcome here."

He clenched his hands at his sides, resisting the urge to reach for her, to reassure himself she was truly safe. "I came to see how you were faring."

She lowered her gaze. "I'm perfectly fine."

How could she say that after what she'd been through? "Are you?" He searched her eyes, desperation seeping into his tone, the same desperation he felt when he realized the depth of the consequences of their plan.

She sighed softly, the mask slipping just enough to reveal a hint of the turmoil beneath. "It's been a long day."

"I can only imagine," he murmured, the words tasting bitter. How his heart pounded when he found her in that lodge. The fear, the rage, the helplessness. "You went through quite an ordeal."

She looked up sharply, a flash of warning in her eyes. "Please, not here."

He straightened, biting back his impulse to respond. His own pain was nothing compared to hers, but it gnawed at him just the same. "Of course." He tilted his head. "My apologies."

Mrs. Kelly returned, carrying a tray with a fresh pot of chamomile tea and a plate of delicate lemon biscuits. "Here we are. Shall I pour, my lady?"

"Thank you, Mrs. Kelly, but I can manage."

As the housekeeper departed, Rockford watched as Lora busied herself with the tea service, the clinking of porcelain providing a welcome distraction for her.

He noticed the slight tremor in her hands and refused to let her struggle further. He covered her hand with his.

Lora raised her chin and stared at her.

"I find I'd rather walk in the garden. It's warm for October. Join me?"

She paused, and he watched as she silently debated. He hoped she would agree with the idea of open space, away from prying eyes.

"Yes, I think I would." She picked up her wool shawl from the end of the chaise and wrapped it around herself.

She accepted his offered arm, and they made their way through the French doors into the gardens.

The Fallsmith garden paths were lined with manicured hedges and bursts of colorful blooms. The soft fragrance of roses mingled with the earthy scent of the late afternoon. A gentle breeze rustled the leaves overhead, whispering secrets only the trees knew. He and Lora went on.

As they walked silently next to each other, he noticed the more they walked, the more the tension lifted from her shoulders. They reached a secluded alcove with a stone bench nestled beneath a canopy of gold wisteria leaves tipped with red.

Lora paused. "Shall we sit for a moment?"

"Of course." He hoped the garden walk was doing its magic.

They settled onto the bench, a comfortable distance apart.

"I appreciate your company, Rockford, but…" Lora hesitated. "There was no need for you to come."

Rockford turned to face her, his expression a mix of worry and admiration. "Lora, I know you've been through an unimaginable ordeal." His voice was gentle yet firm. "I wanted to be here, beside you, give you whatever strength you need. That's what friends do. That's what people…like us do."

Every fiber of his being wanted to reach out, to comfort her, but he restrained himself, aware that his turmoil mirrored hers. He took a deep breath, hoping it would calm him.

She took a steadying breath, pressing her hands together. "I keep replaying moments in my head, but it's like looking through fogged glass." She met his gaze. "Something about his voice… and there was a scent—something I've smelled before, but I can't place it."

All he could do at the moment was listen and be her steadfast anchor. He had sat with many soldiers, letting them talk out their fears, but this was different. This was Lora.

"There were… voices. Muffled, but some things are stuck in my head. One person had a distinctive sound." Her eyes darted to the garden, searching for unseen answers.

His brow furrowed, but he remained quiet, letting her find her own pace.

"And there was a scent… something familiar, but I can't place it. I've encountered it before, but I can't be sure."

He wanted her to remember, not because of the mission, but to stop her torment. His helplessness gnawed at him. He hoped his presence was enough to help her find her strength.

Lora looked down at her hands, fingers twisting together. "There were footsteps… they sounded different. Like someone had a… I don't know. It was an odd rhythm. Now I'm not even sure if I really heard it."

Rockford's gaze softened with empathy. "These are valuable

observations, Lora. Even if they seem fragmented now, they could be meaningful."

Tears welled up in her eyes as she looked up at him.

Rockford moved closer, his heart aching as he watched the tears roll down her cheek. She was a woman of immense strength and pride who rarely showed vulnerability. This rare moment tore at him more than any physical wound ever could. Gently, he placed his arm around her shoulders, hoping his warmth could offer the comfort that his words could not.

"You've done more than enough. We'll piece it together, bit by bit." He pulled her closer, his voice now a whisper. "I should never have gotten you involved in this."

She nestled closer, her lips parted ready to speak, but the distant crunch of footsteps on gravel shattered the moment.

Gently, he released her as Harriet appeared around the bend.

"There you are!" Her stare changed into a relieved smile. "I was beginning to think you'd both gotten lost."

"You were correct, Harriet. I needed to get out." Lora glanced at Rockford. "We've been enjoying the garden."

Harriet's eyes flickered between them. "I see. I hope I'm not interrupting?"

"Not at all," Rockford replied smoothly, rising from the bench. "I was just about to take my leave."

Lora stood as well, her gaze meeting Rockford's. "Thank you for calling."

He nodded, his eyes holding hers. "I'll see you tomorrow." With a polite nod to Harriet, Rockford turned his footsteps, fading down the flagstone path as he made his way to the garden gate.

❊❊❊❊❊❊

SHE WATCHED HIM go, the absence of his presence settling like a whisper of cold air against her skin. She longed for him to stay but feared it would unravel what fragile composure she had left. His visit had been a comfort, a tether to normalcy, but some battles had to be faced alone.

Harriet walked beside her, silent but present. As they reached the door, Lora hesitated, glancing back to where Rockford had stood only moments ago. His concern had been genuine, his touch reassuring, but some battles she had to face alone.

The memory of the highwayman and his threats still lingered, no longer a looming specter but a shadow at the edges of her thoughts.

Taking a steady breath, she stepped into the house with Harriet and closed the door softly behind them.

Chapter Twenty-One

14 October 1822

As Rockford approached the grand entrance of Fallsmith Manor, the crisp scent of autumn mingled with the delicate aroma of blooming roses, a gentle reminder of the changing seasons. Yet, despite the serene beauty surrounding him, his thoughts were consumed by the tumult of the previous day.

The urgency in Lora's message had ignited a fire within him. He'd known that involving her in the scheme to bait Hastings held an element of risk, but he'd never anticipated she would take such bold action alone. Her fierce independence, once merely a characteristic he admired from a distance, was now a source of pride and deeper concern.

He recalled dismounting at the crossroads. His heart didn't begin to pound until he saw the dainty footprints as he scanned the area. He knew they were Lora's. When he found different hoofprints, he knew at once she'd been captured, and it was his fault. Guilt gnawed at him, a slow, insidious weight settling in his chest. The memory of her dainty footprints at the crossroads, the stark contrast between them and heavy boots prints beside them, proof of her capture, flashed in his mind. Proof of his failure. His hands curled into fists. If he hadn't agreed to this charade, if he hadn't let her become involved, she might never have been in danger.

The memory of finding her in that dimly lit room, eyes wide with fear and relief, was seared into his mind. Her whispered plea, the way she clung to him, haunted his every thought. The truth settled in his chest, cold and undeniable, his feelings for Lora were not an act. Perhaps they never had been.

"Good morning, Your Grace."

A familiar voice cut through his brooding, grounding him in the present. Rockford blinked, realizing Axbridge stood before him, patient as ever.

"Good morning, Axbridge," Rockford replied, offering a curt nod. "Lady Lora is expecting me?"

"Yes, sir. She's in the sitting room."

"Thank you."

As he followed Axbridge through the stately foyer, the burden of his deception sat like a stone on his heart. His feelings had deepened, the lines between duty and desire blurred, and for once, he found himself struggling with a task. Each moment spent with her made it more difficult to maintain the charade.

Rockford clenched his fists at his sides, the tension obvious in the rigid set of his shoulders. His gaze lingered on the grand portraits lining the walls, but his mind was consumed by thoughts of Lora, her laughter, and her eyes sparkling with determination. He could not reconcile the happiness she brought him with the deceit he was entangled in. Each smile she gave him was a dagger to his heart, reminding him of the lie he lived.

Axbridge's footsteps echoed through the corridor, but Rockford, lost in his turmoil, barely heard them. He ran a hand through his hair in frustration, the strands slipping through his fingers as if seeking solace in what he had to do.

The realization hit him hard. Soon, he would have to confront the truth with Lora and himself. The battle between his duty and his love for her tore him apart, and he feared which side would ultimately prevail.

Entering the sitting room, his gaze found Lora immediately. She was on the sofa near the window, bathed in sunlight that highlighted the subtle auburn strands in her hair. When she looked up, their eyes met, and a familiar warmth stirred in his heart.

"Good morning," he greeted softly. "I wanted to discuss where we are with the gala plans if you're up to it."

Her eyes searched his, perhaps seeking reassurance, or was he imagining that? She gestured to the seat beside her. "Yes, the gala… it's important we keep moving forward."

He took his place on the sofa, conscious of the respectful distance yet acutely aware of their unspoken connection. She spoke with quiet determination, but her fingers curled around the cushion's edge, gripping it like an anchor. A flicker of exhaustion crossed her face before she smoothed it away. She wore a brave face, and guilt tightened like a vice around his heart.

"Is there anything specific you'd like us to focus on?" he asked gently, hoping to ease into their usual rhythm.

She drew a steadying breath. "I've added the last of guest responses to the list. Let's finalize the list and ensure we have everything in hand."

"Of course." He offered a small smile, producing his notes. "I brought our notes from our last meeting. We can review them together."

As they delved into the details, he couldn't help but become acutely aware of her every movement. The way a stray lock of hair brushed against her cheek and the earnestness in her voice as she spoke about the clinic drew him in.

"You have an incredible vision for this event," he remarked, genuinely impressed by her passion. "Your ideas truly capture the essence of the clinic's mission."

A faint blush colored her cheeks. "Thank you. I believe creating a serene atmosphere will encourage support for our work. The clinic means so much to the community—it deserves nothing less."

He hesitated before adding, "Including certain military and government officials could bolster our efforts. Their support might prove invaluable."

She met his gaze, a flicker of understanding passing between them. "Yes, that's wise. But we mustn't forget our local benefactors, the townspeople who've supported the clinic from the very beginning. It's important we honor those who've been with us all along."

"You're absolutely right." He made a note beside several names. "Their loyalty has been invaluable."

A comfortable silence settled between them, filled only by the soft scratching of pen on paper. Yet, beneath the surface, his thoughts warred. He'd deceived her, led her to believe his courtship was genuine when, in truth, it had begun as a mere strategy. Now, faced with the reality of his growing feelings, he grappled with a profound sense of shame.

"Lora," he began carefully, setting his pen aside. "I can't help but feel responsible for yesterday. If I hadn't involved you in this scheme, perhaps none of it would have happened."

She shook her head gently, a small, reassuring gesture. "Don't blame yourself. I acted on my own because I believed it was necessary. I couldn't risk the highwayman slipping away due to an oversight."

"Still," he pressed, "the thought of what could have happened if I hadn't arrived in time…" He didn't finish the sentence, but the implication hung heavy in the air.

She reached out then, her fingers brushing lightly against his arm. The contact sent a subtle warmth through him. "But you did come," she said softly. "And that's what matters. I knew you would."

For a moment, he allowed himself to simply absorb the sincerity in her gaze, the delicate touch of her hand. He wanted to promise he'd always be there and move heaven and earth to keep her safe. But the words felt too large, too laden with meaning.

She withdrew her hand and glanced down as if collecting her thoughts. "I mentioned to you before that fragments of time I was in the lodge resurface in my mind…"

He leaned in slightly, his attention fully hers. "Anything you recall could be helpful. Even the smallest detail."

"There was a scent," she began, her brow furrowing in concentration. "Like lemon mixed with something smoky. It's distinct, but I can't place where I've smelled it before."

"Lemon and smoke," he repeated, filing that away mentally. "Anything else?"

"His voice had an odd cadence. Almost familiar, but not quite. And he seemed to know things about you."

A chill prickled at the back of his neck. "About me? What did he say?"

"He made veiled references. It felt personal as if he held a grudge."

Rockford sat back, his fingers tightening around the armrest. A slow dread curled in his gut, cold and uncertain. His past was not without its shadows, but this? This was personal. Whoever the highwayman was, he wasn't just playing a game, he had a personal vendetta.

"I thought if we pooled our perceptions, we might piece together who he is and what he wants," she continued, her eyes searching his.

He met her gaze, determination, and something deeper stirring within him. "We'll figure it out," he assured her.

A hint of relief softened her features. "Thank you, Rockford."

He hesitated before adding, "And please, promise me you won't take such risks again. I couldn't bear it if—" He stopped himself, the depth of his feelings threatening to spill over.

She offered a faint smile. "I'll be more cautious."

"Good." He exhaled slowly, tension easing slightly. "Perhaps we can interview the couriers who had encounters with the highwayman. See if any patterns emerge."

"That's a good idea." She reached for a stack of papers. "I've taken some notes…"

As they immersed themselves in the task, he remained acutely aware of her every movement—the way she tucked a loose strand of hair behind her ear and her voice's soft inflection when she pondered a thought. An unspoken understanding lingered between them, a connection that went beyond their shared mission.

He decided then and there to protect her—not just from physical harm but from the shadows that threatened to dim her spirit. Rockford would ensure it ended here, whatever the highwayman wanted, whatever vendetta he pursued.

"Lora." Her name left his lips before he could stop it, barely above a whisper. She looked up, curiosity flickering in her gaze.

He hesitated. The truth pressed against his ribs, demanding to be spoken. But once said, it could never be taken back. His jaw tightened. Not yet.

Instead, he exhaled slowly. "I appreciate your trust in me. It means more than you know."

Her gaze softened, a gentle smile touching her lips. "You've given me every reason to trust you."

The knot in his chest tightened. He forced a smile, nodding. "Shall we continue?"

"Yes, of course."

As they delved back into their notes, Rockford knew the moment to reveal the truth was approaching. But for now, he cherished this time with her, even as his heart battled between duty and love.

Chapter Twenty-Two

T HAT AFTERNOON, THE Sommer Gentlemen's Club exuded quiet authority, its gas lamps burning steadily above whispered conversations and the shifting weight of influence. The Aubusson carpets muffled the measured strides of Sommer-by-the-Sea's and London's most powerful and influential men. Deep burgundy velvet drapes framed the tall windows overlooking Westmore Commons. The subtle scent of cigar smoke mingled with the aroma of aged brandy, creating an atmosphere of indulgent luxury.

Hastings paused at the threshold, allowing his eyes to adjust and his senses to drink in the familiarity of privilege. The hushed conversation provided a rumbling, soothing background. In this realm, deals were struck with a handshake, and reputations could be dismantled with a whisper.

Adjusting the cuffs of his tailored jacket, Hastings allowed a faint smirk to play on his lips. Tonight, he donned his finest attire: a midnight-blue waistcoat embroidered with silver thread, a crisp white cravat secured with a sapphire pin, a recent acquisition symbolizing his rising fortunes. The reflection in the gilded mirror revealed a man of sophistication, but beneath the polished veneer simmered a cauldron of resentments.

Hastings settled into a leather armchair near the fireplace, a glass of whiskey in hand as his gaze casually swept the room. He nodded graciously to several gentlemen who amicably returned his greeting.

Fools, he mused inwardly, casting a glance toward a cluster of gentlemen engrossed in their own self-importance. They think themselves untouchable, yet they all have skeletons waiting to be unearthed. The memory of being snubbed, of whispers trailing in his wake, fueled his determination. He knew that information flowed as smoothly in these halls as the aged whisky in his glass. One by one, they saw the error of their ways. All he had to do was hint at an indiscretion, and oh, how they came around. No longer an outsider, he had clawed his way into their midst, and tonight, he would begin their undoing.

He noticed Sir Becket, a prominent banker with connections to several philanthropic endeavors, engrossed in a game of cards with a few other gentlemen. Rockford, so assured, so untouchable. Hastings had seen the flicker of tension at the mention of Captain Langley. The past still haunted him. Good. Revenge would be slow, deliberate, and oh, so sweet.

Taking up his half-finished glass of whiskey, he approached Becket's table with an affable smile.

"Mind if I spectate for a while?" Hastings inquired, his tone amiable as he approached the card table where Sir Becket and his companions were engaged in a spirited game.

"Not at all," Becket replied, glancing up. "Pull up a chair. We're in need of fresh perspectives, Jackson here claims to have an unbeatable hand."

"Bold claim." Hastings settled into an empty seat. He surveyed the faces around the table, Lord Jackson, with his perpetual air of mischief; Mr. Cranwell, whose shrewd eyes missed little; and Sir Becket, ever the diplomat. "But then again, fortune favors the brave."

Jackson chuckled. "Or the foolish. Care to place a wager on that, Hastings?"

"Perhaps later. I've just returned from a rather enlightening trip to London and thought I'd unwind first. Besides, I wouldn't want to dampen your spirits with a string of victories." Hastings sipped his brandy.

Jackson raised an eyebrow at the mention of London. "Enlightening, you say? Business or pleasure?"

"A bit of both." He kept his reply vague as he leaned in slightly to invite curiosity. "Though, I must admit, the talks in the halls of Parliament were far more intriguing than any entertainment the city had to offer."

"Then, my friend, you do not know where to go for entertainment," the gentleman to Becket's right jested, eliciting a chuckle from the table. "Speak to me before you venture there the next time. I can make some very intriguing suggestions."

"Don't listen to Jackson," Becket interjected with a grin. "We all know that Lady Jackson would never put up with that." The group laughed, as did Jackson, the camaraderie unmistakable.

"Politics can be a labyrinth of intrigue." It was Cranwell's turn to raise an eyebrow, "Anything in particular catch your interest?"

Hastings leaned back, swirling his whisky thoughtfully. "Oh, the usual murmurings. Parliament is abuzz with the latest policies, and socialites are entangled in their dramas... Though I did encounter some rather... intriguing discussions about certain financial irregularities."

Sir Becket exchanged a glance with Cranwell. "That's a serious matter. Embezzlement?"

Hastings offered a nonchalant shrug. "Hard to say without definite evidence. But it's fascinating how funds intended for noble causes sometimes find themselves... misdirected. It's all hearsay at this point, but it does make one wonder about the integrity of some philanthropic endeavors."

The air around the table grew noticeably thicker. Sir Becket's gaze sharpened. "If you have concerns about specific parties, Hastings, it's only right to bring them forward. Whispers can be as damaging as outright accusations." Becket studied Hastings carefully. "In our circles, such matters are taken seriously. Do you have concerns about any organization in particular?"

Hastings met his gaze evenly. "I wouldn't dream of casting

unfounded aspersions. Merely advising caution. After all, with the gala for the clinic approaching, transparency is of utmost importance."

Cranwell narrowed his eyes. "The clinic? You refer to Dr. Manning's expansion endeavor?"

"Indeed," Hastings acknowledged, taking a deliberate sip of his drink. "A commendable initiative. It would be a shame if any shadows were cast upon it due to mismanagement."

An uncomfortable silence settled. The men shifted subtly, unspoken questions hanging in the space between them.

"Well," Jackson interjected, attempting to lighten the mood, "perhaps we should focus on the game. Are you certain you won't join, Hastings?"

He smiled coolly. "Another time, perhaps. I find observing offers its own rewards."

As the game resumed, Hastings watched the interplay among the men. A bead of sweat formed at Mr. Cranwell's temple—a telltale sign of discomfort. Good, Hastings thought, let the doubts take root. He reveled in the small victories, the flicker of uncertainty in Sir Becket's eyes, the way Jackson's joviality seemed forced.

Influence was a blade, one that cut deeper when wielded with precision. A well-placed pause, a half-truth whispered in confidence, and even the most steadfast men began to doubt their footing. They pride themselves on discernment, yet they're blind to the currents beneath the surface.

As the evening progressed, Hastings caught sight of a young man lingering at the room's edge, shifting his weight from foot to foot. His hands clenched and unclenched at his sides, eyes alight with the naive hope of someone eager to belong. Hastings smirked. The young ones were always the easiest to mold. He lifted his glass in a lazy gesture, beckoning the lad forward.

"Mr. Hastings, it's an honor," the man began a hint of awe in his voice. "Thomas Greene, at your service."

"Greene," Hastings repeated thoughtfully. "I've heard your

family name. Traders, aren't you?"

"Yes, sir. My father has dealings in textiles. I've been hoping to expand our connections within the city."

Hastings offered a patronizing smile. "Ambition is commendable. What brings you to the club this evening?"

Greene hesitated. "Seeking guidance, to be frank. Navigating these circles can be… daunting."

"Indeed it can," Hastings agreed, resting a hand on Greene's shoulder. "And one must be cautious. Not all alliances are beneficial."

"I appreciate any advice you could offer," Greene said earnestly.

Hastings feigned contemplation. "Well, for starters, align yourself with those with a proven integrity record. Some look presentable but might lead you astray."

"I see." Greene hung onto his every word.

"Take, for instance, certain philanthropic endeavors that aren't as pristine as they appear."

Greene leaned in. "Are you referring to anyone in particular?"

Hastings gave a subtle nod. "Discretion is key, my boy. But be wary of organizations or causes that have sprung up rapidly, drawing in significant funds without transparent accounting."

"Thank you, Mr. Hastings. I'll keep that in mind."

"Do," Hastings encouraged. "And remember, in this world, knowledge is power."

As Greene departed, Hastings allowed himself a satisfied smile. The eager are so easily led. Another pawn set in motion.

Finding the air inside stifling, Hastings stepped onto the balcony overlooking the moonlit street. The distant sounds of carriage wheels and faint laughter drifted upward. He reached into his waistcoat pocket, fingers brushing against a worn pocket watch—a relic from another time.

Clicking it open, he gazed at the faded inscription: "To my dearest friend, Edward." A shadow passed over his features. Hastings nodded to passing gentlemen, his outward charm masking a deeper purpose. He had waited years for this—the chance to right a grievous wrong. The moment Rockford stiffened at the mention of Captain Langley, Hastings had known. The past was not forgotten. The reckoning was coming.

"Justice," Hastings whispered into the night. "It's long overdue."

He closed the watch with a snap, determination hardening. As Hastings re-entered the club, a rumble of thunder echoed in the distance. The first droplets of rain tapped against the windows, unnoticed by the engrossed patrons. Casting one final glance around the room, he felt a surge of grim satisfaction. The pieces were moving into place.

He thought of Rockford, oblivious to the web tightening around him. *Enjoy your comforts while you can, Your Grace. The storm is coming, and none will be spared.* Tomorrow evening's art auction will be most interesting to watch and listen to. A slow smirk curled at his lips. Let Rockford bask in his illusion of security—for now. The storm was coming, and no one would be spared.

With that, Hastings stepped into the rain and vanished into the night.

Chapter Twenty-Three

15 October 1822

THE CARRIAGE WHEELS clattered over cobblestone, a steady rhythm to Lora's restless thoughts. The cliffs gave way to the North Sea, its waves painted gold by the setting sun. Autumn leaves swirled in the evening breeze, but the beauty of it all did little to settle the unease coiling in her stomach.

Lora's fingers traced the intricate embroidery on her sapphire gown—a nervous habit she couldn't quite stop. She was well aware of how important the night's events were for the clinic's funding and was concerned about the subtle shifts she sensed among society's elite.

Would the whispers she overheard and the glances she felt during the day undermine their efforts? And then there was Rockford. The memory of his warm gaze and reassuring words sent a flutter sweeping through her. She found it both comforting and disconcerting.

The sight of Sommer Castle never failed to stir a sense of wonder in her. Its towering spires reached toward the heavens, silhouetted against lavender and indigo shades that seamlessly blended into the fading azure day. Stone gargoyles gazed ominously from their perches, guardians of centuries past. The ivy clinging to the ancient walls rustled gently, whispering secrets carried on the sea breeze.

As the carriage stopped, the mingled scents of briny air and blooming chrysanthemums swirled around her. The flickering light from the torches danced across the polished carriages. Footmen in navy and white livery with crested buttons assisted guests.

Lora gathered her shawl tightly around her shoulders, the cool air biting softly at her skin. *Everything begins this evening,* she murmured, summoning courage she wasn't entirely sure she felt.

"You're quiet." Harriet studied Lora's profile for a moment before they stepped through the sturdy oak doors and into the castle's vast entrance hall. Though its stone walls bore the marks of centuries, the room conveyed a timeless charm. High ceilings with exposed wooden beams provided a sense of grandeur, while large, arched windows allowed the fading light of dusk to cast a gentle glow inside. The floor was lined with simple flagstones, their cool surface reflecting the soft light of wrought-iron sconces mounted along the walls.

Lora and Harriet decided that to keep the focus on the artwork, the decorations would be limited. They chose a few tapestries and a scattering of potted plants. The results were the correct amount of warmth without overwhelming the space.

Guests mingled quietly, their footsteps echoing softly in the expansive hall as a welcome atmosphere filled the ancient stronghold.

"Are you anxious about the auction? I'm sure Mr. Constable's landscape will sell for a fine price," Harriet said as they entered the Great Room.

Lora offered a slight smile. "I am a bit anxious. We've planned and prepared every detail. Now, there's nothing left to do but wait and hope we raise the funds needed."

Harriet reached over and gently squeezed her hand. "Everything will be splendid. You've worked hard and put in so much effort."

"Thank you," Lora replied softly. "So have you and Rockford. Having him manage all the financial dealings was a welcome relief. I do hope all goes smoothly."

Lora smoothed her gown, deep sapphire silk that complemented her eyes, and took a steadying breath. The murmur of conversations and the soft strains of a string quartet drifted into the foyer, mingling with the salty sea breeze.

Her eyes caught sight of Rockford across the room. His presence stood out amid the bustling crowd, a comforting presence in the sea of faces. She watched as he navigated the crowd with unhurried grace, his dark suit impeccably tailored to his strong frame. A silver pocket watch glinted from his waistcoat, and she couldn't help but notice the hint of a smile playing on his lips.

"Lora," his baritone voice reached her ears, cutting through the surrounding chatter like a soothing melody.

Her pulse quickened unexpectedly. "Good evening, Your Grace." She offered a teasing smile, a playful glint in her eyes.

He offered his arm, and she accepted, the simple gesture sending a reassuring warmth sweeping over her. The tension that had coiled inside her began to unravel. How had he come to have such an effect on her?

"They're staring," Lora whispered, her gaze fixed ahead even as she felt a dozen pairs of eyes upon them.

Rockford leaned in slightly. "Let them. Their opinions are as fleeting as the fashions they cling to."

She managed a small chuckle at that. "Ever the optimist."

They paused before Mr. Constable's serene landscape painting, Wivenhoe Park at Dusk, with its rambling line of the fence and the balance of trees, meadow, and river, demonstrating Constable's ability to make the viewer feel as if they were actually in the meadow.

"I prefer this version of Wivenhoe to the one the Major-General chose for his home. Something about the colors of dusk expresses tranquility to me."

"Do you think so?" she asked Rockford. "The tranquility in this artwork seems at odds with the undercurrents swirling around here this evening. I wish I could step into this scene," Lora mused. "Leave all the whispers behind."

Rockford's gaze softened. "Perhaps someday we can find our

own Wivenhoe Park."

The buzz of the crowd softened to a distant hum as the world seemed to fade away, leaving only the two of them.

Lora's heart thudded softly as she searched his eyes. There was a vulnerability there she hadn't noticed before, a mirror to her own guarded hopes. "Sometimes I feel adrift in all of this," she confessed quietly. "But with you, I find my anchor."

Rockford's gaze held hers steadily. "You are far stronger than you realize. But being your anchor is an honor I cherish."

Her breath caught subtly. Words felt inadequate to express the swirl of emotions in her heart. Instead, she allowed the silence to speak, a gentle smile conveying what she couldn't yet voice to him.

"Lora, I want you to meet someone who might be able to help with the current situation." He gestured to a tall, composed man standing nearby. "This is Thomas Greene. He's Barrington's associate."

Greene bowed slightly. "It's a pleasure to meet you, Lady Lora."

Lora nodded, still gathering her composure. "Thank you, Mr. Greene."

Thomas gave a respectful nod. "I'll leave you to enjoy the auction." With that, he excused himself, blending back into the crowd.

A scent curled around her, sharp, intrusive, unmistakable. Lemon, underscored by a smoky musk. The warmth of the gallery vanished, replaced by the cold, damp air of her captivity. The past surged forward, clawing at the present, dragging her back to that dark room.

"No," she whispered, a wave of nausea threatening. The edges of her vision blurred as snippets of harsh whispers and cold laughter echoed in her mind.

Unconsciously, her fingers dug into Rockford's sleeve. He turned sharply at her touch, concern etching his brow. "Lora, what's wrong?"

She forced herself to focus on his eyes, grounding herself in the present. "It's… the scent… I can't…"

⨯

"HOLD ON," HE urged firmly, steadying her with his grip. He signaled a footman as he headed toward an empty chair.

"My lord—" The man glanced at Lora. No explanation was needed. He retrieved a small vial from his coat pocket and handed it to Rockford.

Rockford quickly opened the vial and passed it under Lora's nose.

She pulled her head up, her eyes wide.

They moved toward a quieter corner. As they did, Rockford heard a muted cough echo behind them, a rasping sound. He felt Lora tense beside him, and he glanced over his shoulder. A man was speaking to Viscount Montague, who was nearby, but Lora was his primary concern. Rockford watched Lora blink, trying to focus. He tightened his grip on her arm.

"I should go after—" Lora turned to follow the gentleman, but Rockford wouldn't release his grip.

"Whoa. Go after him? I think not. As brave as you are, here and now is not the place. And certainly not in your condition." Rockford glanced at Frederic, Viscount Montague.

She looked up at him. "But I'm sure he was one of the men in that lodge."

"Why would the Deputy Secretary of the Board of Control know one of the accomplices to an abduction?" As he turned to identify the man who had been speaking to Montague, he realized the man was gone. Rockford scanned the crowd. "Did you see who it was?"

"No." Lora stood. He gave her his full attention.

"Come, I'll retrieve your wrap and let Lady Harriet know your—"

"You will do no such thing." Lora handed the vial back to the footman with a sincere thank you. Then, she adjusted her gloves. "I was a bit woozy from all the excitement." She placed her hand on his arm, tilted her head, and stared at him. "Shall we, my lord?"

"Very well." He glanced at the Deputy Secretary. "We'll speak to Montague. He spoke to that man before he disappeared." He guided her across the floor.

As they approached the viscount and his wife, Montague hailed someone across the room and hurried away. Montague's departure was too sudden, too precise. A quick glance over his shoulder, the way his steps quickened, it wasn't the exit of a man politely excusing himself. It was the retreat of someone avoiding confrontation.

Rockford's suspicions deepened. He couldn't afford to let his guard down, especially not tonight.

"I do appreciate your concern." Lora's soft words reached him, but his mind was elsewhere. "It makes me feel," She placed her hand on his chest. "Protected."

He brought his attention back to her, patting her hand and letting his worries momentarily fade. "I won't let anything happen to you." He spoke from his heart. His heart. She trusted him. And that was most precious to her and something he didn't deserve.

The king would be here in six days. The mission would be completed, and he'd go back to London. As they neared another group, uneasy looks were exchanged between them before they dispersed. At first, he dismissed the cold glances as happenstance. But as more guests turned away, their conversations suddenly hushed, the realization settled in. This wasn't mere indifference, it was calculated exclusion. And it wasn't just directed at him, but at Lora as well. He had been privy to such slights before, but tonight, they cut deeper.

This second slight only confirmed something was amiss, a shadowy undercurrent he couldn't yet grasp but knew he must uncover.

He glanced at her from the corner of his eye as they moved around the room. Leaving Sommer-by-the-Sea, no, leaving Lora, would be very difficult. The sooner this mission concluded, the better. If he left, it would separate her from his shadow and allow her to recover from the social consequences of their association.

"Perhaps it's time." She tilted his head toward him, "We shared what we've discovered with Barrington. Perhaps then we'd be back in their good graces." She nodded toward the people.

He stared at her, absorbing her insight. She was right. They both were the brunt of the social slights, and it was more than just coincidence.

"Please, don't be so surprised. We've taken a turn around the room, and people have stared and had their quiet little conversation, but no one has stopped to speak to us."

"I agree..." Had she heard his thoughts, too? Or were things that obvious? "We should speak to Barrington," he said. "Something has happened that we know nothing about. We cannot raise any alarms. We don't know who we can trust."

They stopped at the refreshment table. He handed Lora a cup of punch when Harriet joined them.

"You are most brave, Harriet. It appears no one is willing to spend any time with us."

Harriet nearly spilled her punch down the front of her dress. She shot Lora a wry smile, dabbing at her dress. "Well, it's their loss, isn't it? They don't know what fascinating company they're missing."

Before she could steady herself, a figure slipped through the crowd, calculated, precise. Hastings. His attire was immaculate, but his eyes gleamed with something unreadable. A prickle of unease danced down Lora's spine as the corners of his mouth curved upward, not quite reaching his eyes.

"Lady Lora, Your Grace," he intoned with practiced smoothness. "An evening befitting both your reputations."

Chapter Twenty-Four

L ORA MET HIS gaze evenly, suppressing the urge to retreat. She wondered what had drawn her to him. At the moment, she didn't want to be near him. "Your presence adds to the success, Mr. Hastings."

Rockford's hand subtly shifted to rest on the small of Lora's back.

She appreciated his quiet gesture of support. "We trust you're enjoying the auction."

"Immensely." Hasting's gaze flickered between them, a hint of a smirk playing on his lips. "It's heartening to see such dedication to… worthy causes. One hopes they remain untainted by less noble pursuits."

An unspoken challenge hung in the air. Rockford's expression remained inscrutable. He met Hastings' gaze with unwavering confidence. "True dedication to a cause shines brightest when tested. Those who seek to undermine it will find their efforts futile."

Hastings' smile tightened, and a flicker of unease crossed his eyes. He quickly masked it with his usual bravado. "Naturally," he purred, though his voice lacked its usual confidence. "Though appearances can be deceiving, wouldn't you say?"

Rockford held his gaze steadily, his calm demeanor showing an authority that left no room for doubt about his seriousness. "Appearances often reveal more than one intends," he said, his voice low and commanding, making it clear he was not to be trifled with.

"Have you had a chance to see the fine landscape donated by John Constable?" Hastings continued, attempting to steer the conversation back to safer ground. "A true masterpiece."

"Yes, we have," Lora replied, maintaining a cordial tone, her eyes flicking between the two men.

"Excellent," Hastings said. "I must say, it's heartening to see such charitable efforts. Though one hopes all contributions are... appropriately managed."

Lora stiffened, recognizing the insinuation. "I'm confident in the integrity of those with whom I am working," she responded coolly.

"Of course," Hastings said, his eyes glinting with something that unsettled her. "Merely commenting on the importance of clarity in these ventures."

"Clarity is indeed vital," Rockford interjected, his gaze steady. "As is trust."

Hastings inclined his head slightly, the flicker of unease still apparent but masked by determination. "Wise words," he said, his smile returning with a hint of challenge. "Enjoy your evening."

As he moved away, Lora released a breath she hadn't realized she'd been holding. "I can't dismiss the feeling that he has his own agenda." She stared after him. "I don't trust him."

The evening wore on, tension lingering beneath the surface. Lora and Rockford made a point to engage with guests, addressing any unspoken doubts with grace and confidence. Some guests responded warmly, whereas others offered only curt nods or averted their gaze. Yet the whispers persisted, creating an unsettling presence at the edges of her awareness.

"Come, we both need a break." Rockford guided Lora to the terrace doors. "I need to rest my face from smiling. It seems someone has been very busy." They stepped outside.

The night air was crisp, carrying the briny tang of the sea and the faint scent of wood smoke from distant hearths. Above, a tapestry of stars stretched endlessly, a shimmering ribbon across the sky. The rhythmic lull of the waves crashing on the beach provided a soothing pace.

Lora rested her hands on the cool stone of the balustrade, gazing out as the moon wove a silver path across the water. "Moments like this feel almost timeless," she mused. "As if all the world's troubles are held at bay."

Rockford stepped closer, draping his coat over her shoulders. "It would be nice if we could remain here," he murmured.

She turned to face him, her eyes reflecting the starlight. "Perhaps we can, in our minds at least."

He reached out, his fingers gently tracing the line of her cheek. "There's something I need to tell you," he began, his voice barely above a whisper.

Her heart quickened. "And what is that?"

"You've come to mean more to me than I ever thought possible."

Lora's eyes shimmered as she took a deep breath, and a faint blush crept up her cheeks. "I feel the same," she admitted, her voice soft yet steady. Her fingers lightly trembled against his chest before she steadied them.

He turned to face her fully. "Lora, I want you to know that whatever challenges arise, that will never change."

Her heart swelled at his words. "You've been my steadfast ally through so much already. I don't know what I'd do without you."

"You'll never have to find out," he vowed. Hesitating slightly, he gently caressed her cheek, his hand lingering and sending a soothing warmth through her. She looked up into his eyes, seeing a reflection of the emotions swirling within her own heart. "Rockford, there's something I need to tell you."

He waited patiently, his gaze unwavering.

"Over these past days, amidst all the chaos and uncertainties, I've come to realize even more how much your presence means to me." She took a shaky breath. "I care for you deeply, more than ever."

A slow smile spread across his face, genuine and filled with affection. "Lora, you've brought light into my life in ways I never expected. When we first began working on the clinic project together, I thought I was just helping my friend's sister. But it's turned into so much more. My feelings now are clearly sincere."

She placed her hand over his. "Then we face whatever comes next together."

"Together," he affirmed.

A soft rustle of skirts and approaching footsteps broke the moment. Lady Harriet appeared in the doorway, smiling as if she knew exactly what she had interrupted.

⟫⟩⟨⟨

LADY HARRIET APPEARED in the doorway. "There you are! Father was an excellent auctioneer. You would have been proud of him."

Rockford raised an eyebrow. "In addition to him being a brilliant doctor. And how did the auction go?"

"Very well, indeed." Harriet's face lit in a wide smile. "Lady Beatrice won the Constable painting for an outstanding £600. She's a close friend of Major-General Rebow's wife Mary Hester. It appears Mary Hester swoons over the landscape Mr. Constable did for them. This piece His Grace obtained for the auction was one Lady Beatrice was not only surprised to see here but also the prize of the auction."

Lora's eyes widened in surprise. "That's wonderful."

Rockford nodded, his expression softening. "Indeed. It seems the evening was very successful."

Harriet sighed, glancing back at the hall. "Yes, it was, but I can't help but feel there's more to this evening than meets the eye," she murmured, her gaze thoughtful. "But I'm thrilled with the number of people who attended and the auction's success. I've come to share this wonderful news and to tell you the carriages are being prepared."

"Thank you, Harriet." Lora cast one last glance at Rockford. "Thank you, Rockford, for all you've done to make this a successful evening."

Rockford lifted her hand to his lips, pressing a soft kiss upon it. A pleasant shiver ran up her arm, easing the evening's tensions and leaving her feeling cherished and deeply connected to him.

She smiled softly, her heart swelling as she whispered, "Until tomorrow."

Lora and Harriet made their way to the carriage. As they exchanged a warm look, Lora's eyes sparkled with a newfound determination and hope.

As the carriage wheels turned, a quiet determination settled in her heart. Whatever shadows Hastings intended to cast, she would not face them alone. With Rockford at her side, they could withstand anything.

"You seem lost in thought," Harriet observed gently.

Lora offered a small smile. "Perhaps, but no longer adrift. I know where I stand now."

Harriet's eyes held a knowing glint. "And with whom you stand?"

Lora's cheeks warmed. "Yes," she murmured, her fingers brushing the edge of Rockford's coat. "And with whom I choose to stand."

FROM THE SHADOWS, Hastings watched them, his expression wavering with unease. The game was advancing. The chess pieces were moving toward an inevitable finish, a veritable checkmate.

If that were true, why did the sight of them, so in sync, so certain, set his teeth on edge? The fear gnawed at him. This wasn't just about control. It was about losing to Rockford. The sight of their closeness stirred a deep, bitter resentment, one he forced down behind a practiced smirk.

"Enjoy your respite," he murmured, his voice shaded with a barely concealed anxiety. "The tides are turning."

Chapter Twenty-Five

16 October 1822

L ORA STOOD BY the window of her sitting room, gazing out at the garden below. She didn't notice the vibrant blooms that swayed softly in the breeze. Her thoughts were a tangle of the previous evening's events, the art auction, unsettling encounters, and the lingering scent of lemon and smoke that stirred memories she'd rather forget.

A familiar knock pulled her from her reverie. She turned just as the door opened, and her brother, Adam, stepped in, his grin a welcome burst of sunshine.

"Surprise, sister!" He spread his arms wide.

"Adam!" A genuine smile broke across her features. She closed the distance between them swiftly, embracing him tightly. The solid warmth of his hug brought a rush of comfort. "When did you return?"

"Just this morning," Holding her at arm's length and studied her face. "Thought I'd return after my short trip to Brighton. Can't stay away too long, can I?"

She chuckled. "Your timing couldn't be better."

His smile faltered slightly as he searched her eyes. "Is everything all right, Lora? You seem… preoccupied."

She hesitated, torn between unburdening herself and shielding him from her worries. "There have been… some challenges." The words felt insufficient, like calling a storm a passing drizzle. She exhaled softly. "Perhaps we could talk while walking along the cliffs? The fresh air might help clear my thoughts."

Adam's eyes softened with concern. "Of course." He offered his arm with a flourish. "Lead the way."

They crossed the garden and slipped out the back gate, stepping onto the path that meandered toward the cliffs. The North Sea stretched before them, a vast expanse of shimmering blue meeting the horizon. The salty breeze played with Lora's loose wisps of hair, and she inhaled deeply, hoping to ease the tightness in her chest.

"This is one of my favorite places. I understand why Father preferred living here to the house in London," Adam said, his gaze fixed on the distant waves. "Standing here clears the mind, doesn't it?"

Lora leaned close. "It does the same for me. Everything feels simpler out here."

They walked in companionable silence for a few moments. The only sounds were the rhythmic crash of waves below and the crunching of leaves underfoot.

"There is talk about your project to expand the clinic all the way in Brighton," Adam said eventually, casting her a sidelong glance. "How are the plans progressing?"

Lora raised an eyebrow playfully. "Are you teasing me?"

He shook his head, his expression earnest. "Not at all. I was just as surprised as you."

She relaxed, a hint of a smile touching her lips. "Well, we've organized a series of events to raise funds. Last night's art auction was the first. Rockford was incredibly generous. He donated a Constable landscape. It was the highlight of the evening. Lady Beatrice had the winning bid."

Adam's smile broadened. "Thank you for warning me. The last time I saw her, she went on and on about acquiring a Constable. She must be positively glowing about acquiring a Constable."

Lora nodded. "I'm glad the painting found a good home. The proceeds will make a significant difference for the clinic."

They continued along the path, a figure emerged ahead, a man walking briskly in their direction. As he drew closer, Lora recognized Thomas Greene.

"Lady Lora," Greene greeted with a courteous bow when they met. His gaze flickered briefly to Adam. "Good day."

"Mr. Greene," Lora replied with a polite smile. "May I introduce my brother, Viscount Wesley?"

Adam touched the brim of his hat, his eyes cool. "A pleasure."

Greene hesitated, his fingers flexing briefly at his sides before he nodded. "The pleasure is mine, my lord."

"Enjoying a morning stroll, Mr. Greene?" Lora inquired.

"Indeed. The sea air is invigorating. You're looking well, milady." His gaze darted nervously between them.

"Much better, Mr. Greene."

"Well, I shouldn't keep you. Good day." He tipped his hat and continued past them.

Adam watched Greene's retreating figure with a thoughtful frown. "What is this about you not feeling well?"

"Too much excitement and champagne at last night's art auction. Nothing more. I was with Rockford."

"I wasn't aware you were acquainted with Thomas Greene."

"Rockford introduced us," Lora explained. "Why do you ask?"

They resumed walking, but Adam's earlier lightness had faded. "I've heard some... unsettling things about him. In Brighton, his name came up in less-than-flattering contexts."

Lora glanced at her brother, concern knitting her brow. "What do you mean?"

Adam hesitated. "He's been linked to some dubious dealings, associations with unsavory characters. I don't have specifics, but the whispers were enough to raise my suspicions."

A chill prickled at the back of Lora's neck. "I had no idea. He's always been polite if a bit reserved."

"Politeness can be a mask," Adam cautioned gently. "I'll speak to Rockford."

She sighed, her gaze drifting back to where Greene had disappeared down the path. "Thank you for telling me."

Adam squeezed her hand reassuringly. "Anything to protect my sister."

They walked a little further. Her mind churned with the new information about Mr. Greene. If Greene was not to be trusted, what implications did that have for her project? First, Mr. Hastings and now, Mr. Greene.

"We should head back," she suggested softly. "Rockford is meeting me at the house soon. We're supposed to finalize a few things for the luncheon, the next event in our march toward financing the expansion."

"Of course." Adam offered his arm again, and they returned and entered through the garden gate.

"His Grace and Lord Barrington are in the drawing room," Axbridge announced as they stepped inside.

"Both of them?" Lora exchanged a concerned glance with Adam. A knot of anxiety tightened in her stomach, her earlier calm now replaced with a bubbling unease.

Without another word, she hurried down the corridor, the hem of her dress brushing against the polished marble floor. The familiar scent of polished wood and fresh lilies seemed cloying today and failed to soothe her racing heart. Adam kept pace beside her.

As they approached the drawing room, Lora hesitated for the briefest moment, taking a steadying breath before pushing the heavy oak door open. The sight that greeted her only deepened her worry.

Rockford stood by the fireplace, his posture rigid, one hand gripping the mantelpiece as if to anchor himself. The usually warm and inviting room felt chilled despite the crackling fire. Sunlight streamed through the tall windows, casting long shadows that played across his chiseled features. His eyes, stormy and distant, were fixed on the dancing flames.

Barrington sat in a high-backed chair nearby. His fingers

steepled under his chin, his expression grave. The air was thick with unspoken tension.

"Gentlemen?" Lora's voice was gentle but edged with concern.

Both men turned upon her entering, Barrington rising out of the chair. Rockford's gaze softened when he saw her, the hard lines of his face easing just a fraction, but the shadows remained. "I'm glad you're here." His deep voice carried a hint of weariness.

Barrington rose, offering a curt nod. "We have some concerning news that we need to discuss."

Lora felt her heart skip a beat. She glanced between them, noting the seriousness etched on their faces. "What is it?" Her voice was barely above a whisper.

Rockford exchanged a brief look with Barrington before stepping forward. He held out an envelope, the seal broken. "You and I both received these this morning."

Her fingers trembled slightly as she took the envelope, its weight seeming heavier than mere paper should allow. Adam moved closer and glanced over her shoulder.

As she unfolded the letter, her eyes skimmed the elegantly penned words. With each line, a cold dread settled over her.

"They've uninvited me," she murmured, the words tasting foreign on her tongue. "For the sake of harmony and to protect the fundraising project." The justification rang hollow, a carefully crafted excuse to mask a calculated slight.

She looked up, meeting Rockford's gaze. The sympathy she found there threatened to undo her composure.

"I suspected this might happen," Barrington interjected, his voice firm yet laced with frustration. "Hastings has been securing allies in high places, most notably, Earl Marchant and Viscount Montague."

Adam's eyes darkened, his jaw tightening. "They uninvited you?" His voice was dangerously low before he refocused. "Marchant, the Surveyor General of Ordnance, and Montague, Deputy Secretary of the Board of Control? You think they're involved with Hastings?"

Barrington nodded grimly. "It's highly likely. They've been seen in several private meetings. Given their sway in society, their support could significantly bolster Hastings' position."

Rockford's jaw tightened, a muscle ticking just beneath the surface. "They're the ones we've been investigating. They're believed to be part of Hastings' close circle. If they align against us, it would mean we're close to finding the truth."

A wave of dizziness washed over Lora. She pressed a hand to her temple, a headache blossoming behind her eyes. The room seemed to tilt slightly, the rich hues of the drapes and furnishings blurring at the edges.

"First Greene, now this," she whispered, her voice touched with despair. "It feels like everything is coming apart."

Adam stepped forward, his expression fierce and determined in a way she hadn't seen before. "We need to act." He glanced between Rockford and Lora. "If Hastings is consolidating power with Marchant and Montague, we have to expose them before—"

"The king arrives," Lora finished, the seriousness of their predicament becoming obvious. She sank slowly into a nearby chair, momentarily sapped of her strength.

"Agreed," Barrington said, his gaze steady. "But we need irrefutable evidence against them. Without it, any accusations we make could go very badly for us. They hold considerable influence."

"There is another issue." Barrington turned toward Rockford, Lora, and Adam. He took a brass button from his coat and handed it to Lora. "Can you identify this?"

Lora glanced at him and then at the brass piece, the threads still hanging from it. "There's a signet on it." She took a closer look. "A bird of sorts with its wings spread in front of a slanted rectangle, a diamond." She handed it to her brother. "I've never seen it before. Why do you ask?"

Barrington exchanged a glance with Adam before passing the button to Rockford.

"Order of Shadows," was all Rockford said. "It's a clandestine crime organization known for its ruthless tactics and extensive network of informants. They operate in the shadows, manipulating events and people to their advantage. Their influence reaches the highest echelons of society."

"We've encountered them before," Barrington said.

Rockford crossed the room and sat beside her, his presence grounding her against the tide of uncertainty. "They can whisper and maneuver all they like. But we won't let them take this from you."

She took a deep breath, drawing on every ounce of inner strength. "What do I need to do?"

Barrington offered a small, reassuring smile. "Your connections could be invaluable. If you can discreetly gather information from your social circle, it might lead us to the evidence we need."

Lora's gaze dropped to her hands clasped tightly in her lap. "Under the current situation, I'm not sure my connections are as valuable as you think." A hint of bitterness crept into her tone. "Hastings has undermined each of us. Invitations have been withdrawn; whispers follow me wherever I go."

"Not everyone has turned away." Adam placed a steadying hand on her shoulder. "He thinks he has, but there are still resources at our disposal."

She looked up at him, surprised by the fervor in his voice. "I've never seen you so adamant."

He offered a faint smile. "I'll spend some time with some of my contacts. Perhaps there's something I can pick up, people who are discontent with Hastings or have noticed irregularities."

"Rockford and I will concentrate on the financial records and transactions," Barrington added, his strategic mind already at work. He glanced at Rockford. "Hughes is here from London. We can see if he has any information. He's an excellent solicitor with resources that could be quite helpful."

Rockford nodded. "He might be able to trace any unauthorized movements of funds or uncover discrepancies that tie back to Hastings and his allies."

A fragile hope flickered within Lora. "Perhaps Harriet can

help," she mused aloud. "I'm expected at tea today. It might provide an opportunity to gauge where others stand and perhaps learn more."

Barrington regarded her thoughtfully. "That could be advantageous, but you must be cautious. We can't risk anyone knowing we are aware of what is happening too soon."

"I understand," she affirmed. "I'll tread carefully."

The room fell into a pensive silence, the enormity of their predicament settling upon them.

Adam was the first to speak. "We should move quickly. Time is not on our side. The twenty-first is only four days away."

Barrington straightened. "Agreed. Let's regroup this evening to share any developments."

Lora stood, squaring her shoulders. "Thank you, all of you."

As the group began to disperse, Adam approached Rockford. "A moment, if you will. I have a matter I'd like to discuss with you, but not here."

"Of course, feel free to come this afternoon. I have some fine brandy we can share, and we won't have to filch it from my father's study." Rockford clasped Adam's shoulder, a wide, mischievous smile blooming on his face.

The others were gone, but Rockford lingered. "Lora," he said softly, "if there's anything you need, any support, I hope you know you can call on me."

She offered a genuine smile, her eyes reflecting gratitude and something deeper. "I do. And it means more than you know."

He nodded a silent promise passing between them.

Lora allowed herself a moment to absorb everything before straightening her shoulders. There was much to do, and she would not let Hastings unravel everything they had fought for.

"Anna, it's time to get ready for tea."

Anna carefully arranged the gown on the bed, her eyes twinkling with pride. "This soft lavender muslin will suit you perfectly for tea at Miss Harriet's, my lady."

"That will be perfect."

Chapter Twenty-Six

17 October 1822

THE SOFT MURMUR of conversation filled Harriet's sitting room as guests settled into their seats. The lace-covered table, with delicate porcelain teacups and an assortment of pastries, was ready to be enjoyed. The scent of jasmine and fresh roses added to the elegance and warmth of the room.

"Thank you for hosting this, Harriet." Lora smoothed the folds of her gown. She couldn't help but feel a flutter of nerves.

"It's my pleasure," Harriet replied with a reassuring smile. "Today is about friendship and harmony."

As the guests arrived, Lora greeted each with heartfelt warmth, noting the surprise and cautious friendliness of their responses.

"Lady Lora," Lady Weatherby began hesitantly, "it's so lovely to see you. We've missed your presence at our gatherings."

Lora's eyes softened. "I've been quite occupied with the clinic project, but I've realized how much I've missed spending time with all of you."

Over tea, the conversation flowed from fashion to the latest novels. Gently, Lora steered the discussion.

"I must admit, I've been so focused on the clinic that I've fallen behind on the latest happenings. Have I missed any noteworthy events?"

Lady Davenport exchanged a glance with Mrs. Fielding before replying, "Well, there's been quite a bit of talk lately. Mr.

Hastings seems to be very… active."

Harriet tilted her head thoughtfully as she stirred her tea. "Active? In what way?"

Mrs. Fielding leaned in slightly, her teacup delicately balanced in her gloved hands. "He's been visiting several households," she began, her tone casual yet edged with curiosity. "Including mine. He's been sharing some rather… concerning observations."

Lora felt a subtle tension ripple through the room, but she maintained her composure. "Oh? What kind of observations?"

Mrs. Fielding hesitated. "He mentioned rumors about financial irregularities concerning the clinic's funds and suggested that the Duke of Rockford might be facing financial difficulties himself."

A murmur swept through the gathering. Before Lora could respond, Lady Davenport interjected with a scrutinizing gaze. "Mr. Hastings, you say? I've heard he's relatively new to our circles. It's curious that he's so informed about the affairs of our esteemed members."

Lady Weatherby nodded thoughtfully. "Indeed. One must consider the source of such rumors."

Lora offered a grateful glance toward Lady Davenport. "I assure you all, every donation to the clinic has been carefully accounted for. The Duke's support has been both generous and clear."

Lady Davenport smiled kindly at Lora. "My dear, those of us who have known you and the Duke for years can certainly attest to your integrity. It's unfortunate that an outsider like Mr. Hastings feels the need to spread unfounded gossip."

Mrs. Fielding shifted in her seat, a hint of embarrassment coloring her cheeks. "Perhaps I was too quick to lend an ear. It's just that he seemed so certain…"

Harriet seized the moment. "Confidence does not equate to truth. We must be cautious about entertaining claims from those who haven't earned our trust."

The other ladies murmured in agreement. "It's rather improper for Mr. Hastings to involve himself in matters that don't concern him," Lady Davenport added. "Especially when it involves casting aspersions on a peer of the realm."

Lora felt a warm surge of relief and took a moment to reinforce the connection. "I appreciate your faith in us. The Duke and I are committed to the welfare of the community, and it's heartening to know we have your support."

"Between us," Lady Davenport leaned in conspiratorially. "I find Mr. Hastings' motivations rather suspect. He seems overly eager to ingratiate himself, perhaps hoping to elevate his own standing."

Mrs. Fielding sighed. "You may be right. It's been so long since we've had any real intrigue. Perhaps I was drawn in by the allure of it."

Harriet laughed lightly. "Well, let's not give him the satisfaction of causing discord among us. After all, we've weathered far more significant storms together."

The atmosphere in the room lightened considerably. Lora exhaled slowly, the weight of uncertainty easing. For the first time in days, she felt the foundation beneath her steady. Lady Davenport turned to her with a sincere expression. "If there's any assistance we can offer, my dear, please don't hesitate to ask. The ton looks after its own."

Lora's eyes softened with gratitude. "Thank you. Your support means more to me than words can express."

Lady Weatherby hesitated before speaking. "Since we're on the subject, there's also been some chatter about the highwayman and… connections to certain families."

Lady Davenport raised an eyebrow. "Surely you're not suggesting any link between our esteemed members and a common criminal?"

Lady Weatherby quickly shook her head. "No, of course not. But Mr. Hastings implied that perhaps some recent troubles are not entirely coincidental."

Lora took a steady breath. "I assure you, any misfortune I've encountered is purely coincidental." She should have known her incident with the highwayman would be fodder for the gossip mill. "The idea that the Duke or anyone in our circle is connected to such activities is unfounded."

Lady Davenport gave a faint, dismissive wave. "It's hardly appropriate for someone of Mr. Hastings' standing to comment on affairs that are beyond his ken. Perhaps he would be better served tending to matters within his own sphere."

"Quite so," Lady Weatherby chimed in. "One must remember one's place in society. Overreaching rarely ends well."

There were murmurs of agreement around the table.

Lora smiled gently. "I appreciate your candor. If any of you have concerns or questions, please feel free to discuss them with me. Our shared goals are too important to let uncertainty divide us."

The atmosphere shifted subtly as the ladies warmed to Lora's sincerity. Conversations flowed more freely, and snippets of information about Hastings' visits and comments surfaced, providing valuable leads. Lora listened attentively, her heart buoyed by the support she felt growing around her.

As the afternoon tea ended, Lady Davenport rose from her seat. "Thank you for your delightful hospitality, Harriet. I always enjoy our gatherings. It's refreshing to spend time in such pleasant company."

She turned to the others, her eyes twinkling. "Shall we, ladies? We wouldn't want to overstay our welcome."

The group exchanged farewells, soft murmurings of appreciation, and promises to meet again soon. The delicate rustle of skirts and the gentle tapping of heels echoed softly as they made their way toward the door.

Once the last guest had departed, the house settled into a comfortable quiet. Harriet turned to Lora, her eyes shining with admiration. "You handled that brilliantly." She reached over to squeeze Lora's hand. "I could see the tides turning in your favor."

Lora exhaled slowly, relief and lingering concern etched on

her features. "Thank you, Harriet. But I can't help but wonder, what is Hastings truly up to? Why would he seek to damage my reputation?" She paused, her gaze distant. "He will only rile Rockford, and no one wants to witness that."

Harriet gave a gentle nod, her expression thoughtful. "Perhaps he believes sowing discord will weaken your position. But today's gathering proved that you have strong allies."

Lora looked down, her fingers tracing the delicate pattern on the teacup before her. "I just don't understand what he wants to accomplish. Undermining the clinic, spreading rumors… It's as if he's attacking me."

"Whatever his motives," Harriet said firmly, "we won't let him succeed." She leaned forward slightly, her gaze thoughtful. "But have you considered that it's not just you Hastings is targeting?"

Lora blinked. "What do you mean?"

Harriet's eyes sparkled with determination. "Hastings underestimates the strength of your character and the loyalty of those who believe in you. I think Hastings' attacks on the clinic and you are a way of antagonizing Rockford, forcing him to take action."

"Me?" Lora's hand flew to her throat. "But why would he…" She paused, realization dawning. "You think he's using me to get to Rockford?"

Harriet shook her head. "You've known Rockford for years. Do you think he would stand for anyone harming you? You told me how angry he was when he found you in the horrid lodge."

Lora stared at Harriet, her mind racing. "I see what you mean. Hastings must have realized that Rockford and I have a history and a connection."

Harriet put her arm around her and hugged her. "Exactly. Hastings knows that attacking you is a way to provoke Rockford. You don't see it, do you? The way he looks at you, the way he stands at your side without hesitation. He loves you, Lora. Almost as much as you love him."

Lora reached out and squeezed Harriet's hand in return. "I

don't know what I'd do without you."

"Fortunately, you won't have to find out," Harriet replied with a light laugh. "Now, let's consider our next steps. There's much to be done, and I have a few ideas that might help us counter Hastings' schemes. I think we should turn his schemes to our advantage."

⇒⇒⇒◄◄◄

"Viscount Wesley, Your Grace." Mr. Turner stood at the study door as Adam entered.

"Come in, Adam." Rockford stood and gestured to a chair by the fireplace. "Thank you, Mr. Turner." The butler left as quietly as he had entered.

Rockford stood at the cellarette and poured cognac into two snifters. "I hope it tastes as good as it did when we were boys. I remember those stolen sips being the best I've ever had." He handed a half-full snifter to Adam, his gaze steady.

They both chuckled and sipped the golden liquid.

"No, Rockford. This," Adam held up the glass. "Is superior. Now I can appreciate the taste and not liberating the bottle from the cabinet."

Rockford took a seat in the armchair next to his guest. "What is it you'd like to discuss in private? Is there news about Hastings?"

Adam shook his head slightly, then paused, his expression serious. "Lora." Adam held the glass at his knee. "I've noticed a closeness between you two. As her brother, I want to ensure that your intentions are honorable."

Rockford was taken aback, a rare moment of surprise flickering in his eyes before he regained his composure. He met Adam's gaze with sincerity, though unease coiled tightly in his chest. "Adam, I care for Lora deeply. My intentions are entirely honorable. Her happiness and well-being are my foremost concerns."

It wasn't a lie. But it wasn't the full truth, either. His honor demanded that he protect her, yet his actions risked destroying the fragile trust between them. And if Adam ever discovered the truth behind why he started to court her…He'd rather not dwell on it at the moment. The weight of it pressed down on him, but he forced himself to maintain his steady exterior.

Adam studied him for a moment before nodding. "I believe you. She seems happier than I've seen her in some time."

"She brings out the best in me." His voice was soft, almost as if the revelation surprised him. But god help him, beneath his calm exterior, the knowledge of his deception gnawed at him.

Adam took a deep breath. "She's been through so much lately. Hastings' rumors, the pressure of the clinic… I'm worried about her."

Rockford's expression softened. "I share your concerns, Adam." He brought the glass to his lips. "She certainly has a mind of her own." He sipped the cognac, hoping to find some solace.

Adam nodded, his gaze steady. "Yes, I am well aware. Hastings is dangerous, and he's targeting both of you. I know you can handle him."

Rockford's jaw tightened with conviction. "I won't let Hastings harm her. I'll do whatever it takes to keep her safe." He paused. "Did you doubt that I would?"

The question hung in the air, and for a moment, Rockford's composure wavered. Was Adam subtly implying he knew more? The thought gnawed at him, a flicker of fear that his loyalty and honor were being questioned, or worse, Adam had discovered his plan.

"No. Not at all. If Father were in Sommer-by-the-Sea, he would be here asking you these questions. He and Mother left after our gala for London. I knew your answer, but I could not speak for you." Adam emptied his glass and held it up. "This is really fine. We never would have appreciated it when we were younger." He put the glass on the small table between the two chairs and stood. "I can't wait to welcome you to the family."

Rockford stood, the realization of his deception making it difficult for him to breathe. Adam's unwavering trust should have been a comfort. Instead, it felt like a noose was tightening around his throat.

Chapter Twenty-Seven

A T STONEFIELD INN, Hastings leaned back in his chair, a smug smile playing on his lips. The dim light cast shadows that danced around his room, mirroring the dark thoughts swirling in his mind. Across from him, Greene sat, his fingers drummed lightly on the armrest, a barely noticeable tension creeping into his posture.

"It's all coming together, Greene." Hastings' voice was smooth and confident. "Rockford is becoming a thorn that needs to be plucked out. Once he's out of the picture, Lora will be mine. It's a wonder the *ton* has the wealth and power they do. They are meek lambs that are so easily led. A word here, a whisper there, and poof, Lady Lora's friends have abandoned her, left her all alone in this storm. As soon as Rockford is gone, as tragic as it will be." Hastings put his hand over his heart. "The poor girl will be desperate for comfort, and I'll be there to provide it."

"Tragic?" Greene froze.

"Not my doing, of course. But I will mourn his demise. He is the type that would come back from the dead out of spite. No, my friend. He has crossed too many people for his own good."

Greene nodded, a flicker of unease crossing his face.

Hastings' smile widened. "And then there is the money, Lady Lora's inheritance. Her wealth. Her legacy. Soon, it will be all mine. But more than that, Greene, I crave the power and influence that come with it. Lora and her wealth will elevate me to heights I've only dreamed of. Then she'll look at me the way she hungers for Rockford." His breath quickened slightly at the thought of her, and he clenched his fist, feeling a surge of desire. His eyes narrowed. "She knows what to expect...should she choose not to cooperate."

He rose from his chair and walked to the window, looking at the fallow farm below. "Imagine it, Greene. The respect, the control. No longer will we be at the mercy of others' whims. I will dictate the rules." He spun around and faced Greene. "Did you deliver the information to Barrington?"

"I did," Greene confirmed. "He and the others believe I'm helping them capture the highwayman and that he can be found at the old mill."

A sly smile curled across Hastings' lips. "Excellent. He'll walk right into my trap."

Greene swallowed hard. "Rockford, sir? How do we... remove him?"

Hastings' eyes gleamed with ruthless determination. "Rockford has made many enemies. A whisper here, a nudge there. In time, he will fall, an innocent carriage accident, and we will not be responsible."

Greene shifted uncomfortably. "Accident?"

Hastings shot him a sharp glance. "Doubting me, Thomas?"

"No, of course not," he replied hastily. "I just... They're becoming suspicious."

"Let them suspect," Hastings sneered. "By this time tomorrow, they will realize the extent of our plans. And it will be too late."

He paused, his mind savoring the thought of Rockford's downfall. "As for Lora, her spirit may be strong now, but isolation and despair have a way of breaking even the toughest of hearts. She will come to me, seeking solace. And I will give it to her on my terms. You've done well for today." Hastings bent back to work on the documents.

Greene understood that he was dismissed. Yet, as he turned

to leave, a sliver of doubt gnawed at him. He had pledged himself to Hastings' plans, but how far was he willing to go? He nodded, though unease flickered in his eyes before he slipped out of the room.

As Hastings continued to plot, his mind drifted to Lora. The image of her, vulnerable and alone, filled his thoughts. She was a woman of strength, but even the strongest could be broken. He could almost see her, eyes filled with tears, turning to him for solace. The mere thought sent a shiver of pleasure through him.

He could feel the money in his hands, the power coursing through his veins. The wealth she would inherit would be his to command, giving him the means for the influence and control he craved. With her at his side, he would dictate the rules, bending the world to his will.

Greene may have his doubts, but he'll come around. Fear is a powerful motivator, and he knows what's at stake.

Hastings returned to his chair, already wearing the mantle of his successfully on his shoulders. The plan was perfect. The pieces were falling into place. Soon, Rockford would be out of the picture, and Lora would be his.

ROCKFORD RODE UP the drive of Rockford Manor. He dismounted and tossed his reins to the groom. He took the front steps two at a time. As he came to the door, it opened. Mr. Turner was standing beside it.

"Welcome back, Your Grace." Turner took Rockford's gloves. "Mr. Greene has been waiting for you for several hours. I've put him in the drawing room with some refreshment."

Rockford's brow furrowed. "Greene, you say?" He looked toward the drawing room.

"Yes, Your Grace. He seemed quite insistent and… anxious."

"What could be so urgent?" he murmured. Rockford nodded,

handing his coat to Turner. "Thank you. I'll see to him at once."

He turned and headed for the drawing room, his mind racing with possibilities. What could have brought Greene here with such urgency? As he entered, he found Greene standing by the fireplace, his posture relaxed but his eyes focused with intent.

"Greene." One look and Rockford was more curious and concerned. "What brings you here?"

Greene turned to face him, his expression serious, but his fingers twitched against his coat, betraying his unease. "Your Grace, we need to talk. It's about a rumor."

Rockford's eyes narrowed slightly. "What about a rumor? There appear to be many. I cannot keep up with all of them."

Greene took a steadying breath. "Someone has planned an accident. You are their intended victim."

Rockford's heart pounded, a cold chill running down his spine. "What do you mean?"

Greene's gaze was unwavering, his tone firm. "There's no time to explain everything. Trust me, you need to avoid Mill Road. The plan is already in motion. It could happen today, tomorrow—there's no telling exactly when, but soon. Too soon."

Rockford hesitated, his mind racing. The determination in Greene's eyes, however, was undeniable. Despite his usual wariness, something about Greene's demeanor was different today, more urgent, more focused. "Alright. Let's discuss this further in my study." He was ready to hear what Green had to say despite the dread creeping into his thoughts.

As they moved to the study, Rockford's thoughts churned. Hastings' ambition knew no bounds, and now, more than ever, he realized the extent of the danger they all faced.

Once inside the study, Rockford closed the door behind them. "Now, tell me everything you know."

Greene leaned in, his expression resolute. "There isn't more I can tell you. I spent a few hours trying to substantiate it. The answers I'm not getting lead me to believe the rumor is accurate. Even Hastings knows about it. I don't know when or exactly where, but it will be on one of the carriage routes you frequently use. He's hired men to ensure it looks like a tragic mishap."

Rockford's jaw tightened. "And you're certain of this?"

Greene nodded. "As certain as I can be without knowing the precise details. With time running out, I didn't want to waste time trying to get more details. I couldn't live with myself if I didn't warn you. Hastings and his accomplices have created an atmosphere that welcomes this action. They know nothing of the details but sit back and wait for it to happen."

Rockford studied Greene for a moment, evaluating the gravity of his words. There was determination in Greene's eyes, along with a flicker of something else, perhaps guilt or a desire for redemption. That was a feeling he knew well.

"I see." Rockford took his time, his mind working through the implications. "Hastings and his friends have gone too far."

Greene looked away briefly before returning his gaze to Rockford. "I thought I could handle this—just gather information. But Hastings' obsession with Lora has driven him past the point of reason."

Rockford's head flew up. Once again, his closeness with Lora has drawn her into this mess. "Very well. I'll avoid the carriage routes, for now. Hastings and his allies think they've won. It's time they learn what happens when they overplay their hand."

Chapter Twenty-Eight

18 October 1822

LORA SAT AT her vanity in her bedchamber, absentmindedly brushing her hair as her thoughts drifted to the events of the past weeks. Her heart warmed at the memory of Rockford's smile, the way his eyes softened when he looked at her.

A soft knock interrupted her thoughts. "Come in," she called softly.

"Good morning, Lora." Harriet stepped inside, a folded letter in her hand and a furrow in her brow.

Lora stared at her friend's reflection in the mirror. Harriet's face was the same as her tone. Lora swung around. "I'd ask if everything was all right, but clearly, it isn't. It's Asheton or Colin."

"No. Asheton is still visiting all our farmers, and Colin is with Mama." Harriet glanced at the letter. "I received a letter this morning. It's…" She held her breath. "Concerning."

Lora held out her hand, but Harriet didn't move. "Are you going to show it to me?"

She took the letter from her friend and unfolded it carefully. As she scanned the script, her heart sank.

My dear Lady Harriet,

It is with a heavy heart that I feel compelled to inform you of certain indiscretions. It has come to my attention that the Duke of Rockford's courtship of Lady Lora was initiated under false pretenses—part of a calculated scheme rather than genuine affection. As her friend, you have the right to know the truth.

Anonymously yours.

Lora's hands trembled as if the paper burned her fingertips. "No." Her voice was barely a whisper, the single word unraveling under the force of her shock.

She sank onto the edge of her bed, the letter pressing down on her like a physical burden. Her mind raced, a whirlwind of emotions tearing through her—disbelief, hurt, anger. The words swam before her eyes, each one a dagger piercing her heart.

The Duke of Rockford's courtship of Lady Lora was initiated under false pretenses...

The words blurred, twisting into a mockery of every tender moment they had shared. A whispered promise beneath the moonlight. The steady warmth of his touch. The way he had looked at her, as if she were his world. She thought back to the moments when his gaze lingered just a heartbeat longer, the unguarded softness in his eyes when he whispered her name. The way he held her, his touch reverent, as if she were something precious. Had it all been a lie?

She shook her head, but the creeping doubt curled around her thoughts, whispering of deception. "No," she murmured, gripping the letter tighter. "It can't be."

"Where did you get this?" She shook the letter at her friend.

"It arrived this morning by messenger. I couldn't ignore it."

Lora stood abruptly and paced before the window, hoping the activity would calm the storm raging inside her. Memories flooded her mind—Rockford's initial hesitance when they first began spending time together, when he seemed distant or preoccupied. She had dismissed it as the burden of his responsibilities or perhaps his own guarded nature.

Part of a calculated scheme...

The words echoed in her mind. She spun away from the window, catching her reflection. She barely recognized the woman staring back—the usually bright eyes now shadowed with pain. "Why?" she whispered. "What could he possibly gain from deceiving me?"

Thoughts tumbled over one another, frantic and unrelenting. Was it the clinic? Could he gain something from its expansion? Or had she been nothing more than a carefully placed piece in a larger scheme? She clenched her fists, anger coursing through her veins.

"It could be a cruel story," Harriet said softly. "There are those who wish to see you unhappy."

Lora's voice was firm as she replied, "I won't let anonymous whispers poison what I believe in." She took a deep breath, straightening her spine. "But I also can't ignore this. This is a black spot on Rockford's reputation. I must tell him before someone else does."

Lora's gaze snapped back to Harriet. "Who else do you think received a letter like this? If someone wants to tarnish Rockford's reputation or mine, they might have also spread this to others."

Harriet's eyes widened slightly. "I hadn't thought of that. But it's possible. Anonymous letters are a coward's tool."

"Precisely." Lora bit the inside of her cheek as she tried to think. "I can't let baseless rumors destroy everything. I must confront him and get to the truth before this poison spreads further."

Harriet placed a reassuring hand on her arm. "I'll accompany you."

Lora shook her head. "No. This is something I must do alone. Besides, if more letters are circulating, perhaps you could discreetly find out if anyone else has received one. Your connections might help us understand the extent of this."

Harriet nodded thoughtfully. "Of course. I was off to the modiste. The ladies there are often privy to the latest news. I'll see what I can learn." She hugged Lora gently. "I'll return as soon as I can."

Harriet left, and the soft click of the door echoed in the quiet room. The same questions kept going over and over in her mind. Why would he pretend to have a relationship with her? She walked to the window, pushed aside the curtain, and glanced out at the garden without seeing it. What could he possibly gain? Her heart pounded. There isn't any truth to this… She glanced at the note Harriet had put on the table. It was all a malicious attempt to drive a wedge between them.

Now alone, Lora sank onto the edge of her bed. She needed to compose herself before facing Rockford. Her emotions swirled. She couldn't let them cloud her judgment.

She stood abruptly, squaring her shoulders. Enough. "I need to hear the truth from him." She would not cower behind whispers. She would face Rockford, look into his eyes, and see for herself what lay hidden there.

Crossing to her wardrobe, she pulled out a simple day dress. Time was of the essence. As she dressed, her movements were brisk, fueled by determination. She pinned her hair neatly, ensuring that not a strand was out of place.

A soft knock sounded at the door. "Lady Lora?" came the tentative voice of her maid.

"Yes, Anna?" Lora replied, smoothing the skirt of her dress.

"Shall I prepare the carriage for you?"

Lora paused, surprised. "How did you know I was going out?"

Anna offered a small smile. "Just a feeling, milady. Thought you might have need of it."

Lora's expression softened. "Thank you, Anna. Yes, please."

As Anna disappeared to make the arrangements, Lora took one last glance around her room. Her gaze fell upon the letter lying on the vanity. She considered taking it with her but decided against it. This conversation would be between her and Rockford. No anonymous words would dictate her actions beyond this point.

Chapter Twenty-Nine

L ORA MOVED WITH purpose as she descended the staircase, her footsteps echoing lightly against the polished wood. Outside, the carriage awaited, the coachman standing at attention. The sky overhead was a patchwork of clouds, hinting at the possibility of rain, a reflection of the anger building inside her.

She stared out the carriage window as the carriage set off toward Rockford's estate. The familiar scenery passed by in a blur. With each turn of the wheel, she replayed conversations in her mind. The truth was there for all to see. Her fingers twisted nervously in her lap. Rockford needed to know what foolishness was afoot.

"Play me false. Really. Now, this gossip has gone too far. Hastings must be behind this with all the innuendo he was making." she whispered to herself with conviction. The thought of his sincere affection strengthened her tenacity. Every moment she shared with Rockford, the warmth of his touch, the genuine look in his eyes, the tenderness of his kiss, was real.

"What if he denies it?" The question surfaced, but she dismissed it quickly. "Of course, he will deny it. Because it's a lie." She tightened her grip on the letter. Rockford would be as outraged as she was. Someone was out to ruin his reputation, and she would not stand for it.

The carriage jolted slightly over a rut in the road, pulling her from her thoughts. She took a steadying breath. She would remain composed regardless of how Rockford might rant. This letter was a cruel ploy, and they would confront it together.

Moments later, the carriage slowed as it approached the manor. As they came to a halt, a footman hurried forward to assist her. Lora stepped out. Her heart pounded with each step toward the entrance, but she held her head high, feeling like an angel of mercy coming to help him.

"Good day, Lady Lora," Mr. Turner bowed. "Is His Grace expecting you?"

She offered a tight smile. "Perhaps not, but I'm certain he'll see me."

"Of course, milady. Please, this way."

She followed the footman through the familiar halls. They paused outside the door to Rockford's study. "One moment, milady." He knocked discreetly.

A muffled response came from within. The footman opened the door. "Lady Lora to see you, Your Grace."

Rockford looked up from the papers spread across his desk, surprise flashing across his features before being replaced with a warm smile. "Lora." He rose quickly to his feet. "This is a delightful surprise."

She stepped into the room, her gaze steady. "I hope I'm not interrupting."

"Never," he assured, moving around the desk to greet her. "What brings you here?" His eyes searched hers.

For a heartbeat, she hesitated, emotions swirling beneath her composed exterior. *"The Duke of Rockford's courtship of Lady Lora was initiated under false pretenses..."* echoed in her head. She swallowed hard. "Harriet received something absurd that you should know about. I am sure you will know what must be done."

His smile faltered slightly. "Of course. Shall we sit?" He gestured toward the pair of armchairs by the window.

She nodded, allowing him to lead the way. Once seated, she turned to face him fully, holding his gaze.

"What did Lady Harriet receive?"

"An anonymous note making certain... allegations about you."

A trace of apprehension crossed his face. "Allegations?" he echoed cautiously.

She drew a breath, steeling herself. "It claims that your courtship of me was... orchestrated for ulterior motives. That you never truly cared for me."

He stiffened, a shadow passing over his face. "Lora, this isn't what you think. Please, just let me explain."

Her face fell. Explain? The word echoed, sharp as a knife. The urgency in his voice should have reassured her, but instead, it cut deeper. Her heart clenched painfully at his response. The lack of immediate denial struck like a blow. "This is true?" Pain threaded through her words as she dreaded his answer. "You played me false?"

He instinctively reached for her hand, but she recoiled, pulling her hands into her lap. "Please, let me explain," he implored, anguish evident in his eyes.

"Explain what?" she demanded, her composure beginning to crack. "That I was a means to an end? A pawn in whatever scheme you're entangled in?"

He hesitated, guilt and determination etched into his features. "When we met at the tearoom, I was involved in matters of great importance that required discretion. At first, my intentions were...not entirely personal."

She laughed bitterly, tears brimming in her eyes. "Not entirely personal? That's a rather delicate way to admit deceit."

"Lora, please," he pleaded. "What started as necessity quickly changed. My feelings for you grew and became real in a way I hadn't anticipated."

"Real?" She stood abruptly, pacing a few steps away. "How am I to believe anything you say now? Every smile, every whispered word, your kisses, was any of it genuine?"

He rose, desperation coloring his tone. "Yes! More than anything. You must believe me."

She spun to face him, fury and hurt blazing in her eyes. "Believe you? After admitting you deceived me from the start?" Her voice shook. "You let me fall in love. You encouraged me to fall in love with you, and all along…"

He flinched at her words. "I never meant to hurt you. I thought—"

"You thought what?" she cut in sharply. "That I wouldn't find out? That the ends justified the means?"

"I was trying to protect you." He stepped closer, his voice firm. "There are dangerous forces at play. I kept you in the dark to keep you safe."

She shook her head, tears spilling over. "By lying to me? By making me a fool in the eyes of others, in my own?" Her voice broke. "If you needed me to play a part, you should have said so."

He reached out again, his voice thick with emotion. "Lora, I'm sorry. If I could undo the pain I've caused you, I would."

She took a step back, raising a hand to stop him. "It's too late for apologies. And I don't want any."

His shoulders sagged. He was at a loss for the first time since she knew him. "Tell me how to make this right. I'll do anything."

Silence stretched between them, taut and heavy. She drew in a shaky breath. "You can start by telling me the whole truth."

He nodded earnestly. "I will. No more secrets. I swear it."

She studied him for a long moment, vulnerability and determination warring within her. "Why now?" she whispered. "Why not before I had to confront you?"

Rockford hesitated, then spoke with quiet intensity. "Because I was afraid. Not of losing you, but of what I might become without you. I can face any enemy, but not the thought of you hating me."

A bitter smile touched her lips. "And yet, by hiding the truth, you've lost me, anyway."

He visibly paled. "Please don't say that."

She closed her eyes briefly, composing herself. "I see nothing to salvage here."

"Lora—"

"Goodbye, Your Grace," she said firmly, the use of his title deliberate to distance herself from him.

She turned and walked toward the door. Just as she reached for the handle, his voice stopped her.

"Lora, I love you." His voice was soft and passionate. His words trembled in the air.

She paused but didn't turn around. "Some declarations come too late."

She left his study, the door behind her closed with a resounding click. She headed to the entrance. She wanted to run down the hall to get out of the manor, but she took a breath and walked down the cold grand hallway that echoed as she moved away from him.

Descending the front steps, she fought to steady her breathing. The gardens outside were vibrant under the afternoon sun. As she climbed into her carriage, her composure finally crumbled. Tears flowed freely as the horses pulled away, the manor shrinking behind her.

Memories flooded her mind, the warmth of his smile, the touch of his hand, the laughter they shared. Each recollection pierced her heart. Had any of it been real? Or was it merely a well-crafted illusion?

She pressed a hand to her chest, the ache almost unbearable. "I thought I knew him," she whispered brokenly. "Perhaps I never did."

The journey home blurred past, her thoughts a storm of emotions. Betrayal, hurt, love, and longing all intertwined into one. By the time she reached Fallsmith Manor, a numbness had set in.

Retreating to the sanctuary of her room, she sank onto the window seat, gazing unseeingly at the horizon.

"How do I move forward from this?" she murmured to herself.

As twilight deepened, her confidence grew stronger. Rockford would not break her. But whether she could forgive or trust him again remained a question.

A gentle knock interrupted her spiraling thoughts. "Lora, it's me—Harriet," her friend's voice called softly from the other side of the door. "May I come in?"

Lora clenched her hands in her lap, her knuckles white. "Not now, Harriet," Lora managed between breaths.

"Please," Harriet persisted, a note of concern threading through her words.

For a moment, Lora stared blankly at the intricate pattern of the rug, Rockford's deception pressing heavily on her chest. Finally, with a weary sigh, she relented. "Come in."

The door creaked open, and Harriet slipped inside, her eyes immediately searching Lora's face. Without a word, she crossed the room and sat beside her on the window seat, wrapping a comforting arm around her shoulders.

Lora drew a shaky breath. "He admitted it," she said hoarsely, her gaze fixed on the rain-speckled glass. "He played me false."

Harriet's expression softened, her brow knitting with empathy. "Oh, Lora… I'm so sorry."

"I don't know what to do," Lora whispered, her voice quivering. "Part of me wants to hate him, but" she glanced up at Harriet, tears running down her cheek. "… I can't."

"Feelings are seldom simple," Harriet murmured gently. "But perhaps there's more to his story than we know."

Lora turned to face her, anger flashing in her tear-filled eyes. "He lied to me, Harriet. Deceived me completely. How can there be more?"

Harriet held her gaze. "People can make mistakes, sometimes with the best intentions. Only you can decide whether to seek the truth and forgive."

Lora swiped at her tears angrily. "He shattered my trust. Why should I give him the benefit of the doubt?"

Harriet hesitated before speaking, choosing her words carefully. "Because I've been hearing things, rumblings among the social circles. The same rumors are spreading, and it seems the accusations aren't isolated."

A flicker of surprise crossed Lora's face. "It wasn't just one letter?"

Harriet shook her head slowly. "No. It appears someone has been very deliberate in spreading these rumors. Many of the people I've spoken to received similar anonymous letters. The content and timing are alarming."

Lora's brow furrowed, confusion mingling with her hurt. "But what could be the motive? Why go to such lengths to defame Rockford and implicate me?"

"There are a few possibilities." Harriet took her hand and leaned in slightly. "Some suggest it might be out of envy or social rivalry. Rockford's recent actions could have unsettled certain individuals. Others believe it could be tied to financial interests, particularly regarding the art auction and a commission he's rumored to have received."

Lora frowned deeply. "But that's not true. He didn't receive a commission. In fact, he paid the art dealer's commission himself. He wouldn't accept any reimbursement even though I authorized the draft."

Harriet's eyes widened slightly. "Don't you see? If they have that wrong, perhaps other details are fabricated as well. Someone is manipulating the narrative."

Lora's mind raced, the pieces of a larger puzzle beginning to surface. "He admitted to me that he hasn't been truthful," she murmured. "But that still doesn't explain who would orchestrate this or why."

Harriet squeezed her hand gently. "Lora, you know him better than anyone. If you believe there's more to the story, then shouldn't you be the one to uncover it?"

Harriet lowered her voice. "I discovered something troubling. Viscount Montague met with several government colleagues and Hastings around the same time these letters began circulating."

Lora's eyes narrowed, suspicion sharpening her features.

"Montague and Hastings? But Montague is the Deputy Secretary of the Board of Control."

"With responsibility for finance."

She met Harriet's gaze. "What could they gain from discrediting Rockford or sabotaging the clinic?"

"I have to admit, it's difficult to say. But their involvement suggests this is more than petty gossip." Harriet bent close to Lora. "There might be a larger scheme here, perhaps involving political conspiracies and financial gain."

A heavy silence settled between them as Lora grappled with the implications. Her emotions churned. Betrayal and anger had taken second place to a growing determination.

"Thank you, Harriet. This changes everything. If there's a plot against Rockford and possibly the clinic, we must uncover the truth."

Harriet placed a reassuring hand on Lora's arm. "We'll find out what's truly going on, no matter how deeply it's buried."

Lora nodded, a flicker of hope igniting. "But I can't confront Hastings and Montague, not yet. Not until we know exactly what they are planning. I need to be certain before I take any further steps."

Harriet squeezed her hand gently. "We, Lora. We need to be certain. We'll be cautious. Perhaps we can discreetly gather more information. It has worked before. We can speak to those who might know something without arousing suspicion."

Lora took a deep breath, the tension easing. "Thank you, Harriet. I don't know what I'd do without you."

Her friend gave her a warm look. "I have a vested interest in seeing justice served."

A hint of a smile touched Lora's lips. "And what is that?"

"In my heart of hearts, I cannot see Rockford playing you false. There is something more to this, and I will move heaven and earth to help you find what that is. Now, let's consider our next steps…"

ELSEWHERE, HASTINGS SAT in his dimly lit study, a satisfied smile playing on his lips. The news of Lora's confrontation with Rockford had reached him swiftly. His plan was unfolding perfectly.

"The first act is complete," he mused aloud, savoring the words. "Now, for the final curtain."

He reached for a message that had been slipped under his door. *All is ready.*

He tossed the message onto the other papers on the desk. Of course, all was ready. All he had to do was wait. Tonight. Tomorrow morning. It didn't matter. As long as he got the results for which he paid.

Hastings leaned back, his eyes gleaming with malice. "By morning, the Duke of Rockford will be nothing more than a tragic memory."

Chapter Thirty

ROCKFORD PACED HIS study, replaying the scene with Lora over and over, each time more painful than the last.

"I should have told her sooner," he berated himself. "I avoided the truth."

A knock at the door drew his attention. "Come in," he said wearily.

Barrington entered, concern etched on his face. "I came as soon as I received your message."

Rockford sank into a chair. "She despises me, and she has every right to."

"You did what you thought was necessary," Barrington reasoned, his voice heavy with regret. "But perhaps it's time to trust her fully. I should have insisted on it earlier."

"I fear it may be too late." He couldn't look Barrington in the eye.

"Not necessarily," Barrington countered. "There's something else you need to know."

Rockford looked up, a chill creeping up his spine at Barrington's grave expression. "What is it?"

"Simms sent word that there is a rumbling of a plot, something more… lethal," he disclosed. "But still no attribution."

Rockford's jaw tightened. "Greene came to see me. I am the target. Hastings is the mastermind. He's becoming more desperate."

"We need to be vigilant," Barrington warned. "Perhaps stay

out of sight for a while."

"I won't hide." Rockford shook his head and then glanced at Barrington. "But, if anything happens to me, promise you'll protect Lora."

Barrington clasped his shoulder firmly. "We'll both will protect her. But let's not let it come to that. Simms and Watts think they may be close to identifying the major people involved. I'm off to meet them. Do you want to come along?"

"I wouldn't be much help. You go on. I'll see you tomorrow."

Barrington paused on his way to the door. "If it's any consolation, I bear responsibility, too. I counseled you not to say anything to her. I regret that now."

"Thank you for that, but ultimately, the decision was mine."

Barrington nodded and left.

⇒⇒⇒⇐⇐⇐

FOR THE NEXT three hours, Rockford tried to concentrate on the clinic finances, examining ledgers and questioning bank statements. He put down his quill when he felt everything was in good order. Jeffers had brought him dinner, but he had hardly touched it.

He needed to talk things through with someone. Rockford decided to visit Adam. He was the only man to whom he could talk about this.

"Jeffers, have my horse brought around," Rockford instructed.

A few minutes later, Jeffers returned, looking concerned. "Your horse threw a shoe, Your Grace. I'll have the carriage waiting for you instead."

Rockford nodded, accepting the change in plans. The carriage ride along the cliff gave him little solace. The lanterns cast long, wavering shadows, and an uneasy feeling settled in his gut. As they approached a narrow bridge over the swiftly flowing

Sommer River, the horses suddenly reared, neighing in panic.

"What's happening?" Rockford called out, bracing himself as the carriage swayed erratically.

"The reins, the horses are not responding!" his groom shouted, struggling to control the terrified animals.

Before he could react, one of the carriage wheels struck an obstruction, and the vehicle lurched violently. Rockford was thrown against the side as the carriage tipped precariously toward the edge of the bridge.

"Jump, Your Grace!" his groom yelled.

Without a second thought, Rockford flung the door open and leaped into the night. He hit the ground hard, rolling to absorb the impact as the carriage teetered and then plummeted into the river below, splintering into pieces upon contact.

Pain radiated through his shoulder, but he forced himself upright. His groom lay nearby, groaning. Rockford hurried to his side. "Are you alright?"

"Aye, sir," his man winced. "Just a bit shaken."

Rockford scanned the darkness, the reality of the situation settling in. This was no accident. The reins had been cut. The wheel had struck something placed with precision. A trap. Someone wanted him dead, and they had nearly succeeded.

"Stay here," he instructed. "I'm going to get help."

He moved swiftly, driven by sheer determination and the urgency of the situation, which seemed to dull his pain. As he made his way toward town, shadows shifted in the periphery of his vision. Footsteps echoed behind him.

"Who's there?" he demanded, reaching instinctively for a weapon he didn't have.

Silence answered.

His anger flared, fueling his resolve. He quickened his pace, the urgent need to get his groom help propelling him forward. The thought of confronting whoever was behind this filled him with a fierce determination. No one would get away with endangering his life and those he cared about.

⇥⇤

LORA SAT ON the chaise in her room. She read the same page for the fourth or perhaps the fifth time, she wasn't certain. Her mind was a maze of conflicted emotions.

Despite her anguish, worry gnawed at her. She hadn't spoken to Rockford since their confrontation. Part of her wanted to reach out to hear his voice, but pride and hurt held her back.

A soft rustling drew her attention. Turning, she saw Axbridge standing respectfully at the doorway.

"Forgive the intrusion, milady," he said gently. "But there's news of which you should be aware."

Her heart skipped. "Yes, Mr. Axbridge?"

"There's been an incident. The wreckage of the Duke Rockford's carriage was found by the river."

She was on her feet at once. Cold fear washed over her. "Is he…?"

"I do not know, my lady."

Lora's mind raced. "Thank you for telling me."

"Of course, milady." He turned to leave.

Lora barely heard him. Her pulse thundered in her ears. Rockford's carriage, wrecked. She forced herself to breathe, to think. He needed her. "Mr. Axbridge, please have the carriage ready for me at once."

As Axbridge left, she grabbed her cape out of her wardrobe, her thoughts in turmoil. Someone had tried to kill Rockford. The realization shattered what was left of her anger.

"I can't lose him," she whispered, tears welling anew. Despite everything, the thought of him being hurt, or worse, was unbearable.

She pulled on her cape and gloves and hurried down the stairs. Mr. Axbridge stood ready at the door and helped her into the coach.

"Take Lady Lora to Rockford Manor."

Lora looked at her butler from the carriage window and graciously nodded. Her carriage traveled quickly down the silent boulevard that led to the other estates.

Her mind was a jumble. She was afraid of what she would find, but she couldn't stop herself from going. *Let him be safe. Let him be safe. Let him be safe.* Was the cadence the wheels made as they rolled over the hard-packed lane.

Her carriage turned down the manor's drive, and moments later, Lora stood before the grand entrance, her heart pounding.

The heavy oak door opened to reveal the footman, his expression one of polite concern. "Good evening, Lady Lora," he greeted with a respectful bow.

Lora took a deep breath, steadying herself. "Good evening, James. I came to inquire about His Grace's condition. I heard about the accident and… I want to know how he is faring."

James's eyes softened slightly. "Of course, milady. His Grace is in a delicate condition. While he has sustained some injuries, they are not as grave as initially feared. However, the situation is still quite serious. He is receiving the best care possible."

Lora's eyes widened with worry. "Thank you for telling me," she said, her voice catching with emotion. "I… I hope he recovers swiftly."

The footman hesitated for a moment. "Would you like to see him, Lady Lora? I'm sure it would lift his spirits."

Her heart ached to see him, to assure herself that he was truly safe. But what then? What would she say? What could she say? She swallowed hard. "No. I just needed to know."

"As you wish, milady," the footman said with a nod.

She managed a small smile, turned, and returned to her carriage.

James closed the door gently behind her, the echo of its closing resonating through the silent hall.

Outside, Lora paused for a moment, gathering her thoughts before continuing on her way. She could not yet face Rockford directly, but knowing he was alive and receiving care brought her a small measure of relief. Lora hesitated for just a moment before stepping toward the waiting carriage.

Unbeknownst to her, upstairs in a darkened room, Rockford stood by the window, watching. Rockford's eyes followed her retreating form, his heart aching with regret. The sight of Lora, even from a distance, stirred a fierce determination.

"Your Grace."

"Yes." He watched the groom help her into her carriage.

"Lady Lora inquired about your health."

"Thank you."

The footman left, but Rockford remained at the window, watching her carriage disappear down the drive. Her trust had been his guiding light, carrying him through the darkness. He had been a fool to risk it, a greater fool to lose it. His hands clenched at his sides. "Lora, I will prove myself worthy of you—no matter the cost. This, I vow."

Chapter Thirty-One

19 October 1822

ROCKFORD STOOD AT the edge of the estate's lake, the still water reflecting the overcast sky. He skipped a stone across the surface, watching as the ripples distorted his reflection. The cool breeze carried the scent of rain, a hint of the storm lingering in the air and in his thoughts. He held a smooth stone, his thumb tracing the familiar contours. With a swift flick of his wrist, he sent it skimming across the surface, one, two, three skips before disappearing into the water.

How did it come to this? The attempt on his life lingered in his mind like a dark shadow, but it was the hurt in Lora's eyes that haunted him the most. The memory of her face when he'd confessed his deception cut deeper than any physical wound.

Lost in thought, he barely noticed Barrington approaching until he was beside him, skipping a stone across the lake. "Six skips," Barrington noted a hint of satisfaction in his tone.

Rockford managed a faint smile. "Show-off," he muttered, but his heart wasn't in the jest.

Barrington glanced at him sideways. "You used to beat me every time when we were children. You've lost your touch."

"Perhaps," Rockford replied, his gaze fixed on the horizon. "Or maybe I've got heavier stones to carry these days."

Barrington's expression softened. "You're thinking about her."

Rockford sighed, running a hand through his hair. "I can't get her out of my mind. The pain I've caused… it's unbearable."

"Have you heard from her?" Barrington ventured cautiously.

Rockford kicked at the stones on the ground. "She came to the manor last night only to see how I fared. Turner suggested she see me, but she declined," he admitted. "I wouldn't blame her if she never wanted to see me again." He took a deep breath. "But I made my decision." He turned to Barrington. "It appears so has she."

Barrington's gaze softened. "Give her time. Lora is nothing if not resilient. Last night's incident was a close call. If you hadn't jumped when you did, the carriage would have crushed you. How are you truly feeling?"

"A few bruises," Rockford admitted, rolling his shoulder to ease the stiffness. "Dr. Manning was here earlier. We agreed to let it be known that I'm in critical condition. It might buy us some time. Do you have any news?"

Barrington picked up another stone, weighing it in his hand. "Hastings and his associates are making bold moves. Your bank received documents this morning alleging fraudulent activities. They've been asked to seize your assets. Montague is the one pushing it."

Rockford scoffed, anger flashing in his eyes. "Montague? They must be confident to act so openly." Rockford clenched his fists, the stone digging into his palm. The realization sank in—this wasn't just another move in their game. This was an execution. The noose was tightening, and soon, there would be no escape.

"I told Edward about the Order of Shadows. It changes everything. They are getting bolder, especially targeting a peer of the realm. He will handle the financial issues along with Hughes," Barrington assured him. "He'll stall Hastings, but uprooting their entire scheme will take time."

"Time we don't have," Rockford said grimly. "His Majesty arrives in two days. If Hastings poisons him against me before then…"

Barrington placed a hand on his shoulder. "We need to get

you out of sight temporarily. Come, stay with my brother. It's safer, and we can strategize from there."

Rockford shook his head firmly. "Running now would only fuel their accusations. Besides, I can't leave Lora unprotected. Hastings won't hesitate to use her to get to me."

"Then we'll find a way to expose Hastings and protect those we care about," Barrington said.

Rockford looked at him, a glimmer of gratitude in his eyes. "Thank you," he said quietly.

They began walking along the shoreline, the gravel crunching under their boots. The tranquility of the setting was a stark contrast to the storm of emotions that raged inside Rockford.

⟫⟫⟫✦⟪⟪⟪

IN THE HEART of the Fallsmith Manor garden, Lora sat on a worn stone bench beneath the branches of an ancient oak. Sunlight filtered through the leaves, casting dappled shadows on the ground. Memories of sun-drenched afternoons with Rockford when they were young and their innocent laughter came unbidden and mingled with the chaos in her heart.

In her hand, she clutched a letter with Hastings' carefully penned words offering support. She read it again, her eyes narrowing at the feigned concern.

My dearest Lady Lora,

I am deeply troubled by the hardships you face. Know that I am here for you, ready to offer support in any way you need.

Yours sincerely,
Hastings

She crumpled the letter as anger and exhaustion washed over her. "How dare he," she muttered.

Harriet stood by her and waited. She was with her when the

letter arrived.

Lora turned to face her, holding out the letter. "Look at this. Hastings pretends to be my sincere friend, but it feels all wrong."

Harriet scanned the letter, her expression mirroring Lora's disdain. "It's disturbingly convenient, isn't it? Especially after the accident."

Lora nodded. "Hastings can't be trusted, especially where Rockford is concerned. Every moment of kindness, every carefully chosen word, it was all part of his game. And I nearly believed him."

"Have you heard any news?" Harriet asked gently as she put the letter on the garden bench.

"I went to Rockford Manor as soon as Axbridge gave me the news," Lora replied, swallowing hard. "The footman, James said he's resting and that his condition is serious. He asked if I wanted to see him. But I couldn't, not yet." She turned to Harriet, not caring about the tears that threatened to run down her face. "I just needed to know he wasn't…"

Harriet placed a reassuring hand on her arm. "Rockford is strong. Father will not let anything happen to him. He really is an excellent doctor."

"I want to believe that." Lora's voice was a whisper, her gaze drifting back to the ground. "But everything is collapsing around him. Hastings is attacking his reputation and seizing his assets. And now this letter…"

"Then we can't stand idly by," Harriet declared, determination lighting her eyes. "We will take action."

Lora looked at her friend, a spark of hope igniting. "What do you suggest?"

Harriet smiled slyly. "Let's discuss it over tea. I have some ideas that might just turn the tide. The first thing we need to do is speak to your Mr. Axbridge and the other servants."

They linked arms and headed toward the house, leaving the crumpled letter on the bench, a discarded ploy of Hastings' in their renewed commitment against him.

Chapter Thirty-Two

Hastings sat behind the desk in his room at Stonefield Inn. The brightness of the day contrasted with the darkness of his intentions. Before him lay a spread of forged documents, each a carefully crafted piece in his game of destruction.

A knock at the door interrupted his contemplation. He straightened, calling out, "Enter."

The door creaked open to reveal his associate, a thin man with a thick, greying beard, calculating eyes, and an air of perpetual alertness. He stepped into the room, the tension between them palpable.

"James? What are you doing here? Where is Greene?" Hastings' voice was sharp, his eyes narrowing with skepticism.

"Sleeping one off," the associate replied with a smirk. "We were up late last night enjoying the brandy you sent. But don't worry. Everything is proceeding as planned. Rockford's assets are inaccessible by now, and whispers of his 'fraud' are spreading like wildfire."

Hastings leaned back in his chair, a satisfied smile curling his lips. "And Lady Lora?"

His associate's expression turned serious. "She's received your letter."

A glint of triumph sparkled in Hastings' eyes. "Good," he purred. "She'll soon realize that I am her only option."

The associate hesitated. Then leaned closer to Hastings. "You do know there are those close to her who may advise against you."

"Lady Harriet and her ilk are inconsequential," Hastings dismissed with a wave of his hand. "Lora is smart, but emotions cloud her judgment. We'll use that to our advantage."

Hastings leaned in, his voice low and insidious. "You know, your brother's situation is more precarious than ever. Those debts won't just disappear. I've been able to keep the wolves at bay."

James swallowed hard, his eyes flicking nervously to the ground. "I thank you for that, Mr. Hastings."

Hastings' smile widened, a cold gleam in his eye. "Remember, his safety is in your hands."

Rising from his chair, he moved to the window. The mist clung to the landscape, a fitting backdrop to his plans. "By the time they uncover any truth, it will be too late. Their reputations will be shattered, their futures gone. And I will be the one standing amidst the wreckage, victorious." He glanced over his shoulder. "You best go back before you're missed."

The man nodded as he left the room. The door closed with a soft thud, leaving Hastings alone with his thoughts.

Hastings returned to his desk, picking up one of the forged documents. His fingers traced the elegant script, a mockery of the trust and honor he intended to destroy. He relished the sense of control, the power to manipulate and ruin those who stood in his way.

He set the document down with a final, satisfied glance at his handiwork. The path to his enemies' downfall was clear, and he would walk it with ruthless precision.

IN THE COZY warmth of Barrington's library, a small group convened Rockford, Barrington, Adam, Harriet, and Edward, Barrington's brother. Shelves filled with ancient tomes lined the walls, the scent of aged paper lending an air of seriousness to their gathering. A fire crackled in the hearth, radiating a gentle heat that wrapped around them, warding off the chill of the evening.

Edward adjusted his spectacles, his eyes reflecting both wisdom and concern. "I've conducted a thorough examination of Hastings' dealings. His veneer of respectability is paper thin."

He spread documents, ledgers, correspondences, and evidence of embezzlement and fraud across the table. "He's been siphoning funds from investors and creating fictitious companies to mask his activities."

Adam leaned forward, his brows knit in concentration as he examined the documents. "The very things he's accused Rockford of doing." He paused for a moment. "If we present this to the authorities, surely they'll act."

"Perhaps," Barrington straightened in his chair, setting the leather to creak. "Hastings has ingratiated himself in high places. We need conclusive proof and a public revelation."

Harriet drummed her fingers on the table, a spark of an idea lighting up her eyes. "The gala."

The room fell silent, all eyes on her.

"It's the perfect stage." There was a note of excitement in her voice. "Everyone who's anyone will be there. If we expose Hastings, then he won't be able to manipulate the story."

Rockford nodded, his expression grave. "We'll need to be incredibly careful. Any misstep could have things go very wrong."

"I'll help." They all turned toward the door at the soft yet firm voice that interrupted their discussion.

Lora stood in the doorway, a quiet strength about her. "Hastings has used me and Rockford as his pawn. It's time we turn the tables. There are things that I've discovered."

Relief and admiration flickered across Rockford's face. "Are you certain?"

She met his gaze steadily, her determination unwavering. "Absolutely."

He couldn't help but smile, his face softening. "I'm glad

you're here."

Lora hesitated for a moment, gathering her thoughts. "I couldn't stay away. Not when there's so much at stake."

She sat at the table, her hands clasped tightly in her lap, the tension visible in her knuckles. "I did some investigating after I received Hastings' letter, and Harriet left. I found a great deal more than I expected."

Everyone at the table gave her their attention.

"The rumors," she began, her voice steady despite the tension, "about your intentions and my involvement, they're widespread. It seems someone has gone to great lengths to spread these lies." She took a deep breath, her eyes locked onto Rockford's. "There are indications that Hastings and Viscount Montague are involved. Mr. Axbridge spoke with Jason Stonefield. Hastings is staying at his inn. He mentioned Hastings conducting meetings with the viscount and Marchand. There were factory owners from Royston Mills as well. The timing of those meetings aligns with when the letters started circulating."

Rockford gripped the edge of the table. "That supports what Barrington was able to unearth. Montague and Hastings. This was more organized than we thought."

Lora nodded, her gaze unwavering. "It appears so. They're trying to dismantle your reputation and mine with calculated precision. Mr. Axbridge also mentioned that my father complained to Mother about someone nosing about into his accounts."

"There's more." Edward leaned forward, his expression grave. "Hastings and Montague are members of the Order of Shadows. This clandestine group operates in the shadows, pulling the strings to manipulate political and financial outcomes for their own benefit."

A hush fell over the room. "The Order," Edward continued, "has deep connections, and they're ruthless. Discrediting Rockford and sabotaging the clinic are just parts of their larger plan. And Lady Lora," he nodded to Lora. "You're information is quite correct. Your source is beyond reproach."

Rockford reached for her hand, his touch gentle but firm. "Lora, thank you. This is valuable information."

She glanced at their joined hands, her heart filled with conflicting emotions. "I know. But there's so much we need to address."

"Yes, we do," Barrington declared. "Edward and I will coordinate with the local authorities and ensure everything is in place."

Harriet touched Lora's arm gently. "I'll accompany Barrington. There's some groundwork I can assist with."

Lora nodded. "Thank you, Harriet."

Barrington inclined his head. "I'll make final arrangements and report back as soon as possible."

After Barrington, Edward, and Harriet exited the room, an awkward silence settled between Lora and Rockford, punctuated only by the soft crackling of the flames.

Lora stared at the fire, her fingers knotting her handkerchief. "I am glad to see that you are well." She kept her gaze on the fire. "I feared something terrible had happened to you."

"I didn't expect you to join us this evening." Rockford put his hands in his pocket.

Lora turned her gaze from the flames to him, not hiding the softening around her eyes. "I realized that allowing Hastings to divide us only serves his purpose." She moved to the terrace window to get away from the heat. She wasn't certain if it was from the fireplace or her nearness to Rockford.

He exhaled, steadying himself before speaking. "Lora, after everything… you still came." His voice was low, almost reverent. "That gives me hope."

She faced him fully, her eyes reflecting pain and hope. "Trust isn't easily rebuilt, Your Grace. Especially not now."

He nodded. "I understand your hesitation. But, I believe we can rebuild that trust. Not just in our fight against Hastings and the Order, but for ourselves."

Lora studied him for a long moment, then gave a slight nod. "Perhaps. We should go over the plan. I have a feeling these next two days will go quickly."

Rockford's expression shifted, a flicker of regret passing through his eyes as he offered her a tight smile, but he didn't move. "Our primary responsibilities are to greet and mingle with our guests. Be open to having discussions so we can resolve any questions they may have." Rockford paused for a moment. "We'll come from a position of strength. There is no need to apologize to anyone for anything unless you've done something wrong. And we have not; therefore, if necessary, we merely explain. Do you agree?"

"Yes. I do. I assume we use the same tactic with Hastings? He prefers to separate you from others and intimidate you into submission." She crossed her arms, her brows furrowed in concern.

"We won't let that happen." His gaze was unwavering. "We should keep all conversations focused on the clinic. That is why everyone is there. We still want our project to succeed."

"I agree with you." Lora sighed softly. "I think we will be the entertainment for the evening no matter how hard we try otherwise." A wry smile played on her lips.

"You are probably correct, but we control the conversation. We direct the energy. The rest they can put together on their own. If they see how—"

"Enraptured, we are with each other." Lora stood with her back resting against the window casing, staring into his eyes.

A silence settled between them, filled with unspoken understanding. Rockford's breath hitched, and his body reacted to her words and soft tone. The realization of their meaning overpowered and humbled him.

He took a deep breath, his voice softening. "Enraptured with each other?" He echoed her words. He braced his hand on the wall behind her, then leaned forward, closing the distance, creating a private space just for them. His eyes darkened with emotion. "I've never been more captivated in my life, Lora. Every moment with you is a gift."

Her whispered words, "I've missed you, too. More than words can say," trembled with emotion. Even now, the remnants of everything that had passed between them lingered, but in this moment, it wasn't the past she clung to, it was him.

Rockford caressed her cheek, his thumb brushing away a stray tear. "I've missed you too."

His smile. She let out a deep sigh. It was the smile that curled toes. She feared never seeing it again.

He observed her closely, noticing how she shivered in delight and the tension between them melting away. The vulnerability in her eyes tugged at his heart. Gently, he pulled her into his arms, wrapping her in a protective embrace, feeling her softness against his chest. "More than words could ever say."

His other hand found its way to her waist, drawing her closer until their bodies were nearly touching. He leaned in, his forehead resting against hers. "Nothing must ever come between us again," he murmured, his breath mingling with hers. He pulled away slightly, his eyes locked onto hers with an intensity that made her heart race. "Nothing."

"Nothing." Her voice was a whisper, her desire for him intoxicating. Nervously, she wet her lips. His chest rumbled with a deep groan. Breathlessly, she waited for his kiss.

With a bent finger, he raised her chin, his lips hovering just a breath away from hers. "I would do anything for you," he whispered, his voice raw with emotion. His lips met hers in a tender kiss, a soft moan escaping her as he deepened the kiss, pouring all his love and longing into it.

The barriers between them fell away, leaving them bare, with only their genuine connection binding them together.

The touch of his mouth on hers sent a tremor through her entire body. He tempted her with his tongue and teased her mouth open. He swooped in, and she let him claim her mouth. She quivered at the sweet tenderness of his kiss. It was nothing like any of the kisses he had given her before.

He hadn't stopped kissing her. With a slow, steady hand, he began his possession. He kissed the hollow at her throat and then down the gentle slope of her chest where he freed her of her bodice and honored her with kisses.

Every part of her screamed for him. She teetered on the edge, torn between restraint and surrender, until restraint no longer mattered.

He took her hand and encouraged her to explore his body. She touched him in forbidden places and was rewarded with a guttural growl that made her heart hammer and her pulse pound. She was on fire with a liquid heat concentrated between her thighs and gasped at the sweet agony.

He whispered words in her ear that were only for her. They sent a shiver through her, not just of pleasure, but of something deeper. A promise. A vow she wanted to believe. As his hands explored her body, her skin tingled and throbbed as an all-consuming feeling came over her and intensified into small waves.

She reached up and whispered in his ear. His answer was a deep, soft chuckle that made her smile.

He held her closer, kissed her deeper. The small waves became larger and kept building, pounding until an unimaginable need to release swept over her. Wave after wave crashed then slowly began to ease.

He held her, gently stroking her hair and whispering soothing words. As her heartbeat returned to normal, Rockford's warmth comforted her. She slowly opened her eyes, and when their gazes met, she fully realized the profound depth of their connection— the unspoken bond that held them together.

They remained entwined in each other's arms for what felt like an eternity, silently watching the flames dance in the hearth, their hearts beating in perfect harmony.

Chapter Thirty-Three

21 October 1822

THE GRAND HALLS of Rockford Manor buzzed with activity as the household staff hurried about, each person focused on their tasks for the gala. Lora moved briskly through the corridors, her day dress swishing softly with each step. Beside her, Mrs. Turner, the housekeeper, kept pace, her keen eyes overseeing every detail.

"Mrs. Turner, have the floral arrangements for the drawing room arrived?" Lora asked, her voice steady but tinged with anticipation.

"They have, my lady. I've instructed the footmen to place them as we discussed," Mrs. Turner replied, her tone efficient yet reassuring.

They passed through the dining room, where footmen were setting out polished silverware and gleaming crystal glasses, the clinking sounds adding to the masterpiece of preparations. The long table was adorned with fresh linens and delicate centerpieces of roses and lilies, the fragrance filling the air.

Lora paused for a moment, adjusting a slightly off-center painting. "The arrangements look exquisite," she remarked, admiring the artistry of the displays. "Even the table looks like an enchanted garden."

"Thank you, my lady. Mr. Wickham outdid himself," Mrs. Turner replied, a hint of pride in her voice. "And the gardener is putting the finishing touches on the greenhouse as we speak."

They stepped out onto the veranda and proceeded down the path that led them toward the heart of the preparations, the greenhouse. The gentle hum of activity followed them, the sound of busy hands transforming the estate into a magical setting.

Approaching the greenhouse, Lora's eyes widened, delighted at what she saw. The structure had been transformed into an enchanted garden, a vision of beauty and elegance. Arched entrances were decorated with climbing roses and ivy, creating a fairytale-like entryway. Inside, a myriad of blooming flowers in vibrant colors greeted them, their petals dewy and fresh.

Mr. Wickham, the gardener, meticulously placed the final touches on a topiary shaped like a swan. He had arranged the floral displays of lavender, roses, dahlias, and chrysanthemums, all in shades of purple. He looked up as they entered, a satisfied smile spreading across his face.

"I hope you and Lady Harriet found your rooms adequate," Mrs. Turner asked.

"We certainly did. Thank you for making the arrangements. It was very thoughtful of you."

"I'm glad you're pleased, but it wasn't my doing. His Grace told me to make the arrangements. Now, if you'll come with me." Mrs. Turner motioned toward another part of the greenhouse. "We are nearly ready."

"They are beautiful, Mr. Wickham. And perfect." Lora said. "His Grace gave me flowers like these."

"Yes, I know, my lady. It was the first time I ever saw him pick flowers himself. Quite fussy he was." Mr. Wickham nodded. "He specifically asked for these for today."

"He did? How thoughtful." Lora walked through the rows of flowers, her fingers lightly brushing the petals. "It is beyond beautiful, Mr. Wickham. You have truly created an enchanted garden."

Mr. Wickham bowed slightly, his face beaming with pride. "Thank you, my lady. It has been a labor of love."

Candles in ornate holders were strategically placed throughout the greenhouse, ready to be lit as dusk approached. Lanterns, powered by hidden oil lamps, were nestled among the hanging baskets, their twinkling light enhancing the fairy-tale ambiance.

"The guests will be enchanted," Mrs. Turner said, her voice filled with confidence. "This will be an evening to remember."

Lora took a deep breath, feeling a sense of calm wash over her. "I hope so, Mrs. Turner. Tonight, we must show them the beauty and elegance of Rockford Manor."

With a final nod of approval, they turned and headed back toward the manor. The preparations were complete, and all was ready for an unforgettable evening.

"Lora, there you are." Harriet approached from the main hall. "What do you look so pleased about?"

"Everything looks perfect. Mrs. Turner's staff has the kitchen in hand. It's time for the final briefing. Everyone is in the drawing room." Harriet looped her arm through Lora's, her eyes twinkling with anticipation.

As they moved through the corridor, the murmurs of conversation grew louder, filling the air with a buzz of excitement. The scent of freshly polished wood and floral arrangements added to the sense of occasion. They entered the drawing room, where the warmth of a crackling fireplace greeted them.

Taking their seats, they joined Rockford, who looked composed. Adam leaned against the doorframe with a thoughtful expression, and Barrington, whose eyes held a spark of curiosity. The room hummed with nervous energy and determination, every person poised for the briefing to unfold.

"Everyone is clear about their duties?" Rockford looked around the room.

The group nodded, determination etched on their faces.

"Very well, please be here and ready to greet our first guests at 7 o'clock."

As Lora and Harriet made their way to their room, Rockford paused, catching Lora's arm. "We are prepared," he said, his voice filled with conviction.

Lora met his gaze, a fierce light in her eyes. "Indeed, we are."

"Are the accommodations for you and Lady Harriet sufficient?"

"Yes, they are. Thank you for extending the invitation." She started toward the staircase, then turned. "The flowers are beautiful."

Rockford smiled, and she saw the smile that charmed the birds off the trees. She turned and left.

⤜⟫⟩⟩⟩⟨⟨⟨⟪⤛

LORA STOOD IN the room Mrs. Turner had arranged for her. It was a calm oasis in the midst of the evening's hectic preparations. Her emerald silk gown lay draped over a chair, its rich color a perfect complement to her auburn hair. She carefully donned the gown, feeling the smooth fabric against her skin, and adjusted the delicate lace neckline.

As she pinned the last strand of hair, Harriet entered the room, a cascade of sapphire silk. "You look absolutely radiant, Lora." Harriet's eyes sparkled with genuine admiration. "But no jewelry? Your neck is begging to be adorned. An emerald or diamond would be exquisite."

Lora offered a modest smile. "No, no necklace. I'm asking people for money." She fussed with her skirt, smoothing out wrinkles that weren't there.

Harriet patted her opal necklace and nodded thoughtfully. "That is a very good point. Luckily, I am not asking for money." She glanced at Lora. "Stop fussing. You look perfect."

"It's the calm before the storm," Lora murmured, glancing at herself in the mirror.

Harriet approached, her expression serious. "No matter what happens tonight, you are my very good friend, and I am with you."

"Thank you," Lora whispered, embracing her friend tightly.

"I'm truly grateful that you stand with me." She pulled away. "We'd better go downstairs. The first coaches should arrive shortly."

They saw Rockford waiting for them as they descended the grand staircase. His gaze was steady and warm. He wore a finely tailored suit. The fabric emphasized his broad shoulders and dignified bearing.

Lora's heart skipped a beat as she met Rockford's stare. The intensity of his gaze had her pulse quicken. It wasn't only the gala. It was him. It would always be him.

As they reached the bottom of the grand staircase, Rockford turned to her, a subtle warmth in his eyes. He stepped forward and bowed with a graceful flourish. "You look absolutely stunning," he said, his voice low and filled with genuine admiration.

Lora felt a faint blush rise to her cheeks. The soft glow of the chandelier illuminated the gentle smile that tugged at his lips. "Thank you," she replied softly, her eyes meeting his. "You cut a fine figure yourself."

For a moment, the bustle of the gala faded into the background as they stood at the threshold, the air between them charged with unspoken sentiments.

Rockford's smile widened, and he glanced at Harriet. "And you, Lady Harriet, are a vision of elegance."

Harriet chuckled softly, a twinkle in her eye. "Why, thank you, Rockford."

As the carriages rolled up to the grand venue, the team dispersed to their assigned roles, each person moving with purpose and determination.

Lora and Rockford stood side by side in the foyer and warmly greeted their guests. A gentle hum of conversation and the rustle of silks and satins filled the air. Harriet stood at her side, ready to guide the conversations seamlessly.

As guests arrived, Lora exchanged polite greetings, her gaze occasionally meeting Rockford's. "Good evening, my lord. It's wonderful to see you." Rockford followed with a nod, "Do have a pleasant evening."

Once the main wave of guests had been received, Rockford leaned closer to Lora, his voice a soft murmur. "Shall we join our guests?"

"Our guests are aware of our disagreement. Hastings did a very good job of making that known. They are here because they are curious." Lora smiled as they passed by their guests on their way to the ballroom. "They don't know what we're about."

Rockford, who had linked her arm to his, covered her hand with his and leaned in close. "They see two people who are very much in love, willing to swim the widest river for each other."

"So I can tie the legs of your britches together again?" She teased him tenderly.

He paused for a moment, then squeezed her hand. They continued through the crowd, speaking to their guests.

A calm and composed Sir Ellington approached Rockford with a cordial smile. "Rockford, it's always a pleasure to see you." He extended a hand. "I must say, this evening is truly splendid."

Rockford shook his hand warmly. "Thank you, Ellington. I'm glad you could join us tonight."

Ellington leaned in slightly, his tone low so only Rockford could hear. "I couldn't help but hear some rather troubling whispers circulating amongst the *ton*. It seems there are rumors regarding certain financial difficulties. I hesitate to bring it up, but I thought it best to address it directly."

Rockford maintained his composed expression, nodding slightly. "Yes, I am aware of the rumors. I can assure you, Ellington, that while these whispers have indeed reached my ears, they are greatly exaggerated. My assets remain secure, and any temporary inconveniences are being swiftly handled."

Sir Ellington's brows furrowed with concern. "I understand. It's just that such rumors if left unchecked, can cause quite a stir within our circles."

Rockford offered a reassuring smile. "I appreciate your candor and your concern. It is precisely this kind of open dialogue that will help us navigate through any misunderstandings."

Ellington nodded appreciatively. "I'm relieved to hear that. Should these rumors have an impact, and you require any assistance," Ellington stepped close, "or support, you can count on my discretion and aid."

Rockford placed a hand on Ellington's shoulder, his gratitude unmistakable. "Thank you, Lewis. Your support means a great deal to me."

Meanwhile, Adam's keen eyes roamed the room, watchful for any signs of trouble. He nodded subtly at Lora, a silent reassurance that all was well.

Lora found herself near the refreshment table. An enticing display of pastries, custards, and trifles awaited the guests. Silver platters held neatly arranged finger sandwiches and savory pies, while crystal bowls overflowed with ripe berries and whipped cream. The air was filled with the mingling aromas of freshly baked bread and sweet confections, tempting even the most disciplined attendees.

She smiled warmly at Lady Napier as the woman went on about the beautiful flowers in the greenhouse. "Lady Napier," Harriet said. "The beaded flowers on your gown are exquisite. They remind me of Lord Whitfield. Have you met his lordship? He's very astute about botanicals and is eager to discuss the latest botanical discoveries. Let me introduce him to you."

As Lora moved through the crowd, she caught Rockford's gaze across the room. She knew he would not be far away.

On the far side of the room, her eyes briefly flicked to Hastings, who was speaking with Montague. She noticed Hastings discreetly slipping a letter into his pocket.

Lora turned as Harriet came up to her. "Yes, I noticed. But let's not worry about anything. The evening is going well."

The ballroom was a blend of grandeur and warmth. Its ivory and gold décor created an ambiance that was elegant and inviting. Crystal chandeliers hung from the high ceilings. Their light danced off gilded accents and illuminated the intricate molding that traced the edges of the ceiling.

A grand staircase curved gracefully downward at one end of the room, its marble steps polished to a mirror-like sheen. Garlands of fresh greenery intertwined with soft blooms were wrapped around the banister and railing.

Floral arrangements turned the room into an enchanted garden with bouquets of flowers in crystal vases atop pedestal tables draped with fine linens. Tall windows provided glimpses of the moonlit gardens outside, where lanterns glowed softly among the hedges. Soft music from a string quartet nestled in the corner added to the enchantment.

Guests moved throughout the room as silver trays bearing fine champagne and offered trays laden with delicacies, tiny fruit tarts, savory pies, and sweetmeats.

The atmosphere buzzed with energy. Laughter mingled with the clinking of glasses, and the room felt alive, not just because of the glittering décor but also the genuine enjoyment of the guests. It was clear that every element of the ballroom, from the grand staircase to the smallest floral detail, had been crafted to make everyone feel comfortable in the enchanted garden.

Lora and Rockford navigated the crowd separately. Lora moved through the crowd, her thoughts a whirl of anticipation. Yet, every time she caught sight of Rockford's glances, a wave of confidence washed over her. His reassuring smile, a silent promise of support, lingered in her mind like a soothing balm.

From afar, Lora observed him, engaged in conversation, his presence a steady anchor. Their partnership, born from shared trials, was remarkable and steadfast. Whenever she thought about or saw him, a surge of pride raced through her. Despite the challenges they faced, they stood strong, united in their purpose.

A subtle awareness of his presence washed over her moments before he arrived at her side. "A walk on the terrace?"

She glanced at him and nodded. "It has been a tense few days. I could use some relief."

"My thoughts, exactly." He offered her his arm, and they went out the terrace door.

The cool evening air was a welcome relief from the stifling heat of the ballroom. Rockford stood behind Lora and put his arms around her. She glanced up at him. "To keep you warm, my lady."

She eased her back against his chest, feeling the low rumbling of his laugh and how she missed moments like this with him.

They stood in comfortable silence for a while, the stars above twinkling as if sharing their secret. Lora felt a longing she had never known before, her heart swelling with affection for the man who held her so protectively.

Suddenly, they were interrupted by the sound of approaching footsteps. Lora felt Rockford's arms tense slightly, his body shifting as he became more alert. The spell was broken as a familiar, unwelcome voice cut through the night air.

"How charming," Hastings sneered, stepping into the light.

They both turned at the intrusion, surprise tightening her chest.

"Conspirators conspiring. Don't let me stop you." Hastings waved his hand dismissively. "Please, do go on." His smile changed into a leer. "It will be your last. I have learned of your deceit and corruption. Tonight, I will present my evidence of your wrongdoings."

"*You* have evidence, Mr. Hastings. I fear not unless it is something that you have contrived, more precisely, forged. That seems to be your specialty. But beware, your attempts to destroy people and their reputation will not go unchecked." Lora's voice cut through the night air, hard and clear.

"You ungrateful wretch," he spat at Lora, his expression twisted with malice. "You could have had everything!"

She met his gaze unwavering. "Oh, dear. I believe I've struck a chord." The sweetness on her face faded, replaced by a fierce determination. Her voice sharpened as she continued. "What makes you think," she glanced at Rockford, "I don't already have everything?"

"Hastings," Rockford's voice echoed with authority. "It's over. We know what you are up to. Your fun is over."

"You are so self-righteous when you, both of you, have the most to hide." Hastings stepped forward, sneering. "Don't you?"

Lora felt her heart quicken. What did Hastings know? His slick undertone made her uneasy.

People, overhearing the argument, gathered at the terrace door. The hum of curiosity and concern created a tension of its own.

Hastings produced an unopened letter with a flourish. "I have in my possession a piece of correspondence that was mysteriously intercepted. I believe it will shed light on certain... discrepancies. The missing royal correspondence."

Lora's breath caught in her throat. She recognized her father's seal. How did he know about the correspondence? And how had he found it?

"Do you mean the correspondence that was never sent?" Lora's voice was clear and steady. "Before you weave any more lies, let me clarify something." Her eyes locked on him. "That letter wasn't stolen from the courier pouch. I retrieved it from the front hall salver."

Hastings' smirk faltered slightly, but he quickly regained his composure. "A minor detail," he scoffed. "It doesn't change the fact that in this missive, your father's intentions are laid bare."

Lora countered. "You have twisted the truth for your gain, but your plotting ends here."

How did he know where to look? She had tucked it deep in the hollow of the tree. The only one who would know where it was...the highwayman.

Hastings' voice was smug as he stepped in front of her. "Shall we see what secrets this letter holds that made you remove it from the pouch?" He carefully broke the seal and slowly unfolded the parchment, his expression confident as he enjoyed the small drama.

As he read the contents, his smug expression faltered. A flicker of confusion, then disbelief, then something dangerously close to panic. His fingers clenched around the parchment, knuckles whitening. "This is impossible." His voice, once so sure, wavered. "I spoke to the earl myself."

Rockford stepped forward with deliberate ease, plucking the parchment from Hastings' grip before the man could react. He unfolded it, his expression unreadable. "Let's see what has you so shaken, Hastings."

Chapter Thirty-Four

"*Y*OUR MAJESTY,

"*I trust this letter finds you in good health and spirits. As always, I remain grateful for your wise and benevolent leadership over our kingdom. It is with great respect and humility that I write to seek your gracious permission for a matter of personal and familial importance.*

"*My daughter, Lady Lora, has come of age and is at a pivotal moment in her life where the bonds of matrimony could greatly influence her future happiness and well-being. After much contemplation and consideration, I am convinced that a union between my daughter and…*"

Rockford glanced at Hastings then at Lora.

Lora stepped between Rockford and Hastings. She removed the letter from Rockford's hands. The scent of lemon and smoke hit her, unmistakable. She stared at Hastings, then continued reading, her voice softer but steady.

"*I am convinced that a union between my daughter and Duke Rockford would be most advantageous for both our families and the realm at large.*"

Her voice wavered slightly as she read on.

"*It has come to my attention that Mr. Charles Hastings has also sought my daughter's hand. However, his character and past actions render him an unsuitable match. It is not his common birth that concerns me, but rather his reputation for deceit and lack of honor, which would bring dishonor upon our family and jeopardize the stability we seek. Furthermore, please be informed that neither Duke Rockford nor my daughter are aware of this petition, ensuring that this request is made solely from my judgment of their suitability and the benefits to our lineage and the realm.*

With glistening eyes, she continued loudly for everyone to hear.

"Garrett, Duke Rockford is a man of outstanding character, integrity, and dedication to his duties. His reputation as a noble and honorable gentleman precedes him, and I do not doubt that he would be a devoted and supportive husband to my dear Lora. Moreover, their union would strengthen the ties between our houses, fostering unity and stability within our noble community.

"I have not yet disclosed this intention to Lady Lora or Duke Rockford, as I wish to first seek your esteemed approval. I firmly believe that Your Majesty's consent will lend significant importance to this proposal, ensuring its success and acceptance.

"Upon receiving your favorable response, I will joyfully inform my daughter of this arrangement, confident in the knowledge that it carries your royal blessing. Your Majesty's wisdom and guidance in this matter would be deeply appreciated and cherished by our family.

"Thank you for your time and consideration. I remain, as ever, your loyal and devoted servant.

"With utmost respect and regard,

"Earl Fallsmith"

Murmurs of surprise and confusion filtered out from the doorway. Hastings' face was drained of color.

She gazed intently at Rockford, her heart swelling with relief as she caught the unmistakable gleam of pride and passion in his eyes.

Rockford patted her hand. "Keep that letter safe, my love. We will hand deliver it to His Royal Highness." He tried not to smile but was barely successful. He turned, but she held him back and whispered in his ear. "It's Hastings. He's the highwayman."

Rockford searched her face. "How do you know?".

"The fragrance. It's lemon and smoke. And the letter. I hid it in the hollow of the tree where he captured me. The highwayman was the only other person who could have known where it was."

He turned toward Hastings and stepped in front of Lora. "It seems the letter you intended to use against us contains a father's genuine wish for his daughter's happiness."

"It is obvious that Earl Fallsmith is unaware of what you are. You see," Hastings continued, his voice dripping with insinuation, "I've come across some rather... interesting information about France. Toulouse, to be exact. And Langley, Captain Edward Langley. It seems rather convenient how he disappeared without a trace during the Battle of Toulouse. He was the only man who was unaccounted for. It makes one wonder if perhaps there was a reason...a mutual understanding. You see, the man was a traitor to his country."

Rockford's eyes narrowed, a warning glint visible. "Be very careful with your words, Hastings. Accusations of that nature can be dangerous."

Hastings smirked, sensing he had struck a nerve. He leaned in close for only Rockford to hear. "Oh, I'm not accusing you of anything, Your Grace. Just sharing some thoughts. After all, wouldn't it be a scandal if people believed you had a hand in letting a traitor escape?"

Lora clenched her fists, trying to remain composed. She knew Rockford's patience was wearing thin. The guests had a front-row seat and were whispering among themselves.

Rockford's gaze was icy. "Langley's disappearance was a matter of battlefield chaos, nothing more. But I suppose someone like you, with your lack of military experience, wouldn't understand the complexities of such a situation."

"Perhaps," Hastings replied, his smirk unwavering. "But rumors have a way of spreading, and who knows what people might start to believe?

Murmurs spread through the crowd, the atmosphere thick with speculation. Lora's anxiety grew with every whisper.

Hastings continued, his tone shifting. "It is often said that beneath the surface of such grandeur." He gestured around him. "Lies hidden truths. Truths that, once revealed, change our perceptions entirely."

Rockford's jaw tightened, his gaze fixed on Hastings. "You'll face justice, Hastings. And this time, there will be no escaping it. You attempted to destroy lives for your own gain. It ends tonight."

Hastings paused, a cruel smile playing on his lips as he took a few steps closer. "You think you've won? Even now, my reach extends beyond this insignificant town."

"Your associates have been apprehended," Rockford countered. "Your schemes are collapsing."

Hastings' expression flickered with irritation. A scuffle to Rockford's right drew his attention. Marchand and Montague were being led out the terrace doors.

Hastings' head whipped around to Rockford, and he feigned nonchalance. "We should go into your study. Away from prying eyes. I'm sure we can come to an arrangement." His voice was smoother now, but there was something beneath it, an edge of desperation, of realization. "There is always room for negotiation."

Rockford's jaw tightened, but not from fear—his decision was clear. The plan was to expose Hastings to everyone. "Are you afraid of something?"

"I was simply thinking of…" Hastings glanced at Lora, his lips curling. "Delicate feelings."

"I didn't know you were so weak." Lora scowled. "I did have my suspicions."

Hastings' face twisted. His eyes blazed dangerously as he clenched his fists at his side and took a menacing step forward. Rockford stepped in front of Lora and gently pushed her behind him.

"We'll talk here." Rockford's tone left no room for discussion. "You've just opened a royal correspondence. You do know that is treason and punishable by death."

The murmur of the crowd grew hushed as a man in a black coat and hat came through, his presence commanding attention.

He was serious and direct, each step deliberate and unyielding. Thomas Greene was alongside him, their purpose clear in their stern expressions. The man's eyes were sharp and piercing, scanning the room with a calculated intensity. The crowd parted instinctively, whispers quickly spreading like ripples in a pond.

"Who is with Mr. Greene?" Lora asked Rockford as she stared at the pair.

"Stay back, Lora. I don't know what Hastings has planned."

"We said together. Even my father agrees." Her eyes were still focused on the man.

She tilted her head. "I've seen that man before, but I can't place where." Her mind raced through possibilities. London? A gala? A passing encounter? But something about him unsettled her, a sense of familiarity she couldn't explain.

When Rockford didn't respond, she stole a glance and watched as his face turned ashen, his usually steady composure fracturing before her eyes.

Chapter Thirty-Five

THE MAN REMOVED his hat and coat, revealing a clean-shaven face. Rockford's breath caught in his throat. Despite the deep facial scars that a thick grey beard had once hidden, he knew that face. It struck him like a musket shot, impossible, yet undeniable.

Fear, anger, disbelief, each surged through him, twisting together until he could no longer separate them. For years, Langley had been a ghost, a shadow of Rockford's own regrets. And now, here he stood, flesh and blood, as if the past had never let go.

The playful figure by the street vendor who approved of his hat. How could this be?

"Captain Langley," Rockford managed, his voice strained. The man who had seemed so harmless was the specter that had haunted him since the war and now stood before him.

"Good evening, Commander Rockford." Langley saluted smartly, his eyes reflecting regret and determination. He glanced at Lora. "Lady Lora," he nodded respectfully before returning his gaze to Rockford.

Barrington stepped forward, his expression a careful mask. "Captain, why are you here? More importantly, how are you here?"

Langley drew a deep breath. "It's been a long journey to get here, and I owe you both an explanation. The events at the Battle of Toulouse set a series of actions into motion that connect to tonight."

Rockford's jaw tightened. "Go on."

"I was tasked with exposing a traitor while under your command," he said to Rockford. "The man you saw me speaking with on the battlefield was an enemy contact. The traitor was playing both sides. France wanted him eliminated as much as England did. During the process, we had a brief alliance regarding his removal."

Rockford's eyes widened. "Why didn't you tell me?"

"There was no time, and I was sworn to secrecy by Duke Oakdene—"

"My brother!" Barrington exclaimed.

Langley glanced at Barrington and nodded. "Yes, sir. His involvement complicated matters greatly. After the explosion, which was an attempt on my life devised by the traitor, I had to disappear to continue my mission. I couldn't risk informing anyone, not even you, Rockford."

Rockford felt a tumult of emotions, betrayal, and confusion, but all with a flicker of understanding. "And now?"

Langley turned to Lora, a hint of admiration in his eyes. "Lady Lora, your bravery provided the break we needed. The highwayman had been elusive for so long. You hold the key piece of evidence. Please share what you discovered."

She glanced at Rockford, who offered a reassuring nod. Gathering her composure, she faced Langley. "When the highwayman abducted me, I noticed he wore a unique fragrance, a blend of lemon and smoke."

Langley's eyes lit up. "The lemon is from bergamot, and the smoke is from birch tar."

Langley turned to the others, his voice carrying authority. "Bergamot and birch tar is a unique cologne crafted for the Order of Shadows. In addition, I followed you and Hastings to the lodge." He glanced at Rockford. "I kept a watch over her until you arrived."

"You were the specter that followed me after my carriage

accident," Rockford's voice was soft.

Langley nodded.

"There is one more piece of evidence. You see, the criminal is very brazen. He lost two buttons from his coat. One in the lodge which I believe Barrington found. The other was at the tree in the clearing where the highwayman retrieved Earl Fallsmith's letter to His Royal Highness." Langley took a button from his vest pocket and showed it to Barrington.

"Well done, Langley." Barrington put the button he found into Langley's hand, his eyes gleaming with satisfaction.

He shifted his gaze to his left, his voice cutting through the tense silence. "These are your buttons, Charles Hastings."

A collective gasp rippled through the guests, the air thick with shock and disbelief. Lora's eyes widened as she stared at Hastings, pieces clicking into place. Rockford's jaw tightened, fury simmering beneath the surface, his fists clenched at his side.

Hastings blanched, his veneer of confidence slipping. "This is absurd." His voice wavered as he made his half-hearted declaration.

Langley went on, his voice commanding attention. "The buttons, retrieving the letter, and your cologne gave you away, Hastings. Combined with Lady Lora's testimony and the evidence we've gathered, your treachery is undeniable."

"Anyone can purchase that cologne." Hastings remained adamant, though his voice lacked conviction.

Langley produced a letter sealed with a distinctive crest. He held it up for all to see.

Lora frowned and turned to Rockford. "Whose seal is that?"

Langley met her gaze. His expression was grave. "It's from Mr. Thompson."

"Thompson?" Rockford echoed. "Our mentor?"

Langley nodded. "Yes. Years ago, I encountered Hastings at a tavern. He was down on his luck, and I introduced him to Thompson, hoping to help him find honest work. But Hastings betrayed that trust. Thompson uncovered Hastings's collusion with the enemy and documented everything."

He handed the letter to Rockford.

Hastings's face paled further. "You have no proof!" Hastings glanced around desperately, realizing his allies had abandoned him. "You can't do this," he spat. "This isn't over! You may have won tonight, but you have no idea what you've set in motion. My reach extends further than you know, and sooner or later, you'll see the consequences."

Lora and Rockford exchanged a worried glance. Rockford stepped in front of Hastings, "Who else was involved?"

Hastings laughed bitterly. "You'll find out soon enough. Or perhaps you'll recognize the face of betrayal yourself."

Moments later, Greene re-entered the room, dragging a sullen figure behind him.

"James?" Rockford turned to Barrington then back to James. "You've been our family footman for years."

James avoided his gaze. "I never wanted to do it. But... I had no choice."

Rockford's eyes narrowed. "What leverage did he have against you, James?"

James looked up, his face pale. "My brother... he's in debt, deep debt. Hastings promised to clear it and keep him out of debtor prison if I helped him."

Barrington signaled to Peter and Simon. "Take him into the castle dungeon."

"This isn't over!" Hastings shouted as he was led away, his voice echoing down the corridor until it faded into silence.

For a long moment, the ballroom remained still, the weight of what had just transpired settling over every guest. Then, whispers rippled through the crowd, some murmuring in shock, others exchanging uneasy glances. A few stepped away, as if physically distancing themselves from the scandal that had unfolded before them.

Lora exhaled slowly, her fingers trembling at her sides. Rockford stood beside her, his jaw clenched, his gaze steady despite the storm still raging within him.

Then, from across the room, Lord Whitfield cleared his throat, drawing attention. "Well," he said, his voice carrying authority. "I daresay this evening did not unfold as any of us expected."

A murmur of uneasy agreement spread through the crowd.

"But let us not allow the actions of one man to overshadow the greater purpose of tonight." He raised his glass, his expression resolute. "The clinic remains a cause worth championing. If anything, this reminds us why we must stand together, to support those who serve our community with honor."

Lora's breath caught, her eyes flicking toward Rockford. Slowly, a sense of calm settled over the room, as if the guests had found their footing once more.

Whitfield lifted his glass higher. "In light of these events, I propose we all reaffirm our commitment to the clinic's expansion. It is a noble endeavor, and I, for one, am increasing my donation."

A murmur of approval followed, then scattered applause. One by one, others lifted their glasses, their voices rising in agreement.

Rockford glanced at Lora, something unspoken passing between them. This battle was over, but their work was far from finished.

Mrs. Turner appeared at Rockford and Lora's side. "Dinner is served if you'd please have your guests proceed to the dining hall."

Rockford smiled warmly. "Thank you, Mrs. Turner." He turned to his guests. "Ladies and gentlemen, shall we continue our evening? Dinner is served."

The atmosphere shifted significantly as the guests began to move toward the dining hall. Laughter and light-hearted conversations filled the space, the earlier tension replaced with a sense of ease and friendship. The gala was back on course.

Harriet sidled up to Lora, a mischievous glint in her eye.

"Well, that was quite the turn of events. You do know how to keep things interesting."

Lora chuckled softly. "I can't take all the credit."

"Oh, but you should." Harriet squeezed her friend's hand. "I'm so proud of you."

Rockford approached them, his eyes softening as they met hers. "May I steal Lora for a moment?" His voice was gentle yet filled with unspoken emotion.

Harriet grinned. "By all means." She gave Lora an encouraging nod.

Once alone, Rockford led Lora to a quiet alcove adorned with fragrant blooms and softly glowing candles. The distant melody of the quartet played in the background. He turned to face her, taking both her hands in his.

"Lora, tonight wouldn't have been possible without you. Your courage and brilliance shone brighter than any star."

She met his gaze, her eyes reflecting the warm light. "We accomplished it together. I couldn't have faced Hastings without you."

He exhaled, his heart pounding. "These past weeks have shown me something undeniable, you are my anchor, the light that guides me home. Every moment with you is a gift."

Emotion swirled in her eyes. "Rockford…" Her voice was a whisper, barely audible over the soft strains of music.

Lifting her hand, he pressed a tender kiss to her fingertips. "Lora, you are the love I never dared to dream of. Will you do me the honor of becoming my wife?"

Tears welled in her eyes, and a radiant smile broke across her face. "Yes, Rockford. With all my heart, yes."

Relief and joy filled his expression as he withdrew a small velvet box from his coat. "There's something I wish to give you."

She gasped softly as he opened it, revealing an exquisite necklace, a delicate chain holding an emerald pendant encircled by shimmering diamonds.

"This has been in my family for generations," he murmured.

"It was crafted by a medieval duke for the woman who held his heart, much as you hold mine. I want you to have it as a symbol of my love and devotion."

Lora's fingers brushed the pendant as she met his gaze. "It's beautiful. I will treasure it always."

He stepped behind her, fastening the necklace around her neck. The emerald settled just above her heart. "It pales in comparison to you."

Turning to face him, her voice thick with emotion, she whispered, "Rockford, you've shown me a happiness I never imagined. I promise to love and cherish you, now and always."

He cupped her face, his voice reverent. "I vow to honor and protect you, to stand by you through every sunrise and storm."

Their eyes locked, and in that moment, the world around them disappeared. She leaned in, and their lips met in a tender kiss, a silent promise of the life they would build together.

When they parted, their foreheads rested softly against each other, their breaths mingling.

"Together, we'll create a future filled with love and wonder," she whispered.

He smiled, his gaze full of devotion. "Our adventure is just beginning."

A sudden blast of trumpets sounded, signaling the King's arrival. The guests rose from their seats, anticipation rippled through the air. Footmen swiftly opened the doors leading to the ballroom, guiding the attendees to where His Majesty would make his entrance.

Rockford offered his arm to Lora, a joyful twinkle in his eye. "It seems our special guest has arrived," he said.

She took his arm, her fingers curling around his with new-found assurance. "I'm ready to face whatever comes next as long as we're together."

The grand doors opened, and with a regal presence, the king entered. His attire was magnificent, a deep velvet coat adorned with gold embroidery, and a crown that glittered under the chandeliers. His gaze swept the room with a kind yet commanding presence. It was the lady who accompanied him that had the assembly whispering.

Rockford and Lora stepped forward to greet him. Rockford bowed deeply. "Your Majesty, it is an honor to have you with us." He turned to the woman. "And you, too, Lady Harriet."

Lora curtsied gracefully. "Your Majesty."

The king smiled warmly, his voice resonant and welcoming. "Good evening. I apologize for the late arrival. Matters of state, you understand." He paused, his eyes twinkling with kindness as he regarded them. "As well as a little interruption. Lady Harriet has told me a great deal about this evening as well as the admirable cause it supports. But I suspect there's more to celebrate."

Rockford spoke confidently. "Your Majesty—"

The king held up his hand. He glanced at Lady Harriet, who handed him a letter. "I must tell you, Rockford, Lady Harriet made a delightful courier. She stopped my carriage and wouldn't move until I read the thing." He shook his head. "She was very insistent. So, neither of you knew that Lord Fallsmith had made a request on your behalf. I find that very interesting and…romantic."

"We would like your permission." Rockford stood before His Majesty, composed and with a straight posture. "Lady Lora and I wish to announce our engagement."

The King's eyes twinkled. Then, his gaze fell on the Rockford necklace. "You have my permission, and my heartfelt congratulations to you both."

The guests erupted, the room filling with renewed excitement.

The king addressed the crowd. "Let us raise a toast to truth revealed, to noble causes, and the happy couple. May their union bring joy and prosperity."

Glasses were raised as a resounding "Hear, hear!" echoed through the hall.

The musicians began to play, and the dance floor beckoned.

Rockford turned to Lora, offering his hand. "May I have this dance?"

Lora glanced at the king.

"You go on. I need to talk to Barrington. He can fill me in on what has happened."

They moved onto the center of the ballroom. The challenges of the past weeks faded away, leaving only the promise of their future together.

Lady Dorset whispered to Lady Napier. "They make a splendid couple, don't they?"

Lady Napier nodded. "Indeed. Their bond is strong. And to think we nearly let baseless gossip cloud our eyes."

Ellington approached Lady Harriet. "I must say, the clinic's expansion will do wonders for the community. I've always supported your father's efforts. Excellent doctor. I'm increasing my contribution."

Harriet smiled appreciatively. "Your generosity is most welcome. It's heartening to see everyone come together."

As the evening progressed, it became a celebration not just of Rockford and Lora's engagement but of truth, reconciliation, and the strength of the community.

Later, after the king departed, as the gala began to come to an end, Rockford and Lora slipped out onto the terrace. The night air was cool, a gentle breeze rustling the leaves.

Lora looked up at the stars, the night air crisp against her skin. "Everything feels right now," she murmured, the weight of the past weeks lifting. For the first time, there were no unanswered questions, no lingering doubts, only the steady warmth of the man beside her and the promise of the future they would build together.

Rockford wrapped an arm around her. "It does. With Hastings exposed and the truth now known, we can move forward unhindered."

She rested her head on his shoulder. "I'm excited for what the future holds."

He pressed a kiss to her temple. "As am I. We'll accomplish great things together."

They stood in comfortable silence, content in each other's company.

Finally, Lora spoke softly. "Thank you for believing in me."

He turned to face her fully. "It's I who should thank you. Your courage and perception were pivotal. You are, without a doubt, the heroine of this story."

She laughed lightly. "Perhaps we can share that title."

He smiled. "Perhaps we can. But regardless, I am grateful to have you by my side."

"Always," she agreed.

Chapter Thirty-Six

23 January 1823

THE CRISP JANUARY morning brought a delicate layer of frost to Fallsmith Manor, casting a magical shimmer over the estate. The manor's drawing room, warmed by a crackling fire, was transformed into a winter wonderland for the intimate ceremony. Fresh blooms of winter roses and evergreen sprigs adorned the space, their subtle fragrances mingling with the crisp air.

Lora stood in a sunlit room, adjusting the delicate lace of her gown. Harriet's eyes, sparkling with excitement, added the final touches to Lora's veil. "You look absolutely radiant," she whispered, her voice filled with emotion.

Lora smiled, her heart brimming with anticipation. "Thank you, Harriet."

A gentle knock interrupted them. Adam peeked in, his face lighting up with a broad grin. "Is the bride ready?"

Harriet laughed softly. "As ready as she'll ever be."

Taking a deep breath, Lora turned to face her brother. "Well? Do I meet your approval?"

Adam's expression softened with pride. "You look stunning, Lora. Let's not keep Rockford waiting."

As they descended the grand staircase together, every step brought Lora closer to her future. The drawing room was alive with a gentle murmur of voices, the soft music of a small ensemble creating an enchanting atmosphere. Guests, dressed in their finest morning attire, turned to watch, their faces reflecting the joy of the occasion.

Rockford stood by the hearth, his gaze unwavering as Lora approached. His eyes conveyed a depth of emotion, from admiration to unwavering commitment.

Among the guests, Captain Langley stood near the front, his uniform immaculate, medals shining subtly in the firelight. His presence was a testament to the friendship and loyalty that had been restored.

The officiant began the ceremony with a gentle smile. "Dearly beloved, we are gathered here today to witness the union of Duke Rockford and Lady Lora, a partnership founded on love, trust, and shared purpose."

The world seemed to fade away as they exchanged their vows, leaving only the two of them. Their voices, steady and filled with emotion, carried promises of eternal love and devotion.

"I pledge to stand by you," Rockford vowed, his eyes shining sincerely. "In times of joy and adversity, my devotion to you will remain unwavering."

Tears glistened in Lora's eyes. "I promise to support and cherish you," she replied, her voice strong yet tender. "Together, we'll embrace all that life brings."

"By the power vested in me," the officiant proclaimed, a warm smile spreading across his face, "I now pronounce you husband and wife. You may kiss your bride."

Rockford leaned in, their kiss a tender seal of their vows. Applause and cheers erupted from the guests, their joy echoing through the drawing room.

Following the ceremony, the guests moved to the dining room. Tables were laden with a delightful array of breakfast foods, fresh pastries, fruit compotes, and elegantly presented dishes. The air was filled with the mingling aromas of freshly brewed tea and coffee.

Lora and Rockford moved through the gathering, exchanging

smiles and words of gratitude with their guests. The atmosphere was one of relaxed elegance, with laughter and light-hearted conversations weaving through the space.

Mr. Thompson approached them, raising his cup of tea in a toast. "To Rockford and Lora, a union that embodies integrity and compassion. May your lives together be filled with boundless joy."

"Thank you, Mr. Thompson," Rockford replied, clinking cups.

Lora nodded in agreement. "We are grateful for your guidance and friendship."

Adam joined them, a mischievous gleam in his eye. "I believe a toast is in order," he declared, raising his cup. "To the adventures yet to come."

Harriet chuckled. "Always looking ahead, aren't you, Adam?"

He shrugged playfully. "Someone has to keep things interesting."

Rockford approached Langley with a genuine smile. "I'm grateful you could be here." He extended his hand.

Langley shook it firmly. "I glad to be invited. I have thought of you often, my friend, and relived that day. It's good to see you happy. You both have earned every bit of joy today brings."

Lora joined them, her eyes warm with appreciation. "Captain Langley, will you be staying in Sommer-by-the-Sea?"

Langley looked out toward the sea. "No. I've been offered a new commission. A chance to serve and see more of the world." He nodded. "It's time I forged a new path, one where I answer to myself, not to shadows of the past." Then, with a sincere tone, he added, "But know that you have a friend in me, always."

Rockford placed a hand on his shoulder. "And you in us. This is your home whenever you wish to return."

"Thank you," Langley said softly. "That means a great deal."

Finally, it was time for Lora and Rockford to depart. The guests gathered to see them off, waving handkerchiefs and calling out their blessings.

Rockford helped Lora into the carriage, their hands entwined. As the carriage pulled away, they looked back at their friends and family, their hearts full with the love and support surrounding them.

As they journeyed toward their future, Lora rested her head on Rockford's shoulder, a contented smile on her face. "Do you ever wonder what the future holds?"

He reached out, brushing a strand of hair from her face. "Whatever lies ahead, as long as we're together, it will be a grand adventure."

She sighed happily. "Then let's make it a future filled with purpose and love."

He leaned in, their foreheads touching. "To the journey ahead."

"To the journey," she echoed.

※

Barrington and Edward sat in the study, the fire casting flickering shadows on the walls. The letter lay before him, its wax seal bearing an unfamiliar crest. He broke the seal, unfolding the thick parchment with care.

Edward peered over his shoulder, adjusting his spectacles. "What does it say?"

Barrington's eyes scanned the page, his expression growing more serious. "It's in code. But look at the seal." He handed the letter to his brother.

A raven with its wings spread wide over a geometric diamond. Edward glanced at Barrington. "It's from the Order of Shadows." He glanced at the message. "We must decode it immediately."

After hours of meticulous work, the message slowly revealed itself.

"'*The shadows are deep and long. Our work is not yet complete,*'"

Barrington read aloud, his voice tinged with concern. "Here." Barrington pointed to a specific section. "They know about Hastings."

Edward's jaw tightened. "And they're warning us. *'This isn't over.'*"

Barrington nodded, folding the letter with a heavy sigh. "No, it's not. We must remain alert." He glanced once more at the raven's crest, the ink stark against the parchment. "The Order of Shadows never sleeps."

As the fire crackled, Barrington stared into the flames, his determination firm. The fight against the Order of Shadows continued.

The End

About the Author

There was never a time when *USA Today* Bestseller, RUTH A. CASIE hasn't had a story in her head. When she was little, she and her older sister would dress up and act out the ones Ruth creative. Today, Ruth writes exciting and beautifully told legendary historical romances that are both rich and engaging. Her stories feature strong women and the men who deserve them, endearing flaws and all. Her stories are full of, 'edge of your seat' suspense, mind-boggling drama, and a forever-after romance.

She lives in New Jersey with her hero, three empty bedrooms and a growing number of incomplete counted cross-stitch projects. Before she found her voice, she was a speech therapist (pun intended), client liaison for a corrugated manufacturer, and vice president at an international bank where she was a product/marketing manager, but her favorite job is the one she's doing now—writing romance. Ruth hopes her stories become your favorite adventure.

Fun facts about Ruth:

1. She filled her passport up in one year.
2. She has three series. The Druid Knight is a time travel romance. The Stelton Legacy is a historical fantasy about the seven sons of a seventh son. Havenport Romances are contemporary romantic suspense stories. She also writes for the Pirates of Britannia connected world.
3. She did a rap with her son to "How Many Trucks Can a Tow Truck Tow If a Tow Truck Could Tow Trucks."

4. When she cooks she dances around the kitchen.

5. Her sudoku books is in the bathroom and that's all she'll
    say about that!

Social Media Links:

Website:
ruthacasie.com

Instagram:
instagram.com / ruthacasie

Facebook private reader's page, Casie Café:
facebook.com / groups / 963711677128537

Facebook Author Page:
facebook.com / RuthACasie

Twitter:
twitter.com / RuthACasie

BookBub:
bookbub.com / authors / ruth-a-casie

Amazon:
amazon.com / author / ruthacasie

Goodreads:
goodreads.com / author / show / 4792909.Ruth_A_Casie

YouTube:
bit.ly / 3hI5eQr

www.ingramcontent.com/pod-product-compliance
Lightning Source LLC
Chambersburg PA
CBHW070536310726
48976CB00002BA/643